Behildwick Jones

&

The Children of Mud Island ~ Legacy of the Lake

Jeffrey Brett

Behildwick Jones and the Children of Mud Island - Legacy
Copyright © 2021 Jeffrey Brett

For more information, please contact:
Jeffrey   Brett   at   magic79.jb@outlook.com

Books by Jeffrey Brett

HUMOUR, SUSPENSE & MYSTERIES
The Moon, Balloon and Stars
A Moment in Time
Barking Up the Wrong Tree
Matilda's Magic Circle and the Book of Secrets
Rabbits Beside the Track

HISTORICAL FICTION
Shadow of Blame

ROMANCE
Looking for Rosie

PSYCHOLOGICAL THRILLERS
Beyond the First Page
Leave No Loose Ends
The Road is Never Long Enough
A Chrysalis Without Wings

A COLLECTION OF SHORT STORIES
The Little Red Cafe
The Magic of the Little Red Café

POETRY
A Moment in Time

Dedicated to Katie
With much love

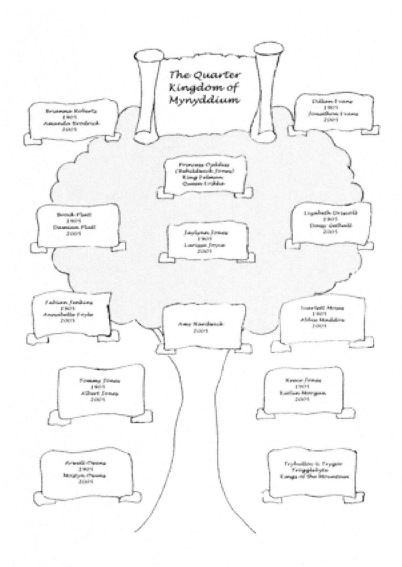

The mountain and
Llandryuid Coal Mine

Mud Island

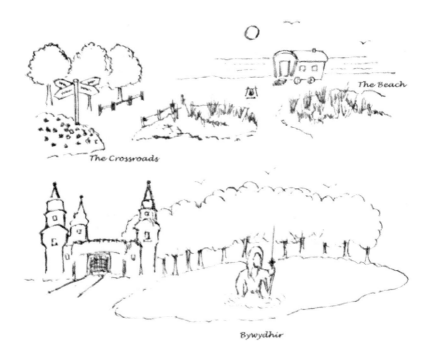

The Crossroads

The Beach

Bywydhir

St Mary's Church

Finiostydd Village

Behildwick Jones
and the Children
of Mud Island -
Legacy of the Lake

Cottage on the edge of the village
belonging to Behildwick Jones

The Dark Wood

Old Jones Farm & Barn

Queen Avallana's Underwater Chamber

Trygor - King of the Mountain
Troggiobytes

Behildwick Jones
&
the Children of Mud Island ~
Legacy of the Lake

There are some fairy tales, derived solely from the imagination of the author, and some that originate from true events from long, long ago.

The secret, is knowing which is which. Who and what is real. Who was present when events took place and where are the characters now, from which the story evolved.

Time stands still for no man, woman or child, but do ghosts exist and do they appreciate time, who really knows.

We see a flicker of light, an oddity that is gone in a flash. Was it indeed somebody walking through or a mysterious visitor stopping to say *'hi'*.

And where do the ideas come from you might wonder? And have you ever stopped to wonder why when you read a story, it sparks a spark of recognition in you. Perhaps you were one of those characters who was there. Maybe, you have a story to tell of your own.

Fairy tale or not. There could well be a Behildwick Jones in the village, that little old lady who lives by herself. She waves although does not speak. And what secrets could she tell I wonder? What secrets could time reveal?

Lastly, have you ever wondered why all the coal mines were shut? I dare you to enter a disused mine late at night when the owl is the only witness that you went inside. Coming back out again however, might be another story. Only if you dare to go in, let somebody know. Why not that little old lady living by herself.

Prologue

Some time, a long time ago

The white horse galloped as fast as it could cutting majestically through the long grass of the field which surrounded the castle with the rider, a young girl waving frantically at the soldiers guarding the battlements who watched her approach.

'She's coming back,' cried an archer high above in the tower next to the portcullis. Down below those protecting the gate lay aside their swords and shields as they began straining hard to raise the heavily fortified gate. With the portcullis raised high enough to allow horse and ride through they held the chain steady. Moments later the echo of hooves thudded over the wooden drawbridge. Pulling back on the bridle the rider halted the horses gallop. Leaping from her saddle she ordered that the portcullis be secured.

'Be quick good men and secure the castle once again,' she cried, 'all is not well beyond our walls.'

A boy arrived from the stable block to take charge of her steed as the rider ascended a flight of stone steps nearby.

Watching from the window of their private quarters the king and his queen were relieved to see that their daughter had returned unharmed.

'There would be no denying Felman that Oyddiss is of your blood. She is bold and fearless although I do wish that occasionally she would wear a pretty dress and act like a princess rather than a teenage boy.'

King Felman grinned as he observed, watching the portcullis drop back down. He had wanted a son, an heir to take over his crown with his passing, but his daughter was as good as any male youth in the castle.

Giving his beard a stoke he replied. 'Oyddiss is like a bird Erikka and she cannot be caged.'

With admiration he had watched her dismount, her sword in the scabbard hung low at her side. The soldiers adored her. 'And she rides like the wind.'

Erikka however was less impressed. 'And she distracts your soldiers. You need to talk to her Felman. Oyddiss is blossoming into a young woman and the change in her body is becoming noticeable.' She heard her husband laugh. She turned to face him. 'And when you talk to her, do so as her father not like you do with the men. Be firm.'

Felman sensed another moral battle about to commence. Oyddiss could so easily wrap him around her little finger.

'Remember…' continued Erikka, 'this our daughter. Put aside your tales of bygone escapades that you like to fill her head with and instead take a stand, make her understand that she is a princess not a warrior to defend the land. Her place is here inside the castle.'

Felman heard her footsteps as Oyddiss was almost at their chamber door. Eagerly he awaited her arrival.

Unenviably he accepted that Erikka was right and circumstances beyond the castle walls had changed and become more dangerous. Staring at his wife he knew that he was lucky. She was as wise as she was beautiful. A moment later there was a thud upon the timber panel of the door as Oyddiss burst in.

Erikka watched with dismay as her only daughter undid her belt holding her sword and scabbard before her. From a toddler she had found little time to amuse herself with dolls preferring a wooden sword that the carpenter had crafted for his princess. Running along the battlements she had pestered and challenged her father's soldiers to duels much to their amusement. On her thirteenth birthday her father had presented her with a white horse.

'Father,' Oyddiss announced, 'the settlers are on their way to the castle and from the looks in their eyes, they're unhappy and hungry... the children are hungry!'

Erikka walked over to Oyddiss placing a soothing hand over her daughters arm.

'You should not burden a young mind with such troubles Oyddiss. Your father knows only too well the struggle that befalls the people of the village. We were talking over a solution when you returned.'

Oyddiss went to her father. 'But the look in the children's eyes father... the dark shadows will haunt my dreams forever. Please, I beg of you to help them.' She went to the window to look out at the courtyard below. 'Raise the portcullis and give them grain, flour and potatoes. Fill their aching stomachs. Our store overflows with enough food to share and leave enough for the castles need.'

Felman looked at Erikka before going to his daughter's side. Her words of wisdom from someone so young made him proud. A restless breeze entered the chamber coming in through the window. Time was changing and so was the unease throughout the lands of his realm. Autumn was only weeks away.

'One day Oyddiss you will make a very fine queen. You possess qualities already that you will need to rule your quarter kingdom, when I am no longer around. I am unhappy to see you so vexed and I aware of the villagers plight, but they have their elders, their council to deal with such matters.'

Oyddiss was about to respond, but her father held up the palm of his hand indicating that he had not yet finished.

'As often the case an easy solution will resolve any problem. I am grateful for what you tell me, and that youth sees what old eyes miss. I will help.'

Erikka stepped forward hugging both her daughter and husband. She too had experienced unsettled nights worrying about the hungry children. A good uninterrupted sleep was overdue. She noticed however that he had not got around to telling her about going riding by herself.

Felman coughed to clear his throat.

'Your mother is worried Oyddiss about your rides to the Whispering Woods and poverty in man can harbour hatred. Deep seated anger and seeing their children starve can produce acts of violence. Go for your daily ride, but only if you are accompanied by members of my personal guard.'

Oyddiss wanted to object, but her mother put a solitary finger to cover her lips.

'You must remember Oyddiss that as a princess you will one day be queen. You are the most precious jewel inside this castle. We have high walls and a strong portcullis to keep you safe. Listen to what your mother tells you, she knows best!'

Oyddiss reluctantly knew that he was right. Had she been born a boy, it would probably have been different. Her mother added her opinion.

'Keeping you safe Oyddiss is so important and come the day that you are queen the villagers and other citizens in Mynyddium will depend upon you to keep them safe. As from tomorrow other riders will accompany you. That is my final word.'

Felman was glad he had not said it was his final word. Looking down at the bailey where soldiers were talking to the gathering of settlers the other side of the portcullis, he called Oyddiss to the window.

'I am going to give the responsibility to you to distribute the grain and vegetables, bread and fruit to the villagers. Consider it your first royal duty.'

Oyddiss punched the air in triumph. She kissed her mother and hugged her father before running back down the stone staircase to the courtyard beyond.

'Raise the gate,' she ordered and somebody find the key to the stores.'

In their chamber King Felman and his queen watched their only daughter help with the distribution of food. She called upon the help of the kitchen hands to give the children oat biscuits, bringing a smile to her own and their blackened faces as they filled their empty stomachs. Kneeling low she engaged the children in conversation.

'Behold your majesty,' said Erikka admiring her daughter. 'The transformation from child to a young woman, to a future queen.'

King Felman watched on with pride. Oyddiss had a free spirit that would endear her to many. Like his daughter the children of the village would not forget this day.

Standing near to the door of the grain store one of the village elders saw the king and queen watching. He bowed low, a tribute to their generosity and kindness.

'At the moment, all is well with our kingdom Erikka although I felt an ill-wind blow in through the chamber window when we were talking with Oyddiss. A time of uncertainty is fast approaching. I feel it in my bones.'

Erikka looped her arm through her husbands, but her attention was elsewhere as she watched a young lieutenant on the ramparts taking an interest in Oyddiss below.

'Changes are afoot both inside and outside Felman.' He too noticed the lieutenant.

'He has grown into a handsome young man,' Felman admitted patting the back of his wife's hand, 'do you think I was unwise in promoting Castilleon so young?'

'You would have to ask the Captain of the Guard the answer to that question my king.'

Felman saw the wry smile crease her cheeks. 'What?' he asked.

'King you are, but did you know that your daughter has taken to walking the castle garden in the evening for exercise?'

Felman shook his head. 'No. Is there a reason she needs more exercise after such vigorous rides on her horse?'

Erikka chuckled. 'Wise you are Felman and generous, but do you not remember when you looked at me like that when we were young and you were just a prince.'

Felman remembered. He watched Castilleon watching his daughter.

'Oyddiss knows her own mind and she will find her rightful place in the world, including having her heart broken perhaps. At times, she can be stubborn like her father so Castilleon will have to tread carefully along the pathway to love.'

'Did you?'

Felman laughed. 'I went to see your mother without you knowing to seek her council.'

The look of shock made him laugh once more.

'As long as Oyddiss has you around, she will always have wise council.' Erikka kissed her husband on the cheek.

'What did I do to deserve that?' he asked.

'No reason, other than I love you and for talking to Oyddiss.' She kissed him again only this time on the lips. 'And that is for making her deal with the villagers. Your wisdom is what makes you a great king.'

Neither noticed that the young lieutenant had disappeared from the battlement, but minutes later they saw him standing alongside Oyddiss. His daughter looked happy, so he was happy and tomorrow he would ride out with the princess where together they would visit the village and talk with the elders, taking a cart loaded with fresh baked bread and oat biscuits for the children.

Maybe that evening he would take his queen for a stroll around the castle garden as well, like he had when they went courting.

Chapter One

A long way forward in time

Pushing aside the feathery fronds hanging down from the large willow tree the children began arriving in pairs until at last the group had gathered.

The eldest girl Brianna Roberts already a week into her thirteenth birthday was the envy of the younger girls who so desperately wanted to be her age. Wanted to be like Brianna and being a teenager was important. Being a teenager was a magical age of excitement and adventure. Much more interesting than being a boring nine, ten or even eleven.

In an odd sort of way Brianna herself felt different. Characteristically, she had developed a confidence, took on the challenges the days could throw at her bouncing them aside with a teenage arrogance. Nothing she felt could penetrate the wall of belief that she had. Nothing other than Dillan Evans. A good two inches taller and older than her by nineteen months. Maybe a little handsome into the bargain, not that she would tell him and especially as he considered himself the leader of the group.

'At last...' said an agitated Brock Platt who had been irritatingly scuffing the heels of his boots against the church wall. 'Are we going or are we going to stand around here until the sun goes down?'

Standing almost beside Brock, Lizabeth Driscoll sighed. 'One day Brock Platt your mouth will be the undoing of you. Girls need time at the beginning of a day to make sure that everything looks just right. Unlike boy's who forget to comb their hair.' Brock ran his fingers through the loose strands covering his forehead. Keeping a style wasn't a priority.

'And what was so important to make them so late?' he replied.

'Just things, girl things. Nothing that need concern you. Although my mum said they would in time!' Brock frowned oblivious to what she meant.

Brianna, second in command, or least as the girls in the group saw her, stepped in between the two. 'Maybe it is time that we left.' She raised her eyebrows at Dillan who nodded back that he agreed.

Sensing a moral victory had been won Brock Platt punched the air victoriously.

Brianna checked with Jaylynn Jones, going through their bag of provisions, the various items contained within having been dropped in by each member on arrival. Provisions that had to last them through until tea-time.

'Some of the apples look a little over-ripe,' whispered Jaylynn as she sorted the fruit, apples, peaches and pears. There were two large onions, a string of carrots and a misshapen loaf of bread, the end of which resembled a face in distorted agony. Best of all was a whole fruit cake baked especially for the occasion by Scarlett Moses grandmother.

Fabian Jenkins put his contribution a screw top metal canister containing fresh milk, on the church wall. There was enough in the canister for them each to have a drink.

'I milked the cows myself,' he said, 'this morning…' None doubted his word.

Each had put something in the collection except Brock, although none questioned why. His father, a miner had been badly injured in an explosion underground three years back. Retired early because of his disability he could only hobble about using a pair of walking sticks. Others further down the throat of the mine had not been as fortunate to escape.

Hard times was not uncommon in the valleys, but regardless of the difficult challenges felt my many families the community spirit was high and people pulled together, helped one another. Not to be outdone Brock produced a large menacing looking knife.

'It were my father's afore the accident.' He proudly showed it the other boys. 'He could skin a rabbit in under a minute using this. He still can, it's only his legs that are naff. I brought it along to help cut the fruit.'

Dillan grinned.

'Well done, Brock. The knife is a valuable contribution.'

'It'll be needed to cut the cake,' somebody said.

With that the young of Finlostydd village began walking away from the church leaving the sunshine that had cast a long shadow over the stone wall. The adventure was about to begin and none would envisage the day ahead.

The rear of the group consisted of Tommy Jones, Reece Brynn and Arwel Owens who always took up their position at the back protecting the girls in front. The boys outnumbering the girls by six to four. Throughout the village they were known as the children of Mud Island. More often than not their adventurous exploits had come to the unwanted attention of the local constable.

Today however, was different. Before arriving at the church Dillan had checked and made sure that Constable Armstrong was still sipping his early morning coffee before commencing his patrol. Keeping to the back alleys and leafy lanes their leaving went unnoticed.

Avoiding the stinging nettles that were overgrown in places, the group meandered a way through the bog treading carefully over loose boulders and using overhanging tree branches to help make their way around the island. There was a dirt track leading to the disused mine, but this way the adventure had begun and it meant overcoming the sticky bog.

'Did we have to come this way?' asked Scarlett, 'the bottom of my boots are already caked in mud!'

Brock Platt turned around to reply. 'Constable Armstrong only ever uses the track. Now stop your bleating Moses and keep up.'

'My nanny says the bog has claimed others in the past that didn't watch their step.'

Alongside Scarlett, Jaylynn Jones agreed. 'I don't like the way that the reeds want to grab your ankles and the mud bubbles every so often. It's like the bog is alive.'

Where the route narrowed, they had to follow one behind the other with Dillan leading and Brianna immediately behind, both thought to be the best trackers.

Other than natural obstacles and the Constable the only risk that each was wary of was a rival gang who lived in the next village, but deemed that Mud Island and the spoils to be found belonged to them. Many a battle had been fought and won, but their number was growing in strength.

'Pass the word back,' Dillan told Brianna. 'I heard that the gang from Treharron were seeking to get to the mine before us. Tell everyone to keep their eyes peeled.'

Having heard the warning Brock grinned as his hand ran down the cold steel of the knife. 'Let them try. They'll get a shock if they come too close.'

They were close to the old disused mine.

'Something doesn't feel right,' Scarlet whispered to Lizabeth.

'I know,' replied Lizabeth as she shivered,' it's as though the sun has no warmth today and yet it's as bright as it's been all summer. Today feels spooky.'

They continued treading down tentatively on the loose boulders beneath their feet.

'We're almost there,' announced Dillan. 'This is the old track was used by the miners when the mine was first opened.'

Hearing the encouragement from their leader they continued to forge ahead. Leaving the mystery of the island they emerged back out into the sunshine unhindered and accosted, much to their surprise. So far everything was going as planned.

Ten minutes later the group stood silent before the metal fence that had been erected after the mine had been closed for the last time. Hanging down lower at one end the signboard above the main gate announced they had arrived at their destination, the disused Llandryuid Vale coal mine. Under the name was stencilled Duffy and Rea Corporation, the owners.

'Is it haunted?' asked Scarlett Moses. Her eyes scanning left and right, looking for signs of unusual movement.

'Only since that explosion underground claimed the lives of fifteen miners,' replied Brock.

'The rock face looks perilously unsafe.' Added Brianna.

Sensing that some were questioning their courage Dillan stepped in. 'It's okay. The mine is just lonely and sad. That's all.'

'But the miners,' Scarlett replied searching the darkness beyond the entrance which was guarded by boards. 'Their bodies were never found.'

For once Brock was sympathetic of Scarlett's apprehension.

'It happens sometimes.' He said. 'According to my grandad the cause of the explosion was never determined. Some same it was gas, others dynamite. The fall underground was so dense the rescuers couldn't get through.' Scarlett shivered once again.

'Then why are we here?' asked Jaylynn Jones.

Standing next to Jaylynn, Reece Brynn continued staring ahead. 'I guess, because it's there and we're the first to come here. We're like those explorers of the past.'

'And we all agreed.' Injected Brianna, sensing an argument brewing.

Dillan took charge of the trepidation spreading through the group. 'What say we just take a peek inside? We notch it up alongside our other exploits and go look for something else to discover this afternoon, something in the sunshine.'

There followed a lot of mutterings and nodding of heads.

Reluctantly Scarlett and Jaylynn conceded, agreeing although still wishing that they were elsewhere. Brianna thought it best that she keep an eye on the three younger girls. They were never normally this anxious. Dillan and Brock could do the same with the younger boys.

Ignoring the warning signs that had been tied to the fence they crawled through the gap that had been created by Dillan and Brock. Soon they were all gathered on the other side. All around were discarded coal trucks, twisted metal and broken shafts of wood. A bird in the branches of a tree the other side of the fence was chirping loudly.

'It's only a Redstart,' said Brock.

'It's bigger than I imagined it would be,' exclaimed Tommy Jones looking up. 'The mountain, I mean!'

'They're all big Tommy,' whispered Arwel Owens who was stood alongside.

'Come on…' urged Brock. 'Remember, we are the sons and daughters of miners past and present. Coal dust runs through our veins. Let's see what treasures lie hidden in the storeroom before we enter the mine.'

On the far side of the compound were several disused huts. One had belonged to the mine manager and his foreman. The tool store, shower block and horse stables were nearby. Each building was badly neglected and looked unsafe having been rocked by the explosion underground.

Brock ran across the compound kicking up a cloud of white dust in his wake. Moments later with reckless abandon he disappeared inside. A banging on the glass he invited the others to join him.

'Look at all this stuff...' he enthused, rummaging through wooden chests, cupboards and lockers. 'This hasn't been used in years, but it's still in a good state of repair.' He retrieved an old lamp from a locker. Searching through the drawers of the desk nearby Brock found a box of flint starts. The boys found other lamps, but most were damaged. Dillan located some heavy metal shovels.

'We'll need these if we going to remove the planks over the mine entrance.' He handed out the shovels to each of the boys.

Exiting the store hut the sun was now overhead. Arwel Owens thought that he saw a movement in the trees beyond the fence, but he didn't say anything for fear of being ridiculed. The last time that he thought he saw something odd it had turned out to be a deer

'It's going to be a hot one,' Brock remarked, as he placed his shovel down examining where the wooden planks had been fixed to the edges of the mine entrance.

Looking up at the sun Jaylynn nudged Brianna's arm. 'If the sun is overhead, why do I have goose bumps on my arms?'

Brianna felt her arms feeling the same prickly explosion beneath the skin. 'It's probably only anticipation of what's inside.' She replied.

Jaylynn wasn't happy. She watched as Dillan and Brock inserted the heads of their shovels in the first plank, then heaving hard with all their might they herd the plank give. Like a squealing animal caught in a trap the plank resisted, creaked and groaned. After others inserted their shovels to help the plank finally relented and sprang away. Brock stuck his head through the gap.

'Coal dust, that's all there is.' He said as he pulled his head clear.

They continued removing the planks until the gap was large enough for them to crawl through. Stepping back Scarlett was nervous.

'Maybe, this wasn't such a good idea.' She said holding onto Lizabeth Driscoll. 'I can almost feel the eyes of the ghosts watching us. We should leave the dead alone!'

Brock sighed despondently. 'Oh, come on Scarlett. Today is Monday the twenty-fourth of July, nineteen hundred and five. It's the first day of our summer holidays and we've been planning this adventure for a long time. We've no teacher or parents breathing down our necks. For once let's be reckless and have something to remember this holiday by. All old mines look haunted. It's only because they are so dark inside.'

Jaylynn was on Scarlett's side.

'It's almost six years to the day Brock when the mine claimed the lives of the doomed miners.' Jaylynn declared. 'I'm with Scarlett on this one. We should put back the planks and do something else.'

'What are you looking at?' asked Dillan having noticed that Brianna was reading an inscription, inscribed into a weather dirtied brass plaque.

'It was put here by the mine owners to commemorate the lost men.' She ran her finger over each the names on the plaque. 'We know some of these families Dillan.' Using the spent oxygen from her lungs she breathed out onto the plaque rubbing away the dirt with the cloth of her cuff.

Brianna repeated the process several times until it was clean, at least legible.

Dillan dabbed at one of the names inscribed. 'That was my cousin's eldest brother.' He too gave the plaque an extra hard rub.

'Perhaps we should respect the dead Dillan and leave them to their resting place?'

Brianna could sense the unrest amongst the girls and the younger boys.

Brock however was unperturbed. 'Oh come on... we all know somebody inscribed on the plaque. The same as we know the names chiselled on the headstones in the church cemetery. If we stopped to consider the dead every time we went exploring, we'd never anywhere except the back lanes of the village.'

Despite their trepidation several nodded. Brock was right. The dead had, had their time and now it was their time. The school holiday had only just begun and Dillan had promised that after exploring the entrance to the lift shaft the rest of their adventures would be less daring.

To make life easy for the girl Brock placed the head of his shovel under the end of another plank and pushed as hard as he could. The wooden board sprang away from its housing with the resounding echo of a pistol shot. Smiling at the younger boys he was their hero.

Peering in through the hole created by Brock the long shaft to the lift looked like looking down the inside of a dragon's throat.

'It smells musty, like the leftover ash from the fire the night before!' Somebody said.

'It smells like my older brother's socks when he's been wearing them for several days.' Replied Reece Brynn. Several tittered knowing his brother.

'What happened to the pit ponies?' asked Scarlett.

'I guess that they were sent to other mines,' Dillan responded. 'Or maybe they were retired to live out the rest of their lives amongst the grassy knolls of the valley.'

'Dragons…' exclaimed Tommy Jones. 'What about dragons. Legend says that they live in the mountain?'

Brock who was closest to Tommy punched his arm. 'Myths and legends. Really Jones. You've straw between your ears if you still believe in fairy tales. We left those stories behind at the nursery!'

Tommy came back fast and fierce. *'No… you're wrong!'* His eyes were fixed solely on Brock as he rubbed his arm. 'My dad says that there are flies that can breathe fire as well.'

Brock laughed. 'Your dad means fireflies you numbskull, not dragons. Fireflies look like little flames when there's a lot of them together, but just the same as fairies don't come out from a secret door at the bottom of a tree at night to weave a daisy chain.' He thumbed his thumb sideways. 'The girls do that.'

'So we won't be finding any ugly witches or trolls lurking in the dark then?' asked Arwel Owens.

Brock gave a shake of his head. 'Stay close to me. If any jump out from a crack in the wall, I'll gut them so fast, old Dai Williams will want to give me a job cleaning his fish.' Brock looked over at Tommy. 'That includes dragons!'

With the miners lamps lit they went inside wary of every flicker as the flames from the candles danced on the narrow walls either side of the long passage. Beneath their feet and buried in dust, dirt and rubble was the old coal truck rails. Several times Tommy gasped as the shadow from his lamp produced a dragon's head, quickly disappearing into a dark recess cut into the rock.

At the end of the passage they came to a large chamber where on the far side stood the workings of the lift which had taken both men and beast below the level of the surface. Brock went over to look down the shaft.

Holding onto the supporting wood he lent forward. 'That's a long way down.' He scuffed at a stone with the toe of his boots kicking it down into the abyss. Two, maybe three or four seconds later it landed. 'A bloody long way down.' He announced.

Coming alongside Jaylynn said she thought the darkness below was moving.

'Don't be daft Jones. It's just you and your imagination.'

Standing near to Dillan, Brianna felt the goose pimples creep down her arm from her shoulder blades. *Something don't feel right Dillan,'* she whispered. *'I'm not sure what. I think we should leave. Some of the young ones are getting jittery.'*

'Now won't don't seem right?' asked Brock having come upon them from behind. He was fed up with the persistent whining, knowing that it would ruin the day.

'This being here…' explained Brianna as she cast the light from her lamp around the chamber. 'We should have taken note of the notices on the fence and at the mine entrance.' She showed Brock her arms. 'And I don't goose pimple unless something isn't right.'

Brock rubbed his forearms as an unexpected chill breeze made him feel cold.

'Old mines are always spooky Brianna.'

'No Brock,' she replied, 'I have this weird feeling that we're being watched.'

Brock swept his lamp left and right, behind and forward.

'I don't see anybody other than us!'

'First we enter the confines of the mine works ignoring the warning signs. Secondly, we break down the boards guarding the entrance designed to keep us out and thirdly...' Brianna paused, 'thirdly there is something very wrong inside the mine and I am not talking about ghosts or dragons.'

Brock was about to respond when Brianna raised her hand.

'Before you ridicule me Brock Platt, please hear me out. Some of the others have felt a presence too. Yes, old mines and the deep shafts can be draughty throwing up the unexpected gust of cool air, but this is a disused mine and since the collapse six years ago it has been sealed shut. If the men who went down tom rescue the trapped miners couldn't get through, where did that cooling breeze originate?' Dillan and the others looked on nodding. Brianna talked sense.

For once Brock didn't respond. It wasn't that he didn't have an answer, more that he too could the sense in what she had said.

'Brianna's right...' agreed Dillan. 'The air is coming from down below and not behind us, like it should be!'

Brock pointed. 'You mean the lift shaft?' Dillan raised his eyebrows and agreed. Brock went over and looked down. Nothing had changed, it was still very dark and menacingly uninviting. 'Well we came, we saw and we conquered. I say we go back out. What about going to the river?'

The mutterings that issued forth were unanimous. They turned as a group looking at the entrance which was ablaze with sunshine.

'The river it is…' said Dillan as he stepped forward.

Suddenly from nowhere a gust of fresh air made the candle flame in the lamps dance violently. One of the girls screamed almost dropping her lamp.

'What caused that?' Arwel Owens asked, wondering how the air had gotten in through the glass.

'I don't know,' cried Brianna, *'but let's get out of here!'*

Running towards the entrance the passage was suddenly flooded with a pungent foul-smelling odour. It made some cough.

'That's awful…' said Scarlett, cover her mouth with her hand. 'What is it?'

'It smells like sulphur.'

'I told you…' exclaimed Tommy, 'a dragon lives inside the mountain!'

Dillan did his best to ally Tommy's fears. 'There's no such thing and dragons are myth, nothing else. Come on keep up.'

And then it happened. At first the ground started to tremble beneath their feet followed by fragments of rock falling on both sides and overhead. Small shards, splintered rock made them protect their faces as the intensity of the rock fall continued to grow.

'It's an earthquake!' Brock cried, urging those behind to hurry.

They stopped running when they heard the mountain roar as loose earth, vegetation and rock started to cover the entrance blocking out the sunlight.

'It's not an earthquake,' shouted Dillan. *'It's a landslide. Quick back the way that we've just come. The passage is filling up fast.'*

Within seconds they were trapped.

Back in the lift chamber the smoke from below was choking. Brianna raised a finger and pointed, grabbing Dillan's arm.

'There…' she pointed, 'look!'

Rising and growing in size was a monstrous shadow rising from the lift shaft below.

'What is it Brianna?' asked Jaylynn Jones. 'I don't like this and I'm scared!'

Dillan put a protective arm around Brianna pulling her in close. The others were huddled together. Brock had his knife out at the ready.

'Whatever it is, I'm ready.' He said.

Despite his courage the tension in the air was wound tighter than a bed spring as the younger ones stood behind the three older members of the gang, Dillan, Brianna and Brock. To make matters worse two of the lamps had gone out.

Behind them the rumbling had stopped and the passage was now a quarter full. Jaylynn Jones looked back. *'We've no way out, we trapped,'* she cried.

'Aye, you'd be that missy and much more!'

The voice that emerged from the top of the lift shaft was old and gurgling, raspy. Sitting crossed legged where the shadows had concealed the back of the old lift the creature presented itself.

Defensively Brock stepped forward, his knife pointing at the creature. *'And who the hell are you?'* he asked. *'And where'd you come from?'*

The funny, ugly looking creature with its long strands of unkempt hair, bulbous lips, big round eyes and potbelly, grinned back rolling its tongue covetously across its mouth as it eyed the group. Lying beside the creature was a burnt torch crudely made from twigs and moss. It had been extinguished but was still smoking and small wisps of smoke were rising to the ceiling overhead. Dillan whispered to Brianna. *'That's the sulphur we could smell.'*

The creature remained momentarily silent as his staring eyes went from one to the other of the group, studying them very closely. When he did speak, he spoke only three words in response to Brocks question.

'Hell… young master.'

'Yeah, and I'm the devil in disguise,' replied Brock thrusting his knife even closer.

The creature smiled. 'An interesting interpretation young master and perhaps not as far from the truth as you would expect. As to who I am, well…' he stopped mid-sentence, his eyes coming to rest upon Brianna Roberts. She felt the shiver cut through her body like a sharp sword.

Chapter Two

When the mountain had ceased shaking and the earth beneath his feet had stopped moving about young Gavin David let go of the wire fence that he had been holding to stop himself falling.

Unable to grasp the enormity of what he had just witnessed he stood motionless, his eyes fixed and staring, his mouth open as his mind tried to absorb the facts.

A month shy of eight, it was almost too much to take in. He had seen a large chunk of the mountain come tumbling down and where there had been an entrance was no longer visible, completely gone, swallowed up by rock and earth. He could feel his heart beating fast.

Looking at where there had been wooden shacks and sheds, they too had disappeared.

The last thing that Gavin remembered seeing was the flicker of the lamps a long way down the passage. He heard the mountain roar and somebody scream. He recalled calling out for his cousin Jaylynn moments before the entrance was obliterated. The second time he called her name was no more than a whisper.

'She's gone. I've got to get help!' He said forcing his legs to turn around and run. *'Jaylynn and the others are trapped. They'll need help!'*

Running as fast as his legs would carry him Gavin ignored the wicked stinging nettles and brambles covering the bog as he launched himself over spats of oozing mud. He ran around avoiding an adder that had been sleeping in the undergrowth abruptly woken by the earth moving. In the distance he saw the church spire and chimney tops of the houses. His lungs hurt as he ran, he thought they would burst, but his need to get back was ever the more important.

When the old woman suddenly appeared from behind a tree and grabbed his arm bring an instant halt to his running Gavin struggled to make her let go although she was surprisingly strong for her age.

'Here... leave off,' he cried. 'I've got to go for help, let me go!'

Hearing his explanation the old woman held on ever tighter.

'Stop wriggling damn you. Tell me boy, what did you see?' She had a determined look in her eyes. 'What makes you run so fast back to the village?'

Gavin looked again, he recognised the face.

'You're the woman who lives at the edge of the village. Please lady I must go, it's urgent!'

The woman relaxed her grip, but did not let go.

'You... you're Behildwick Jones,' he stammered. 'You're supposed to be a witch, have a large cauldron and a black cat!'

The sides of her mouth creased into a smile.

'I do have a cat, but no cauldron and I cannot cast spells. My name is Behildwick Jones. Now please young man, tell me who are you and what it was that has scared you half to death back at the mountain?'

Pointing back to where Llandryuid Vale had once prospered Gavin told the woman his name and what he had seen and how his cousin and the others were trapped inside the mountain. Clutching her chest she finally let go of his arm.

'Are you hurt? Gavin asked.

Behildwick Jones gave a shake of her head. 'Only my memories hurt me, Gavin.' She smiled, it was a nice smile. 'You're too young to understand so do not concern yourself. Now go, run like the wind and tell your mother. She will know what to know what to do.'

Gavin was about to leave when she grabbed his wrist. 'I once knew a young girl called Josephine who married and became David. When she was your age, she was good at running too!'

Gavin left. To know his mother when she was his age, the old woman had to be really old. It was strange because she didn't look it.

The moment that Gavin was lost from sight Behildwick Jones turned and faced the top of the mountain. With outstretched arms, she felt the warm tears flow as she cried, crying out.

'Why are you never satisfied?' Her head fell forward in agony. *'Why can you not let others live in peace?'*

Soon the mud flats would be awash with people from the village as they came to help rescue the trapped children. Behildwick Jones wanted to help too but she was afraid that many would blame her for what had taken place. Lowering her arms she wiped her cheeks dry. No amount of magic would help, even if she did know a spell or two.

*****

Gavin David burst through the door of the kitchen, the perspiration running down his face. Gasping for breath his mother came though from the front room.

'Whatever's wrong Gavin?' she asked seeing his perspiration turn to tears. 'Have the older boys been tormenting you again?'

Wiping her hands down the front of her apron she poured him a glass of home-made lemonade making him sit at the table to drink it. Gavin pushed the beaker aside.

'No. The mountain, it blew up!'

Josephine David smiled at her young son and his vivid imagination.

'Is that what scared you. I heard the loud bang too Gavin. You know that sound and that it'll be the miners over at Gwynedd, just using dynamite to explore the rock face. I thought that you'd be used to that by now.'

Gavin swallowed down a mouthful of lemonade to help clear his throat.

'No. Not Gwynedd… I'm talking about Llandryuid Vale!'

Josephine David felt her insides suddenly sink as her eyes opened wide.

'Llandryuid Vale… are you sure Gavin?' She sat down next her young son. 'That old mine was closed down and nobody digs for coal there any longer!'

Gavin nodded slowly but emphatically. 'It was Llandryuid mum, the works beyond the mud flats.'

'You shouldn't have been there, it's dangerous. The bog is riddled with snakes and the mine is haunted.'

Gavin nodded. 'By the fifteen dead miners.'

'That's right.'

'I was following Jaylynn and the others.' Gavin started to cry, the shock coming out at last. *'They're inside mum, and they're trapped!'*

Josephine David felt her insides churn as an imaginary cold dagger pierced her heart.

Taking the hot water from the stove she grabbed Gavin dragging him from the kitchen going to her neighbour next door. Soon word had got around that there were children trapped in the old mine. When news reached the men working at the Mallgwylly mine at Gwynedd work was immediately halted. The pit ponies had wagons attached, filled with tools for digging.

Assembling his workforce Emmelyn Wynn the foreman of Mallgwylly spilt the men into three groups. One hour digging, another moving away the fallen soil and rock, while the third group rested for an hour before returning to take over from the team digging.

A long line of women and children helped where best they could with the older women brewing hot tea and heating soup over a makeshift fire to keep everyone's energy levels up high. Many at the mine had been there six year earlier although none spoke of that day as they kept on digging, shifting and taking a short rest.

With the sun dropping on the horizon the men from Mallgwylly looked at one another. Come the darkness the children from Mud Island would have been inside the mine for almost twelve hours.

'We'll dig and move away the earth until nobody can stand any longer,' said Emmelyn Wynn, his broad shoulders, arms and hands caked in earth, his skin scratched by the sharp stone.

As he expected, there were no replies. Sinking his shovel into the earth once again Emmelyn grinned to himself. He knew that there wasn't a man, women or child who would go home until there was no longer any hope. Even the youngest child had brought along his toy wheelbarrow.

Wiping the sweat from his brow Emmelyn Wynn watched as Owain James, the vicar roll up the sleeves of his shirt before he picked up a pick.

'Acts of God come in all shapes and sizes father, but none as testing as a mountain.' Exclaimed the foreman.

'Do not be so despondent Mr Wynn,' the vicar replied, 'the good lord will send down divine inspiration to help with the dig.'

Emmelyn Wynn, a deeply religious man looked up at the late evening clouds. The night was drawing in faster than expected. 'I don't dispute that Mister James, but did he have to send down so much sod and all in one go!'

Owain James wiped the dirt from the back of his hand. 'The tone of your voice suggests this was not the work of the lord?'

'As far as I know dynamite wasn't invented by God.'

Owain James looked up at the enormity of the landslide.

'You mean this was a deliberate act of sabotage?' His question was no more than a whisper.

'Did you not hear the explosion? We thought it was the mine engineers blasting elsewhere in the valley. There is treachery here vicar, trust me.'

A young man when the last tragedy had befallen the old mine the rescuers had not stopped digging for a week, not until the heavy rains had made digging impossible.

Taking a bible from his pocket, Owain James said a prayer for the children trapped inside the mine.

Adding *Amen* he read the page where the bible had opened. *'The lord is near to the broken hearted and saves the crushed in spirit.'* Owain James felt his head drop low, his despair hanging heavy on his soul.

*****

Hidden between the trees where she could not be seen the lonely woman had been watching all afternoon and into the evening. Having been woken from her midmorning nap Behildwick Jones had recognised the rumble of the mountain.

Making her way through the mudflats she had seen a young boy running towards her. Gavin David had confirmed her worst fears.

. The whispers, children's bedtime stories were true, although none knew it. Many in the village had been scornful of her fantasies. The tales of trogglebytes, the mountain dwellers, and of brave knights who fought to the last to save their king and queen. For centuries she had kept quiet and on this dark, dark night all she could do was watch and grieve.

'The mountain always wins,' she whispered.

Behildwick Jones was about to turn away when she recognised the face of a young boy packing a wheelbarrow with rocks. Gavin David was determined to do his bit and help rescue his cousin. In time the experience would haunt his dreams for a very long time.

Scooping up a handful of dirt she put her hand to her nose, remembering when in more carefree days she had ridden her horse through the fields beyond the castle walls. In some ways nothing had changed. Dropping the dirt she started to cry, not for her memory, but for the children.

Chapter Three

Brianna felt the unease creep up her skin as the creature continued to stare at her. She especially didn't like the way that his tongue went from side to side of his mouth as though tasting her flesh. Sidling around Dillan she stood behind where she wasn't so visible.

Letting out a loud reverberating laugh the creature introduced himself.

'Welcome to my world,' he pulled himself up standing roughly the same height as Brianna and Brock Platt. It was only Dillan who was taller. 'I am Trygor and this here is my mountain.' Pointing down the seemingly bottomless lift shaft, he grinned. 'And that is where I have come from.'

Putting his hand on her hip and keeping her behind him Dillan took a step forward. Intentionally he reached out and helped lower Brock's knife, hoping that the gesture would ease the tension between the two. Trygor acknowledged that it was a sensible move.

'That's better young master.' He was wary of the boy with the knife whose eyes told him different. 'There's no need for hostilities. I only came up from below because I heard a girl scream. I thought that somebody needed my help.'

'Do you live in the mountain alone?' asked Dillan.

'Sometimes my existence is a lonely one young master. Sometimes my responsibilities are great.'

Brock stared at Dillan, it was a strange reply.

Trygor craned his head around the group looking back up the passage leading to the entrance.

"It's a nasty affair when the mountain decides to roar.' He tutted loudly. 'There's a lot of broken mountain inside and it'll take many men at least a week to get through, if the gas don't get you!'

'What gas?' Jaylynn asked.

Trygor smiled at the girl, his manner friendly. 'Why there'll be many gases down here young missy. Most are dangerous, deadly. Some you can see, some you can smell. Some you can't do either. That don't mean that they are any are less the deadlier.' Inhaling hard Trygor demonstrated. 'One minute you are struggling to breath,' he fell to the ground throwing up a small cloud of dust, 'the next you are lying amongst the coal dust wishing that it was all over.'

Brock wasn't taken in so easy by the creature's explanation.

'And you would know this, would you?'

Trygor grinned. 'I've been lucky young master. It's what I've seen happen to others. It's not easy escaping down here, not unless you know where the passages lead you.'

'So there is a way out?' asked Dillan.

Trygor nodded. 'Aye young master, there's always another way out!'

All the while the girls had gathered around Brianna. They also could feel the creature looking at them. With a sigh Trygor tried another approach.

'Look, it would suit both our needs if we could all be friends. The mountain only roars when it's angry.'

Tommy Jones was still convinced, despite Brocks ridicule, that there was a dragon.

'And why is it angry today?' Dillan pursued.

'It gets angry when unwanted visitors come snooping around.' There was a menace to Trygor's reply that none thought friendly. So much for being friends thought Brianna.

'Did you make it angry?' she asked.

Trygor frowned. 'How could I do that missy? I might not look like you, but in many ways we're not unlike one another.'

The thought made Brianna and some of the others shiver. Dillan squeezed her hip for encouragement.

Stepping from behind Dillan, Brianna had suddenly found her courage again.

'And how exactly would that be, may I ask?'

Trygor thought his ploy might work. It pleased him that it had.

'In a time long gone, I had hair as shiny as yours, eyes that were not as dark as the darkest coal and a future to behold, but time and events are unpredictable. You could say that I was forced to live here in the mountain, although not by choice.' He swept his short but strong arms around the inside of the chamber. 'In time the mountain changes you!'

'Have you a mirror?' asked Brock. 'Have you seen yourself lately?'

'What's a mirror?' asked Trygor.

'Something whereby you can see your reflection.' Brianna replied.

Trygor was pleased that she had decided to show herself once again, he liked her. She was more wholesome than some of the others in the group.

Dillan sensed that Trygor wasn't telling them everything.

'You say that you heard a girl scream and yet the mountain roar was so loud. You must have very good hearing?'

Trygor pulled back the hair on both sides of his head to show them his ears. Some of the girls uttered *'urgh'* when they saw his misshapen and dirty ears plus long lobes.

'I hear many things young master. I hear the bats as they sleep, the creatures that live in the coal seams and the cries of a young girl in distress.' He removed his hands letting his hair fall back down covering his ears. 'I hear when *'outsiders'* come trespassing.' He saw Scarlett Moses start to cry.

'There's no need to be afraid little missy. I only came to help. Each one of you is so beautiful compared to an ugly old mountain troll like myself. Beauty is such a rarity.'

Brianna tucked herself behind Dillan once again.

Trygor stepped forward, but stopped seeing Brock raise his knife.

'Spend a week inside the mountain while others come to search for you, and you will look different young master. There are things inside the mountain that need to be considered. The lack of fresh air, running water, no food.' He had noticed their sack of provisions. 'Soon you will begin to question your sanity. Wondering why you came. You will grow suspicious of the others, even the girl who hides behind you. Soon you will change. Your eyes will become dark, accustomed to the lack of light, your hair will grow and you will be wary of every sound.' Trygor turned to face Brock. 'Not even your knife will save you!'

'It would take more than a few weeks to end up short, wrinkly, overweight and hairy.' Brock replied, his insults making some nod. 'You call yourself Trygor. It's an unusual name and you're an unusual mountain troll.'

Picking the fluid sediment from its nasal cavity the troll flicked it aside at the disgust of the girls.

'I'm a trogglebyte,' Trygor replied proudly. 'You must have told the stories about the folk who lived in the mountain.'

Brock shrugged. 'Legends and myths, but that's all they are.'

Trygor laughed. In the lamp light the trogglebytes eyes seemed to glisten all the more brighter.

'And where exactly do you think that the stories originated young master. I am living proof that they are real.'

Tommy Jones eyes opened wide. 'The stories...' he stammered. 'If they're real. Is there a dragon?'

'Aye young master. You heard it roar today. What creature do you think processes the power to bring down the side of a mountain?'

Tommy shook his head. He refused to look at Brock knowing that he had been right all along.

'You tell us that this is your mountain... how is that so?' asked Dillan.

Sitting down crossed leg Trygor placed his hand over the dying embers of the moss torch. Unaffected by the burns that he might receive he crushed the life from the torch.

'A long time ago before any of your oldest relatives were born, I came from a village similar to your own. Men however, powerful men always want more. Eventually their oppression leads to rebellion and fights become battles. The victor takes the spoils for themselves. My people, my family were forced to hide inside the mountain, living under the shadow of the sun.

'They could only hunt at night for fear of being caught or slaughtered during the day. Soon their eyes became accustomed to the darkness, but children's bellies grew big for the want of food. The men had to hunt to survive, to keep everybody inside the mountain alive.

'Without sunlight, the people in the mountain changed. Babies born of their mothers were different. Much smaller, shorter and their eyes were always black. Even young children had wrinkles. Not just old women.

'In time, the men won small battles going out late in the evening. The victories grew in confidence and so did the menfolk. We became known as the mountain trolls, trogglebytes.

'In time, the people inside the mountain found other sources of water. They would steal cattle, crops and pick berries. Soon the children grew and their bellies shrunk to a normal size, but over the centuries the older ones died and soon only the children were left. I am the last of my kind.'

'So are there others, like you, living in other Welsh mountains?' asked Brock.

Trygor nodded. 'Probably, but their numbers would be few. The mountain is a hostile place to live. In time trogglebytes will become the topic of legends again.'

'Was it you who set the fire below, sending the smoke up the lift shaft?' asked Brianna.

Trygor liked the tall girl, she had pluck despite being very wary of him.

'The fire was to cook my breakfast, I thought that it had gone out. Smoke has a bad habit of finding its way along the lower passage and up a shaft when you least expect it.'

Dillan went to look down the lift shaft.

'Did you feel the landslide down there?' He asked. 'When the dragon roared?'

'The mountain often roars young master. I don't always take notice. Today was different because I heard the girl scream.'

There was something, in fact lots of things that Brianna didn't like about the trogglebyte. One was that he always had an answer and another was that his tongue was forever moving around inside his mouth. Trygor had the look of a hungry man. It was one aspect of his character that she didn't try to think about.

Dillan remembered Jaylynn Jones screaming and calling out, but then things started happening too fast for him to worry why. His responsibility had been to get them to safety.

Looking around the inside of the chamber Dillan realised that he had failed.

Squeezing his hand and sensing his angst Brianna wanted Dillan to know that she was there for him.

'We'll find a way, we always do,' she whispered.

Dillan smiled back although he wasn't convinced, they would.

Trygor had heard her whispered words. He admired her faith and courage. Smiling at the anxious faces that were looking his way, he knew different.

Chapter Four

They were trapped and Trygor, the trogglebyte knew it.

Brianna and Dillan, Brock and the others knew it too. It was only the older ones that sensed Trygor knew more about the dragon roaring.

'You say you hunt only at night. Have you been down to the village?' Brianna asked. She watched for any change in his expression. An indication that he was lying.

Rolling his tongue over his lips several times, his eyes remained focused as did his expression. Trygor had quickly recognised that the girl was no fool. And neither were the two older boys.

'Anything that crosses my path.' He replied.

As soon as it had been said, it was Trygor's turn to watch. He didn't respond to whether or not he had visited the village.

'It's mainly small creatures. Field rabbits, mice, voles and earthworms. I like juicy things with meat on them.'

'What about chickens, sheep, goats, pigs and cows?' asked Fabian. He was aware, being a farmer's son that such animals had been disappearing without an explanation. It included the odd dog and cat.

'A trogglebyte moves slowly because our legs are short. Catching larger creatures is difficult.'

He saw the look of suspicion in the boy's eyes. 'I only takes what is necessary young master.'

Dillan hadn't missed the *'our'* in his reply. Neither had Brianna.

Both, including Brock noticed that although dirty the trogglebytes clothes looked to have been fashioned from animal skins. Trygor's was a mix of fox fur and sheep wool, possibly cat.

'It's a long time since I've had anything so young and tender.' He suddenly announced.

'You mean like us?' Scarlett Moses announced. Her stare set hard, demanding a reply.

Trygor feigned the shock as he crossed his hands over his chest.

'Nay missy, not you. I was merely saying that to have something plump and fresh would be most welcoming. I've not had a good hot meal in ages!'

Dillan who had been surprised at Scarlett's insinuation interrupted.

'But, you said that you'd lit the fire to cook your breakfast?'

Trygor had been right in his assumption of the trio. They were sharp besides bright.

'Have you ever swallowed live earth-worms young master, believe me it's not easy and they leave you full of bad wind all day long. Cooking them first not only stops them wriggling about, but the fire makes them bigger in the pot!'

Several of the girls and the younger boys pulled anguished faces, repulsed by the thought of eating earthworms.

Brock went to look back down at the deep shaft. He extended his knife in Trygor's direction just in case.

'Six years ago this very mine suffered another big explosion or dragon's roar as you call it. Fifteen men were trapped behind tonnes of rock. They were never found and yet somehow you managed to find a way to survive. You say you go hunting every night. There has to be another way out of the mountain?'

'Aye, that there is young master. I could show each of you where the mountain opens up again. Where you would see the stars overhead. Trygor would do this because you are his friends!'

Brock narrowed his eyes. He didn't trust the trogglebyte. The look in the mountain trolls eyes were as black as anything he had ever seen. It was difficult knowing what was going through the trolls mind.

A gust of fresh air suddenly exploded into the chamber having emerged from the shaft below. Breathing in deep Trygor spread his arms wide proving that had not been lying.

'I'll go with,' declared Brock. 'The others can stay here. If what you say is true, then I'll come back and get them. I want to make sure that this isn't a trick!'

Trygor contained his anger. He had wanted them all to go down the lift shaft. Thinking fast he nodded.

'Aye young master. I would take the same precaution. The entrance is on the far side of the mountain where the rock never slips.'

Brock felt a strong hand stop him from stepping onto the lift cage. He turned seeing that it belonged to Dillan.

'Wait,' he demanded. He looked at Trygor. 'If you've lived here for so many years alone and you know many of the mountains secrets, including the passage that leads to the outside, why didn't you help the trapped miners escape?'

Trygor had been expecting the question.

'Aye I knew about them young master. I heard their cries, but I couldn't get to them. When the mountain roared that day, it brought down the rock so fast that many were crushed underneath. I could see through where there were small gaps, but the wall of fallen rock was too thick and their fate was already sealed. I did try young master, and my hands bled where I had tried. Soon all were dead. I gave up trying.'

Dillan recalled his older cousin's brother had been one of those lost.

He let go of Brock's arm allowing him to step into the lift cage. The cage rock as the pair steadied themselves for the descent into the darkness below.

Assisted by Reece Brynn and Fabian Jenkins, Dillan released the cage pulley system. Slowly the cage started to drop. The last the group saw of their friend was his white face looking back up at them.

'Do you think he'll be alright?' Lizabeth asked, as the rope continued weaving itself through the huge pulley wheel.

Brianna reached out and held her hand. 'If I'm certain about anything, it's that Brock Platt could fall into the mud flats and still rise as clean as a whistle.' She sent up a silent prayer hoping that it was received.

When the pulley wheel and rope stopped the lift had reached the bottom of the shaft. They heard the echo as timber and metal hit the ground below, but nothing more.

'I should have gone as well,' said Dillan, peering down into the abyss.

'No, you're our leader,' argued Brianna. 'We depend upon you Dillan to make the awkward decisions. Brock can look after himself and remember that he has the knife.'

*****

When the bottom of the lift cage hit the bottom of the shaft tiny coal dust segments made Brock cough and splutter. He felt the trogglebyte step clear of the cage platform and then nothing. All around it was very dark and Brock could barely see his outstretched hand in front of his face.

'*Where are you?*' he called, thrusting his knife left and right. '*Show yourself!*'

What seemed like ages, but was only seconds Trygor spoke. He grabbed Brock's wrist dragging him clear of the cage.

'I only checked went ahead to see that the rock fall had not blocked the passage.'

'Well next time take me with you.' Brock was clearly unamused.

Trygor let go of Brock's wrist. 'I didn't want you having an injury young master. The rocks down here can be extremely sharp and treacherous. Come on follow me, we have a way to go.'

It was hard keeping up with the trogglebyte and Brock could only do so by straining his ears listening for the trolls footfalls. Every so often Trygor stopped running and waited.

'I thought you said trogglebytes couldn't move fast?'

'It's just that I know these passages young master. We've not far to go. Around the next bend and then you'll see!'

Chasing behind Brock could only imagine the fear that must have haunted the lost miners as some lay injured knowing that they would never be rescued. On either side the walls were damp and moss hung from rock ledges. Ahead Brock saw the glow of a light.

'Are we there?' he asked, his hopes rising.

'Almost,' replied Trygor.

Brock ducked low and beneath an arch cut into the rock. When he emerged the other side, he was in a large cave. All around was moss lamps burning brightly.

To the left of him was a fire surrounded by three old women, the ugliest women that he had ever seen. Stepping aside to see his arrival he saw a large cauldron bubbling away above the fire.

Suddenly from deep cracks in the walls of the cave they emerged, coming out in their dozens. Trogglebytes some fat, some lean, none were tall, but each with a hunger set deep in their eyes. Eager to taste his fresh young flesh.

Chapter Five

Sitting high upon a tiered throne made entirely of black stone Trygor had his arms outstretched wide. A gesture of his success.

'Welcome to my inner kingdom young master...' His grin was as wide as his arms showing two lines of blackened and missing teeth.

Trygor's greeting met with the approval of his subjects who were edging towards Brock who was stood with his knife weaving left and right, ahead and behind.

'Keep back,' he warned. *'I'll gut you where you stand!'*

The nearest trogglebytes laughed, including that of their king.

'Don't be shy young master. They just want to look. You must appreciate they are eager to see what I have brought for them.'

Brock's eyes were alight with raging flames only not those of the fire.

'I knew all along that you had been deceiving us.' His reply was tinged with venom.

Looking around he saw that he was surrounded. Trygor stood up, stroking his beard thoughtfully.

'Making the mountain angry comes at a price young master. A forfeit has to be paid. That is how things are done in our kingdom. Look upon it as suppressing the beast, to appease many!'

'One day there'll be another battle and you'll be crushed. All of you!'

Some standing close backed away, his words ringing in their ears.

Trygor thumped the side arm of his throne.

'You and your friends have made the mountain angry. A penitence had to be found to quell the vexation of the beast.' Trygor pointed at Brock. 'You must forfeit your life. It is the only way. A sacrifice must be made to address the balance.'

'The hell I will,' Brock angrily replied. 'Some here will die before I do.'

Trygor threw his hands into the air.

'That as might be the case, but we deal with death in a different way to you young master. We shall dine on your friends as well, all except the tall girl. She will become bride.'

Brock edged himself slowly back warning those near not to tempt fate. When he felt the crunch beneath his feet he stopped and looked down. Crushed underfoot was the remnants of a man's rib cage. He heard laughter as he recognised other bones. Each human.

Suddenly the trogglebytes pushed one another aside until a human passage had been created emerging on the far side of the chamber where a stack of bones was piled high.

Even from where he was stood looking Brock counted fifteen skulls.

'You evil monster!'

'Do you recognise anybody?' Trygor asked, his laughter echoing about the walls of the cave.

Suddenly one of the three ugly women who had been standing next to the cauldron appeared before him. With ease she pushed aside the knife aimed at her chest, prodding and probing as she examined the boy's shoulder. Turning to look up at her king she nodded, her toothy grin lop-sided. Licking her lips to make them moist, she announced to the crowd.

'We need more wood to build the fire!'

Chapter Six

Brock knew that it would not be long before he was overpowered, there were just far too many of the trogglebytes to fight.

With each second that passed Brock wished that he had not been so insistent upon coming into the mountain that morning. His arrogance had almost certainly placed him in a position where death was imminent.

Despite his predicament Brock thought about his friends, Dillan and Brianna, the younger ones and Lizbeth Driscoll. He wished that he had tried that bit harder with her. As a girl she was alright and he would have liked to have walked out with her. Brock envied Brianna and Dillan.

Stalling for time, he yelled above the cries to take him down.

'You're no better than a bunch of cannibals.'

Trygor raised his hand and instantly the crowd ceased jostling.

'That is a strong accusation young master. The roar of the mountain is a sign.'

Brock pointed at Trygor.

'You make the mountain roar, not nature!'

Trygor paced back and forth.

'The falling rock did bury the miners who were lost. We dug hard to help, but in the end our hunger, our efforts needed to be rewarded. We killed the injured pit ponies.'

Brock pointed at the crushed bones beneath his feet. These bones are human!'

'In the end, everybody dies young master. Man or beast.'

Trygor descended the stone steps coming close to where Brock had his knife thrust out at the king of the mountain's chest.

'It was your ancestors that made us this way. We did not ask to live in the mountain. We were forced to live where the sun never shines. Our bones are chilled with the merciless winds that blow in the winter.

'Our children want to go outside, to play and be like other children they see playing in the village, but look at them. How they look is not their doing. *Outsiders* would make fun of them, but our children are fierce warriors, some even hunters. We cannot take that risk.

'We steal to live. You have mothers to cook food. We have three old hags. Our meat is old, tough. The vegetables are wilting. You dare to call us cannibals. Now there are lots of dogs in the village and farms. We only kill outsiders when we are desperate.' Trygor walked around Brock touching his clothes as he went. 'Your cloth is soft unlike our furs. You changed your destiny when you entered the mine today. We are simply taking back what is owed to us.'

'Who owes you what?' Brock had no idea as to what Trygor was talking about. 'Mining for coal goes back as far as the Romans. The seams don't belong to you.'

'We steal to eat, we do not interfere with your homes. We expect you to do the same here inside the mountain.'

Suddenly it dawned on Brock.

'It was you who brought the side of the mountain down and it was you who trapped the miners. The dynamite, you stole dynamite from the miners store.'

Trygor chuckled to himself.

'We used dynamite today, but with the lost miners we let the gas take its toll. We let them get to the coal seam before we threw a flaming torch their way. The explosion killed some, the falling rock did the rest.'

'Soon the rescuers will dig their way through and they'll find my friends. At least they'll survive.'

Trygor sat down on the bottom step leading up to the throne.

'Like the time before, six years ago, there will be another explosion only from within. The fate of your friends is sealed like your own.'

Accepting that fighting would be useless Brock placed the knife through his belt. 'Was there a way out?' he asked.

Trygor pointed to three deep cracks embedded into the far wall. 'Yes. It's knowing which one to take.'

The three old woman who did the cooking stepped out from between the ranks of the trogglebytes.

Trygor gave the order for the men to release the *stink damp gas* at the bottom of the lift shaft. 'Save the oldest girl. If she dies, you will die as well!'

Three trogglebytes ran past Brock disappearing under the stone arch carrying metal canisters under their arms.

Trygor ordered that more wood be added to the fire wanting the water to be boiling. Eager to begin the three old hags began tearing at Brocks shirt. Sensing that a meal was coming young children helped throwing sticks and broken branches beneath the cauldron.

'Shall we bleed him first?' the ugliest of the three hags.

Enthusiastic cries echoed around the chamber as Trygor nodded.

Placing the blade of a sharp knife over Brock's left shoulder the ugly hag sliced through the skin drawing a line down to his chest, cutting through muscle and sinew. Brock's cry was muffled, refusing to show the trogglebytes that he was a coward. Held on either side by strong hands he saw the children coming close, their long wispy tongues licking the blood that had run seeped from the wound.

Pushing the children aside, the old hag was satisfied. 'He is ripe and ready for the pot.' She exclaimed.

'Then let the feast begin.' Roared Trygor to the delight of the packed cave.

Brock closed his eyes knowing the end was nigh.

'Leave him be… or these children die, here and now!'

Trygor was the first to turn towards the stone arch where he saw the tall girl and one of the younger boy's holding two of the trogglebyte children, at their throats were sharp shards of stone.

Trygor raised his hand at the three old hags. 'Let fair hair go.'

Brianna whispered something in the ear of one of the children. The child pointed at one of the old women.

'This is a surprise young missy,' said Trygor. He was pleased to see that she was unharmed. 'I had sent three men to help your group. Did you not come across them?'

With her free hand Brianna pointed at Brock.

'Is this what you call helping?'

Tommy Jones raised the shaft of a pickaxe above his head for all to see. Gasps of surprise rang out amongst the watching crowd. *They're taking a long rest at the moment,'* he said.

Trygor had seriously underestimated the *outsider* children. They were more resourceful than the miners. All around anxious faces waited for their king to make a decision.

'You are but a child yourself missy. You would not hurt another, would you?'

Brianna however was in no mood to play games. Like Brock she had come to realise their fate the moment that the rock face had blocked the entrance. Neither had she believed anything that Trygor had told them.

'What have I got to lose king of the mountain, only my life?'

Trygor wanted to tell her that he proposed in making Brianna his bride, although he guessed now wasn't the right time to let her know his plan. 'Sooner or later young missy, we all die, including the children that you now hold.'

There were various shouts of protest in the cave, but Trygor silenced the protestors pointing indiscriminately into the crowd. The mood in the cave had changed. A rebellion now would be disastrous. He turned to the three old hags.

'Release the fair-haired boy,' I said.

Reluctantly they did as he commanded. Snatching back his knife he considered cutting the old hag who had cut him.

'One day,' he warned, 'mark my words you ugly old crone. I will tie you to a spit and roast you alive!' Weak from the loss of blood he staggered across to where Tommy and Brianna stood waiting. Pulling the trogglebyte children back through and under the stone arch Brianna had one last message for Trygor.

'We will release the children unharmed when we reach the safety of the lift cage. If you or any trogglebyte follow us, although I don't want to, I will harm them. If I am to die this day, it will be with my friends and not here with you.'

Trygor sat on his throne.

'I agree.'

'Know this trogglebyte king, you are nothing except a foul loathsome toad. You are the essence of evil, but the shadows will come for one day. When that day comes, good will conquer evil.'

Holding onto her child Brianna, Tommy helping Brock, let his captive go. Seconds later all four disappeared into the darkness. Others went to rush the arch, but Trygor ordered them to stay.

'Be calm…' he advised, *'they are going nowhere.'*

'But they have Riaragon!'

Trygor sighed. 'Yes, but the girl will not harm Riaragon. Her soul is not tainted, poisoned like that of ours. I will send others to release the gas. We will collect their lifeless bodies and still have our feast. We have waited this long. We can wait another couple of hours.'

A short while later young Riaragon ran back into the chamber and into the arms of her father. She was unharmed and happy to be back. Once again Trygor had been proved right. The rebellion which had been simmering had been averted, but he had lost a bride. His mood was dark.

*****

Together they placed Brock against the cage side where he had some support. Tugging hard on the hoisting line Brianna knelt alongside. Instantly the bottom of the cage started to lift away. Brianna was surprised not to hear the sound of running feet coming their way.

'Why didn't they come?' asked Tommy.

'They don't need to Tommy,' replied Brock. He coughed. 'They know we're trapped. They've already laid extra explosives along the passage that hasn't been affected. The first sign of the rescuers and the dragon will roar once again.'

Tommy wanted to smile, but now was not the time. 'You were incredibly brave,' he said, tearing a sleeve from his shirt to help cover Brock's wound.

'Incredibly stupid. I thought this would be the adventure to top all adventures. All I've done Tommy is got us killed.'

Brianna lent over and kissed them both. 'Without you Brock, life would have been boring. In the half-light from the lamps above she smiled at Tommy. 'I could not have faced Trygor alone. For someone so young, you have the heart of a knight facing a dragon.'

From above they heard Lizabeth Driscoll call out that she could see them ascending the shaft.

'Thank you, both of you. I would surely have died had you not come to rescue me.'

Brock handed Tommy the knife.

'You had best look after this. I'm in no fit state to fight anybody now.'

Brock suddenly slumped sideways, but Brianna caught him before his head hit the floor of the lift cage. Resting upon her shoulder Brock laughed. It was weak, but a laugh all the same.

'Did you see me naked?' he asked.

Brianna felt the smile crease her face. 'No more than when we were young and we would go swimming in the river.'

'Thanks Brianna. Promise me that if anything happens to me, you will tell Lizabeth that I thought she was nice.'

Brianna held on tight to Brock as the lift came to a sudden halt with a jerk.

'Tell her yourself…' she whispered, 'we're here now.'

Surprisingly Lizabeth was the first to get to Brock as other willing hands helped to make him comfortable. Seeing that Lizabeth wouldn't leave his side, Brianna knew that it was a message that didn't need delivering.

She went to Dillan pulling him to one side.

'Trygor, he's the trogglebyte king. It was he who caused the mountain to collapse today. They did it on purpose!'

Dillan looked over to where Lizabeth was attending to Brock.

'How do you know?'

'Tommy and I heard everything that was said inside the trogglebyte cave. We were fortunate that two young children happened to come along the passage when they did.'

'Why?'

'I had no idea or plan how to get Brock free.'

They was aware of Reece Brynn standing close by.

'Then why haven't they come chasing after you?'

'Because they have no reason to hurry.' Brianna replied. 'They won't get through in time, will they?' The question was aimed at Dillan.

'I don't think so.'

Taking Brocks knife Dillan cut through the rope looped through the pulley. They watched it fall along with the lift cage. When it landed it did so with an almighty crash reverberating along the passage below. They thought that they heard a cry from the bottom of the shaft, but they wasn't sure.

'Well that's one less trogglebyte that we have to worry about.'

Dillan knelt down beside Brock resting his hand gently on his friends shoulder. Lizabeth was still at Brock's side.

'At last the bleeding has stopped.' Instead there was a horrible, long mauve line where the knife had cut through the skin.

'The gas Dillan… watch out for the gas!'

Brock was very weak and his warning came as no more than a whisper.

Lizbeth looked at Dillan. 'Do you think he'll be alright?' she asked.

Dillan nodded. 'Yes. Brock is as strong as an oxen. He'll be alright once he's had a rest.'

'What did he mean about the gas?'

Dillan shrugged. 'He's confused as well. Look after him Lizabeth.' He went over to where Brianna had been talking with the younger ones.

'The gas, is it true?'

'Yes. On our way to find Brock Tommy dealt with the trogglebytes who had been sent by Trygor to activate three canisters of stink damp gas. Trygor intends to kill us all Dillan.' She didn't mention the cooking cauldron.

'The black gas. That's what my dad calls it.' Some of the others had started to distribute the food. He thought it was a good idea that they ate before anything happened. 'Come on, we might as well join the others.'

*****

At the bottom of the lift shaft Trygor peered up through the gloom at the roof of the chamber high above. Next to where he stood were a solitary pair of legs protruding from under the broken cage.

'Cut them,' he ordered, 'and take them back. The old hags will have something to cook and feed the children.'

'What about the *outsider's*?' one dared to ask.

'We'll release the gas and later go around the other way. They've not found the secret passage.'

Trygor wondered why. Sons and daughters of miners they should have known that there was always an escape route out.

Using rusty swords, relics left over from their days fighting the castle soldiers they hacked at the dead trogglebytes legs. Only the king received a burial fit for his position. Other's served the needs of others. Nothing was left to rot or go to waste.

*****

Coming to sit beside Lizbeth, Brianna handed over a piece of cake. Brock was sleeping.

'He likes you. Did you know that?'

Lizbeth blushed. 'I like him too. Odd really because we've always been at one another since we were young.' She gently replaced a loose strand of his hair that was covering his eyelid.

'Maybe if you told Brock when he wakes how you feel, will make him feel better again.'

Lizabeth looked across where Dillan was sitting amongst the younger boys.

'And what about you. Will you tell Dillan?' she asked.

Brianna managed a smile. 'I think he knows already.'

Lying on an improvised pillow made of the sack Brock was drifting in and out of consciousness. He was no longer inside the mountain but swimming and splashing Lizbeth. The sun was high in the sky and the day was warm and bright. Mumbling in his dream he told her that everything would be okay.

Brianna went back to join Dillan.

'Brock's not too good, is he?' Dillan asked.

'No. He's lost a lot of blood. He's quite weak. If we don't get him to a doctor, I fear that he might die.'

'I think we're all going to die.'

Brianna lay her head on Dillan's shoulder ignoring the sniggers from the others.

'This was supposed to have been our best adventure. We should never have come here Dillan. I would have liked to see the sun one more time!' She kissed his cheek. *'At least, if I am to die here today, I will be with you when I do.'*

Brianna closed her eyes, tasting the gas as it began to fill the chamber.

'Cor, who brought the rotten eggs,' exclaimed one of the younger boys.

Dillan held her tight as Brianna rested her head against his chest hearing the beat of his heart. A heart that belonged to her. Opening her eyes one more time she saw that Lizabeth was already sleeping alongside Brock, the cake untouched.

When she closed her eyes, she felt Dillan kiss her.

A long way away she heard a woman crying although it wasn't her mother.

One by one the children of Mud Island went to sleep overcome by the gas. They had grown up together, bickered at one another and played hard. Never to grow old it seemed right they died together.

*****

Clutching her chest Behildwick Jones let her tears fall. It was over and soon they would be at peace.

Passing beyond the mudflats to where her cottage sat waiting on the edge of the village, the torment raging within her was as painful as ever. Again the mountain had roared loud and been victorious.

Once again, the evil immorality of Trygor had destroyed what didn't belong to him. One day she vowed, she would avenge the spirits of the dead.

Chapter Seven

Going Forward - A hundred years

Amanda Brodrick removed the birthday cards from her bedroom window sill gathering them together. Counting the number she had one more than the year before. Tying a length of silk ribbon around the bundle she lifted the lid of the wooden box where she kept her keepsakes finding a suitable space where they would be safe and looked at, perhaps another day in the future.

Lying on top of the bed covers she felt relaxed placing her hands behind her head. Where exactly had the last year disappeared too, she wondered. The jump from thirteen to fourteen had flown by without much happening.

'I hope the next is more interesting,' she said aloud, not getting a reply back.

Beside the bed lay a leather book which her mother and father had got as an extra present. It was to help record her most treasured moments, her thoughts and dreams. Inside the cover her mother had inscribed *'Remember Amanda that with age comes responsibility. A knowing that you belong.'*

Lying on her bed she read the inscription. It had seemed a strange thing to say.

'One day, I'll prove my dreams did come true.' It was no more than a mumble to herself, but Amanda had big ambitions. She wanted to be a somebody in the world. A scientist, an astronaut, maybe a lawyer. As yet she was undecided. Closing the cover of the book she swung her right knee over her left resting them on the wall as high as she could get them up.

With her head slung back, her eyes viewing the room upside down she caught sight of the ballet dress that had been kept on the hook, hanging in a protective bag for when she would wear it next. At the moment her interests were elsewhere.

She put the book down on her bedside cabinet then with the agility of a gymnast cat she swung herself around and over onto the floor behind landing with both feet level. No, she had no desire to be a gymnast. Too much training and consuming of her free time. At least with ballet the lessons had only happened once a week. In the sunlight coming in through the bedroom window she noticed that over washing had made the tutu fade in places.

Her thoughts were interrupted by the sound of two boys fighting one another on the grass verge outside of her bedroom window. Their presence was heralded by a cry from the bathroom along the landing.

'Amanda... your suitors have arrived.'

She shook her head from side to side with abject disdain. It was bad enough that Jonathon Evans and Mostyn Owens were always fighting, but why she wondered, did they always have to perform under the ever-watchful eye of her older sister. Emma always took great delight in pointing out that they were only outside, fighting to prove who had the right to ask her younger sister out. It was intensely irritating and embarrassing. They were both acting like morons.

With a sigh Amanda remembered Jonathon escorting her home the last Friday night. Under the porch light he had asked if he could kiss her goodnight. The request, having arrived out of the blue had taken her by surprise.

When it was over, she had quickly said goodnight and gone inside. Wiping her mouth with the back of her forearm she thought she had been attacked by a wet cod. Sensing a shiver embrace her body, it was an experience that she didn't wish to repeat, least not with Jonathon.

Having discussed the experience with Emma at breakfast, her older sister had laughed telling Amanda that there was more to come. Watching the two boys from her bedroom window Amanda could shake her head. The next time she kissed anybody, she would control the moment.

Bursting into her bedroom Emma was dressed only in her underwear.

'Up until now those idiots have only been interested in football or seeing who could climb the tallest tree.'

Emma disappeared as swiftly as she had arrived. Checking herself in the mirror Amanda could see the changes. She decided to go downstairs knowing the next to shout would be her mother.

With her hand on the catch of the front door she gave one last flick of her hair to make sure that it didn't have that just brushed look. With her collar up and her sleeves pulled up to her elbows, she looked every inch the tomboy. What they saw in her she didn't know. Whatever it was she did wet the end of her fingertip, pasting down her eyebrows. It was always best to look somewhat feminine. Another of Emma's useful tips.

Leaning over the landing bannister Emma had been watching.

'Remember. Don't wiggle your arse, it's like a red rag to a horny bull.'

Amanda turned up the palms of both hands.

'What can I do about it Emm? If I'm nice to one, the other gets jealous. It's already becoming so boring!'

Emma replied laughing.

'Tell them somebody else has asked you out, only don't admit who. You'll see their ego deflate faster than a balloon going pop.'

Amanda looked up at her sister whose breasts were struggling to stay inside her bra. Given another three years, maybe four she would be like Emma. Pulling the door shut she walked over to where they were still rolling about the grass verge. Like a pair of grinning hyenas they stopped sensing somebody was watching.

'Can't you find anything more beneficial with which to use your energy?' she asked. The sarcasm in her voice telling each of them that she was less than amused.

'It's what we do…' replied Mostyn Owens. His reply sounded feeble.

Amanda looked at Jonathon Evans expecting better.

'It's what boys our age do.' His response was even more irritating.

With a shake of her head Amanda turned away walking towards the end of the road. Instantly they were up and dusting themselves down.

'Well if you're coming, you'd best make it quick,' she advised. 'The others will think we've ducked out of going.'

Standing, watching from the landing Mary Brodrick watched her daughter take a firm stand putting both boys straight. The last year had seen changes physically and emotionally. She smiled seeing Amanda walk on ahead with Jonathon and Mostyn running behind like a pair of dogs jostling over a juicy bone.

'If she does entertain one or the other, I hope they're prepared...' announced Emma emerging from the bathroom. 'Amanda certainly knows her own mind.'

Going next to the bedroom Mary Brodrick was surprised to find it unusually tidy. It was so unlike Amanda to keep anything organised. When she next looked her younger daughter was flanked on either side.

Mary Brodrick remembered when Emma had been Amanda's age. She recalled the anxiety, the tears and growing pains. She laughed to herself remembering how her father had lost weight worrying about his eldest daughter. He was about to lose some more.

Picking up a framed photo that Amanda treasured Mary Brodrick struggled to keep her tears back. *Amanda, you look so much like Brianna.* Mary Brodrick said a silent prayer. *'Please, wherever you are, watch over your young niece. She possesses your wild spirit for adventure.'*

Turning the corner at the end of the road the trio disappeared from sight.

Mary Brodrick knew that Amanda and the others in the gang would gather outside of St Mary's church. The grey stone edifice seemed to offer a place not just for worship, but solace. Many in the village went there often to pray for the souls lost inside the mountain.

'At last...' bellowed Daisy Gethall. 'Come on we've been here ages.'

'Hush your noise Daisy,' Mostyn responded. 'The church bell hasn't chimed nine yet.'

Daisy Gethall noticed the telling stains on the knees of their jeans.

'Still fighting over Amanda. It's a wonder she's not sick of you two!'

Amanda didn't look at either boy. A year older, she had a position and reputation to uphold.

'Well, are we going to Joneses farm or not?' she asked.

'Tell me, why are we going?' Daisy was keen to know. She looked up at the sun. 'It's a long walk and it's going to be a warm day.'

'We're going mutton head,' replied Mostyn, 'because we agreed to go.'

Daisy looped her arm through Larissa Joyce's crooked elbow.

'Huh, the only reason you and Jonathon agreed was because the place is abandoned and you're both eager to sniff about and see what you can find. I doubt there'd be anything there that would interest me or Larissa.'

Mostyn had been ready for another of Daisy's sudden change of heart.

'Fair enough. Stay here and babysit one another. If we do find anything worth having, we won't cut you in with what it makes at the market!'

Looking at one another Daisy and Larissa agreed to go along. Mostyn knew they would. Daisy however, had only half rolled over with the idea.

'You've a very short memory Mostyn. I thought that you as much as any here would remember the original gang that ruled Mud Island. Your great uncle was one of the children lost when the side of the mountain slipped down. Visiting old Joneses farm could be deemed as disrespectful. You know the feeling throughout the village and that the dead should be left to rest in peace!'

Larissa nodded, adding her support.

'I don't fancy touching anything there. It could be cursed.'

Mostyn wasn't so quick to respond. Larissa spoke sense and some of the others were in agreement with her sentiment.

'Maybe we should leave it…?' Jonathon said, his spirit for adventure diminishing. His own family had also lost somebody to the mountain.

In the porch of the church portraits of the twelve children had been etched into a brass plate, their memory never be forgotten. On the opposite side were the names of the lost miners.

'If we don't go now,' said Mostyn emphatically, 'the bulldozers will obliterate the place and they'll be nothing left except rubble. If need be I'll go by myself.

Like most decisions where the group was undecided, they flipped a coin, heads they go and tails they stay away. It landed on the ground heads up.

'Alright…' agreed Daisy reluctantly. 'But I'm not going inside the farmhouse, only the barn.'

*****

During the past hundred years very few changes had taken place and surprisingly the mountain had not roared since the ten children had been lost inside. The only significant change were the arrival of new generations.

Owain James had tried hard to bring together his parish following the tragedy that had befallen Finlostydd, but some wounds ran too deep that even religion could not heal. In nineteen hundred and seven he took a missionary post in Africa, never to be heard of since.

In the intervening years several vicars had filled his shoes and the present occupant was one Oswald John James. A nephew of the original Owain James, twice removed. He had arrived at Finlostydd hoping to continue his great uncle's work and restore the family name.

There had been only one other noticeable event and that concerned the disappearance of Angharad Jones, the wife of the late Benjamin Jones. Together they had managed the farm.

There were many rumours regarding her sudden disappearance, only having gone into the back garden late one evening to fetch in the washing she had vanished without so much as a trace, the only evidence was an upturned washing basket and a clean bedsheet that lay on the grass.

Benjamin had been a cantankerous husband and farmer, known for his strange ways. Some believed that he had murdered Angharad and disposed of her body. Where exactly nobody knew as farms had many places of opportunity, deep wells, cess pits, pig sty's and even the dark wood nearby.

Finlostydd like many other villages had had its fair share of heartache and pain, and many of the residents believed in ghosts. When Benjamin Jones was found dead by the visiting doctor who had gone to check on his patient's health, some of the residents said that at last the devil had come to claim his soul. It was a story that Daisy Gethall.

'Somebody has already been here!' Exclaimed Larissa Joyce rattling loose the chain connecting the gate to the wooden post.

'Don't be soft...' Mostyn barked back. 'Old Jonesy never kept anything locked down, except his wallet.' There was a titter throughout the group as Larissa glared back. 'He was always losing the odd cow, horse, sheep, pig, goat and chickens.'

Mostyn recoiled the chain and pushed aside the gate. It was heavier than he had expected it to be. It hit a large boulder embedded into the ground, the gate shaking until it settled.

Daisy wasn't impressed.

'Are you purposely trying to wake the dead Owens?' she asked.

Chapter Eight

I n places the paint was peeling from timber panels and the wallpaper also had objected to being abandoned for so long. Discoloured with age it had begun peeling at the corners. Everywhere looked dishevelled, unloved and unkempt.

In the kitchen the aga had long since warmed the pipes running through the farmhouse. Hung over the fireplace a solitary framed photograph showed the wedding day of Angharad and Benjamin Jones. Some say it was only day that he was caught smiling. Hanging at an angle Jonathon respectfully put it straight.

'It's not as if they'd care.' Mostyn Owens remarked.

'We're invading their home. It's the least I can do.' Replied Jonathon.

Mostyn huffed as he continued rifling through the drawers of an old sideboard. He found a collection of spent tobacco tins, unpaid bills and odds and ends, but nothing of value. Disgruntled he went upstairs followed by Albert Jones.

The stairs creaked under their weight, a reminder that they also had seen better days. Jonathon decided to stay on the ground floor. Looking around the kitchen he was surprised at how spartan it all looked. Angharad had gotten by with the minimum of luxury or modern appliances to help.

Moving around, he set things right blowing away the dust and cobwebs where necessary. Daisy's trepidation ringing in his thoughts. Jonathon didn't believe in ghosts, had never seen any, but the farm didn't feel right. Not only cold, but unwelcoming. Maybe old Jonesy hadn't quite departed.

Hearing Mostyn and Albert scurry from room-to-room overhead Jonathon decided to go back outside where the warm sunshine enveloped his face. He closed his eyes absorbing its heat.

Walking through the long grass he found a wooden peg. The washing line had been snapped in the middle and hung down limply at either pole, a reminder of the day Angharad had disappeared. He felt a cold shiver pass through his shoulders. Looking towards the wood nearby Jonathon wondered if her spirit wandered between the trees.

'We didn't come to snoop,' he whispered, 'just to satisfy our curiosity.'

'They put people like you away, who talk to themselves.'

He recognised the sound of Amanda Brodrick's voice. She came and stood alongside.

'This place is creepy.'

'I was just thinking the same. I was looking at the wood wondering if old Benjamin did bury his wife there.'

'I had the same thought a few minutes ago. It's odd, but it feels cold here despite the warmth in the sun.' She showed him her bare arms that were pimpled in goose bump mounds. 'Where's Mostyn?'

Jonathon thumbed towards the upstairs bedrooms.

'Ransacking the wardrobes I expect.'

Amanda shook her head empathically. 'Does he have any scruples?'

'No.'

They watched Albert Jones climb up onto the abandoned tractor letting his imagination plough the field, farm side of the wood.

Suddenly there was an almighty loud crash from inside the farmhouse. Amanda and Jonathon ran back in through the open kitchen door. They found a bed leg sticking through the ceiling above.

'What the hell are you doing up there?' Jonathon bellowed.

'Nothing...' Mostyn snapped back. He was annoyed having to explain anything to a boy not much older than himself. 'The floor joists must be rotten through. Albert was standing on the bed to look on top of the wardrobe, when the floor gave way.'

'We came to look around, not destroy the place.'

Mostyn muttered something realising that Amanda was in the floor below. *'Sorry!'*

'I suggest you come down,' Jonathon advised. 'And tread carefully. I saw woodworm on the newel post. The place might be riddled with it.'

They heard Mostyn and Albert move onto the landing.

Suddenly there was a cry from the barn. It was calling for Jonathon to come and look.

'Now what,' said Amanda.

'I don't know, but we'd best go look.'

They ran to the barn where they saw Amy Hardwick up in the hayloft. She was the only one not to have a family connection with any of the lost children from nineteen hundred and five, having moved into the village two years prior.

'What's wrong, who cried out?' Jonathon asked.

Amy pointed. 'At the back of the barn... Abbie's found a trapdoor.'

Jonathon stood beside Amanda as they stared at the faces of the others. Embedded into the floor of the barn were two large wooden doors. Each had a metal ring attached. Jonathon tried to lift one of the doors, but despite his best efforts the door hardly budged.

'Old Benjamin must have possessed colossal strength to have managed it by himself.' A hand reached down to help. 'Thanks Albert, where's Mostyn?' Jonathon asked.

'He's still looking around the farmhouse. I left him going down into the cellar. He reckons Jonesy must have had a shotgun knocking around.'

'It makes sense. He would have needed something to deter the foxes from his chickens.' Jonathon sensed a foreboding with Mostyn's insistence on finding at least one thing that he could take home and make their going to the farm worthwhile. 'He's changed...' he said. 'We used to be good friends, but more recently, he has a different agenda to me!'

Albert agreed.

'He always seems so angry nowadays. Mostyn could snap your head off as much as look at you. It was he who ordered me to climb on the bed and look at the top of the wardrobe.'

Together they tried to lift the door, but it still wouldn't relent. They let go of the two inches that they had succeed in lifting it. It fell back down into the metal frame with a resounding crash sending up a cloud of dust and old straw heads.

'*Urgh...*' exclaimed Larissa Joyce spitting out small husks from her mouth. *'Get that awful smell... it's like a dead animal is under the door!'*

Amanda laid her hand over Jonathon's arm.

'Maybe we should leave the trapdoor alone. Something doesn't feel right. I can feel it in my bones.'

They watched Amy Hardwick climb down from the hayloft.

'There's definitely something strange about this farm Jonathon,' Amy said. She pointed up at the hayloft. 'There are some dead carcasses up there. It's difficult to say what, but they look like dogs and cats.'

Katlin Morgan, related to Reece Brynn put a hand to her mouth. 'We lost our cat a year ago. It went out one night to chase field mice and never came back home.'

'Blimey, what'd you swallow a poetry book over the weekend?' asked Albert smiling at Larissa.

Mostyn suddenly appeared empty handed. He looked down at the trapdoors. 'What's down there?' he asked.

'Nothing,' replied Amanda. 'We were about to leave.'

Mostyn detected an urgency in her tone. Something told him that she wasn't telling the truth.

'You've no idea, have you?'

Jonathon gave a shake of his head.

'The doors are stuck fast. They've probably not been opened in ages.'

Amanda helped Jonathon stand.

'Come on, let's get out of here. This whole place is creepy!'

Rummaging around a pile of old farm tools Mostyn found a long metal shaft that looked as if it had once been attached to a plough.

'This'll do,' he said.

He inserted the narrow end through the iron ring and asked Albert to help. Others joined Jonathon in lending their weight to the shaft. Slowly the door started to rise.

'Bloody hell,' said Mostyn, 'this is heavy.'

The door fell back down, but they gave it their all with another try. This time the hinged door gave up the challenge. They managed to get it open as another cloud of obnoxious gas invaded the inside of the barn.

'Quick, somebody put the head of a spade under the door near the hinge,' ordered Mostyn. Daisy Gethall did the honours. They left the end of the shaft inserted through the iron ring.

Mostyn hid his nose in the crook of his elbow.

'Christ, did something die down there.' He peered into the darkness. 'Maybe, it's old Angharad!'

'That's not funny and it's in extremely bad taste.'

For the second time that morning Mostyn Owens apologised to Amanda.

He took another look.

'There's a metal ladder attached to the hinged wall. It's too dark to see how far it drop down.'

Abbie Maddox suddenly screamed. It made them all jump. She was pointing at the darkness.

'I saw them.'

'Saw what?' asked Amanda.

Abbie took a step back.

'Horrible looking eyes. They were big and looking at us.'

Mostyn laughed out loud. 'It's the bogeyman.' He shook his hands, pacing back and forth like an Egyptian mummy.

'I've seen a shaft like this before,' said Albert.

'Where?' asked Jonathon.

'When I accompanied my dad to Sedge Henderson's farm. He's got one similar only he uses the underground pit to store his sacks of potatoes. It's not as deep or dark as this one!'

This time it was Daisy who let forth a piercing scream.

'Quick, close the trapdoor, there is something down there!'

Jonathon, Mostyn and Albert looked. Suddenly a pair of eyes appeared, emerging from the darkness. They were as Abbie had described, big and staring. There was also a tongue, longer than normal and it was licking bulbous lips.

'Be quick,' came the cry from behind. *'Somebody remove the spade and close that door. Hurry.'*

Damian was closest. He yanked hard and the spade head came away. The heavy door crashed back into the metal surround. They heard an agonised cry from beneath the door then nothing. As a group they turned to see an old woman blocking their exit.

'I know you,' said Amanda, 'you're the lady who lives in the cottage at the edge of the village.'

'Do as I say and drag that old cart over here and put it over the trap door. You really have no idea what evil lives at the bottom of that shaft.'

The boys did as she asked. When the heavy wheels rolled into place, covering both doors their unexpected guest released a long sigh of relief.

'What the hell was that thing?' Mostyn asked.

'A trogglebyte.'

'What's that?' asked Daisy.

The old woman stared at the one at a time. It was incredible they were so like the other group.

'That my dear, is a creature from your worst nightmare.'

'That accounts for that awful smell,' said Mostyn screwing up his nose. He was surprised to see the old woman look so alarmed. He watched as she took a step back.

Suddenly the air inside the barn seemed to grow colder.

'Cor, it's like a bloody fridge in here!'

'Please, come forward children…' said the old woman. 'It has been a long time since you last saw the light of day!'

There were gasps all round as ten others stepped from the shadows in the barn. Slowly they became whole again losing their transparency.

'They're ghosts,' Daisy whispered. She felt her jaw fall and her eyes open wide.

'Yes, they are my dear,' replied the old woman, 'only these ghosts you know.'

Amanda Brodrick tried but the tears started to fall. Looking directly at the oldest girl she recognised the face from the photograph in her bedroom.

'You're Brianna… Brianna Roberts. We're related.' She slipped her hand into Jonathon's needing to feel his strength flow through her.

Brianna Roberts smiled back. She had her hand looped through the arm of the boy standing next to her.

'And you are Amanda. I have been watching you grow. You possess some of my spirit.' She looked at the hay cart covering the trap doors, nodding her approval at the old woman. 'That was a wise move. There were more trogglebytes coming up the ladder. We should all leave here as soon as possible.'

Behildwick Jones agreed.

'Come let's make haste, this place is not where we should be right now. If you follow me, we can go somewhere much safer.'

They followed Behildwick Jones down the drive of the farm leaving the gate pushed shut, not that they would ever return. Some places were never meant to be visited. Walking alongside one another, ghost and living established a comfortable bond.

'It's so good to see the sun again,' said Brock Platt. Happily walking alongside him was Lizabeth Driscoll.

Chapter Nine

Amanda Brodrick had been dead set against the boys opening the trapdoor in the old barn, but once the deed had been done there could be no going back.

Walking alongside Brianna Roberts the pair had talk incessantly, girlie things ignoring the difference of a hundred years, styles, fashion and technology. Some things never changed and for teenage girls talking about boys was always interesting. The one subject that they avoided was how Brianna and her friends had died at the hands of Trygor and the trogglebytes.

Walking a short way behind Behildwick Jones had overheard their conversation. Watching them walk and talk, it reminded her of when she had been that age and she too had talked about boys, one in particular, a teenager who would eventually become a lieutenant in her father's royal guard.

Screwed to the front gate was the name *'Bluebell'*, an apt name as many of the flowers adorned the front garden either side of the path.

When Behildwick Jones unlocked the door inviting them in Amanda Brodrick grabbed Mostyn Owens arm.

'Don't you dare mention anything about her being a witch or owning a black cat. If you do, I will never talk to you again… I mean it!'

'Well the cottage looks normal.' It was all he said going inside.

Taking in a deep breath Brianna held onto Dillan's hand.

'Will we ever be free of the mountain,' she whispered.

'One day,' Dillan replied. 'I have a feeling that this old lady can help.'

Surprisingly the front parlour was spacious enough, although the ghosts didn't need a lot of room. Sensing their unease Behildwick Jones opened the conversation. She saw the boy looking at the miniature cauldron beside the fire.

'I hope you never see a real one!'

There were nods all round.

'So now you know who I am. I have lived for longer than you know and watched children being born, growing and die. Some were good friends. Some of my friends belonged to your own families.'

'How comes you have not introduced yourself to us before?' asked Larissa Joyce. She shuffled over in her chair giving Amy Hardwick more room.

'I wanted to my dear, but I couldn't. It was necessary to keep everyone of you safe.'

She noticed the frowns and looks of confusion.

'Long ago, long when others also believed that I was a witch, I lived here with my cat where I too was confused and alone. Today brought back bad memories, but I felt compelled to help.'

'How?' asked Amanda.

'When I saw you pass my cottage heading for the farm, the feeling of dread was like a cold sword passing through my heart.' She swept her hand around the room encompassing all present. 'I think that by now you believe in ghosts. I do. Today, one came to see me in my sleep. I was told that you were walking into danger.'

Some of the girls shivered remembering when the eyes had appeared beneath the trapdoor.

'A very long time ago I had an encounter with an evil, despicable trogglebyte who lives in the mountain.'

'Brock Platt pulled his knife from his belt. 'You mean he's still alive.'

Behildwick Jones nodded. 'Yes, I am sorry to say.'

'One day,' muttered Brock. The other's agreed.

Behildwick Jones continued.

'For centuries the trogglebyte king has tried, but fortunately been unsuccessful in his efforts to find me.'

'Why?' asked Jaylynn Jones.

'Because I killed Trybulloc, his father, and the former king of the mountain before Trygor sat himself upon the throne.'

The children couldn't believe that the old lady sat before them could do anything so brave. She was able to read their thoughts and the expressions on their faces.

'Let me tell you a story and perhaps then you will understand.'

They jostled, shuffled and settled themselves ready for her to begin.

'A very long time ago I known as Oyddiss, born a royal princess. King Felman, the king was my mother and Queen Erikka, my beautiful mother.

'The land surrounding the mountain and the valley below was known as the quarter kingdom of Mynyddium. Long before I was born, the land was divided into four kingdoms, shared equally amongst four kings. .

'Beyond the castle walls the villagers were always restless and there was often skirmishes between the soldiers guarding the castle and the men in the village. One particular village known as Troggle, the men and women were particularly stubborn and rebellious. They earned the name trogglebytes.

'At night, they would go to other villages stealing chickens and sheep. Eventually my father and the elders of the villages attacked joined forces. They forced the trogglebytes into the mountain caves. At the time it seemed a suitable place for them to dwell as their hearts were dark and as black as pitch.

'Like you, I was a spirited teenager your age. I had my own horse and each day I would go riding to the wood and alongside the mountain. My mother was concerned that I took risks.

'The older I got the more the trogglebytes resentment grew. They continued their night raids at times killing a villager who happened to cross their path. Least we think that is what happened because people besides cattle would simply disappear.'

'Like Angharad Jones,' said Mostyn.

Behildwick Jones agreed with a nod. There was no smile attached.

'For a whole week, mostly at night they tried to breach the defences of the castle, crossing the moat and scaling the high walls, but our soldiers were some of the best trained through the land. I know this because I was friendly with a handsome young lieutenant.'

She see Amanda Brodrick nudge Brianna Roberts arm. The pair passed a knowing smile to one another.

'We would meet late in the evening under the orchard trees inside the castle gardens. One summer evening I walked around and beneath the trees coming across Castilleon who I found unconscious. After a struggle I was taken by force by a band of trogglebytes before other guards arrived to help.

'Inside the mountain it was extremely dank, dark and very inhospitable. Inside the mountain I met the most evil king ever, Trybulloc. He was big and brutish to his people. He had one son Trygor. I soon learnt that kidnapping me had but one reason and that was to destroy my father and make him pay for the trogglebytes hardship.

'When word was received by my parents, it near broke their hearts. Something else I didn't know was that Trybulloc planned to make me his bride. He said he would kill my parents, including Castilleon and destroy the castle. With my hands emotionally tied, I saw no way to escape the mountain. To save the lives of many, I agreed.'

'Noooo,' cried Lizabeth Driscoll. Brock put a comforting arm about her shoulders.

'I had no choice. Three toothless old crones dressed me in a cloak made from dead bats wings and on my head was placed a crown of braided ivy. Made ready for the wedding ceremony, I was taken to the great chamber where they gather for their meals and other events. Gathered on either side for the wedding ceremony I saw dishevelled men, women and children, who were to become my subjects. What was unnerving was that they all had eyes as dark as coal. Some licked their lips as I walked on by. I felt a great pity for the women and children, but not the men.

'Long had it been known throughout the quarter kingdom that Trybulloc had a fierce temper. He would rule his subjects using both cunning and trickery. I never did not find out how many wives he had taken before my own ceremony, or indeed *how many had died through his cruelty. With Trygor amongst the crowd, one at least had borne him a son. As evil and ugly as his father.*

'*What I didn't know was that before the ceremony Trybulloc had his men attack the castle. They had used the cover of the muddy stretch of land to the side of the valley, which you children know as Mud Island. Back then the island was a treacherous and unforgiving place, full of dangerous reptiles and bogs. During the attack King Felman was killed and my mother taken prisoner. Castilleon's life I believe was saved that because he was out searching for me. Many living in the village believe that Mud Island is haunted by the ghosts of those killed in the attack.*

'*With Trybulloc waiting atop of his throne stone I climbed the steps with a dread in my heart. At his side was one of the old crones. In one hand she had a long-bladed knife and the other a garland of raven's feathers. Trybulloc had on a similar cloak and his crown.*

'*Trybulloc grabbed my hand and the old crone draped the cloak over our wrists. Spouting a strange incantation, the old crone gently sliced the blade of the knife across Trybulloc's hand creating a small cut, she grabbed at my hand to do the same, but there was no way that she was cutting me. With my free hand I lapped her hard and grabbed the knife from her hand, the shock making her fall down the stone steps.*

'*Trybulloc and all gathered were momentarily shocked by my attack. He forgot about the knife I was holding, that was until I plunged it deep into his chest. With an agonised cry Trybulloc fell from the throne stone into the arms of his son.*'

'How did you escape?' asked Daisy Gethall fisting the air, pleased that girl power still ruled.

Jeffrey Brett

'I ran as fast as I could to the back of the chamber where there were three cracks in the chamber walls. I'd heard some talking the day before and that one of the passages led to a secret entrance.'

Brock looked across the room at Brianna Roberts and Dillan Evans. It was the promise of a way out of the mountain that had made him go with Trygor.

'I chose the passage on the right of the three. I didn't realise that I still had the knife in my hand. Stumbling along as best I could, I could hear the cries and shouts, above them all was Trygor. His cry was baying for my blood.

'Eventually, I'm not sure how long precisely, but I reached an entrance. Outside the moon was out and the sky was full of stars. I never thought I would ever see another night sky nor day of sunshine. Running down what looked like a goat track I tripped and fell down rolling through the long grass. I didn't stop falling and tumbling over until a clump of bushes a long way down the mountain halted my descent. By this time I was almost at the bottom.

'I saw a group of trogglebytes appear at the secret entrance armed with swords and torches, but hiding behind the bushes I could not be seen. I was surprised when they turned away, disappearing back inside. I would not have envied them their fate. Trygor's temper was as bad as his dead father's.

'Using the stars to guide me I made my way back to the castle arriving just after daylight. To my horror the castle was a burnt-out shell. There was nothing left of my parents bedchamber except a charred corpse, my father. I could not find my mother. I did find a dying soldier who told me what had taken place.'

'What about Castilleon?' asked Abbie Maddox. 'Had he not returned to the castle?'

'No. Hearing that my father had been killed and my mother kidnapped, Castilleon went straight to the mountain to rescue her. Many blamed my tryst with the dashing young lieutenant for the downfall of the castle.'

'But you weren't to blame or know that the trogglebytes had already laid siege to the castle and left Castilleon unconscious in the castle garden.' All eyes fell upon Albert Jones.

Behildwick Jones smiled back.

'Thank you, but guilt is not any easy emotion to forget. I still remember the faces of the dead, even now.' She lowered her head and those closest through that she wiped away a tear.

'Everything changed that day. Trygor's only quest was to hunt me down and make me pay for what I had done to his father. I was found wandering the kingdom and ended up in Finlostydd. I was taken in by a kindly widow who looked after me. It was she who gave me the name Behildwick Wick. She cut and dyed my hair with leaf sap. For a while I resembled one of the old crones back in the mountain, but it would have fooled many. She told everybody that I was a niece who had come tom stay. When she died, I carried on living in her cottage. I've been at Bluebells ever since.'

'And Castilleon never came looking for you again?' Daisy bent forward waiting for a response.

'No. The last I saw he was unconscious in the garden. I can only imagine that he too was captured by the trogglebytes. They would have surely killed him being of the king's own royal guard.'

'From that night forward Trygor has been searching everywhere for me perhaps now you understand why I could not approach or talk with any you until today.'

Mostyn was curious. 'What made you come to the farm today?'

'The mountain had already claimed so many lives and I could no longer standby and have it claim any more innocent souls. The farm however hides a deadly secret and by lifting the door to the deep shaft in the barn, you have unwittingly released a terror that has lain dormant for several centuries.'

'How old are you exactly?'

Sitting opposite Amanda glared across at Mostyn.

'I don't honestly know.' Behildwick Jones, shrugged. 'Several hundred years at least.'

Ignoring Mostyn Amanda wanted to know. 'Is there anything that we can do to help?'

'Live long and prosper would please me the most.'

'And you believe that Trygor is still alive?' This time it was Dillan who asked.

'Immortality Dillan.' She held up her hand. 'Oh, I know each of your names.'

'Wow…' said Daisy. 'Amazing.'

Her response made some laugh.

'Immortality to answer your question. Long ago the mountain had a spring that was believed to have prolonged life. The waters were given to the king and his family so that there was always an heir to rule. Trybulloc also knew of the spring and so would Trygor.'

'Do you have any friends?'

Behildwick Jones gave a shake of her head.

'One or two, but so many of my friends are buried in the gardens surrounding St. Mary's Church.'

'Does anybody living know that you're a princess?'

Behildwick Jones smiled.

'Only my best friend. She agrees with me that Princess Behildwick doesn't sound quite right... does it?' she asked.

'By rights... you are the queen of Mynyddium. The heir to the quarter kingdom.' Everyone looked at Scarlett Moses. Some nodded, she was right.

'I understand that we have only one queen ruling now. Elizabeth, a nice name and that all four kingdoms' belong to her. Destiny is a fickle journey Scarlett and at times without mercy. Maybe it is better that I stay plain old Behildwick Jones. It's safer for me.'

'We could tell the police,' said Albert, 'they'd get a search party together and hunt old Trygor down.'

Several laughed including Behildwick Jones.

'It's a thoughtful and nice idea Albert, but there are dark forces at work here.'

'Did you ever find out what happened to your mother?' Amanda's voice was no more than a hush.

'Over the years I have heard many different stories. Some say that her being taken as part of a fairy tale, but that is only because those telling were drunk. I met a traveller passing by one day who told that he she had been killed along with a young soldier. Both had been captured by a king named Trygor. It was all that he could tell before he went on his way.'

'But she might still be alive if she drunk the spring water?'

'That is true, but cut down by steel is one of the ways that you can die. It has something to do with the metallic imbalance. Both elements originating from the earth. Good and bad, if you see what I mean.'

'No, what do you mean?' asked Albert.

'The spring water was pure. The metal in the sword was fashioned to kill.'

'Oh,' said Albert. 'Now I understand.'

The ghosts of the lost children of mud island, the original gang, had been relatively quiet having listened to Behildwick Jones and her amazing tale. They too had a story to tell of their own, a story very few knew about. Brianna Roberts suddenly got up and walked over to where Behildwick Jones was sat next to the fire. She took the princesses hand in her own.

'The traveller did not lie. Your mother was captured the night that you escaped. She did live on for a number of years under the tyranny of Trygor until such time when she made her escape only she picked the middle passage. She died peacefully through natural causes. The trogglebytes found her but she had already passed into spirit.'

Behildwick Jones nodded very slowly. 'She chose her time and place, not Trygor. That pleases me to hear that.' She did not mention the time up until her death.

'Have you spoken to her?'

'Yes,' Brianna replied. 'We would cross paths occasionally. She was accompanied by Castilleon.'

Behildwick Jones held her hands to her chest.

'I have always though that he must have died. Hearing that he has, is no easier a release from my burden.'

'He remains as loyal as ever.'

Behildwick Jones took a hanky from the pocket of her dress to wipe dry her eyes.

'I am so sorry,' she apologised. It has just been a long time waiting to hear of their fate.'

Mostyn suddenly fisted the air in front of him.

'Well, take it from me princess or Behildwick Jones. What you did to the king of the mountain took a great deal of courage and you're well wicked in my book!'

Behildwick Jones looked at him, the surprise and confusion showing in her eyes. Amanda quickly intervened.

'It's not what you think. *'Well wicked'* is a compliment in modern terminology. It's slang meaning you're cool. Admired and Mostyn thinks highly of you!'

Behildwick Jones was still a little confused although bemused.

'I was wicked killing another Mostyn and I do suffer the cold winters, but I am happy to hear that we could be friends.'

Another fist in the air presented with a *'rock on.'*

Amanda scrunched up her nose alongside Behildwick Jones. 'Don't bother. It's another compliment.'

Looking around the room, it was the first time in centuries that Behildwick Jones had been with so many. It was good to hear them speak, hear their laughter, even Mostyn's odd sayings.

'So what happens now?' Jonathon asked.

It was a good question and invoked a number of options.

'Kill Trygor seems to be a priority and halt the evil from spreading any further.' They looked at Tommy Jones, but his face was set serious.

'Well, it would bring his reign of terror to an end and the princess could live out the rest of her life in peace.'

'It was the first time also for a very, very long time that Behildwick Jones had been referred to as a princess.

'That would not be easy.' It was Brock Platt who responded first. 'Trygor may look like a stunted unkempt oaf, but remember that he is no fool. With eyes as cold and black as coal there is no telling what he is thinking or has planned. Older and wiser to do battle would be like sailing a small boat through a tempest.'

Behildwick Jones agreed.

'Brock is right. Trygor is an unpredictable monster. If anything needs to be resolved with the king of the mountain, it should I who delivers the final blow. Call it family honour.' She noticed the look of disappointment on the young teenagers face. 'You are still very young and have your whole life ahead of you Mostyn. You should not be thinking of committing such atrocities. Killing takes a strong stomach and how many years pass, the memory remains as fresh as a spring breeze.'

'But the trogglebyte in the barn, I saw it look your way. Will it not go back and tell Trygor?'

'He probably picked up your scent as well Behildwick...' Brianna sighed.

'All the more reason that I should keep you safe.' She paused, before resuming with a new thought. 'Perhaps the time has come for me to leave the village and remove the risk.'

There were lots of shakes of the head.

'Where will you go?' Amanda asked.

'Somewhere that I have never been before. Somewhere that I feel is part of my destiny and somewhere I must visit before I do die.'

'Then we should come with you.' Announced Amanda. 'Given that we are young and inexperienced is not an excuse. Our eyes and wars are sharp and Jonathon and Mostyn are good fighters. I can vouch for that.' They both lowered their heads in shame.

Even the ghosts agreed that Behildwick Jones needed protecting.

'The journey could be long and perilous!' She hoped it would dissuade them, but she had not accounted for their spirit of adventure.

'It'll prove our worth,' said Mostyn. He stood, looking at Jonathon. 'Are you in or chickening out?'

'You betcha I am.'

Behildwick Jones took it that it meant yes.

Chapter Ten

When Iskard had seen the trapdoor coming down upon him, he had quickly put up his arm to fend off the descending impact, but the weight of the door was great and it had thrown him from the ladder.

Tumbling through the darkness to the ground below Iskard knew that it had been a mistake to have not taken a foot hold. He crashed onto the rocky surface hearing the breaking of bones, his bones. His cry echoed through the passages. He lay in dread knowing that when help came, it would be the end.

Casting his eye over the badly injured trogglebyte Trygor had little sympathy.

'What was you doing opening the trapdoor without my authority?' he asked.

'I was hungry Trygor, I thought I could catch rabbits and bring some back for the pot.'

There was no telling what Trygor was thinking his coal black eyes looking up, then back down at the injured trogglebyte.

'So what made you fall?'

'There were children in the barn. New children and...' Iskard hesitated.

'Go on,' said Trygor, the suspicion hanging in his tone.

'And a scent my king.'

Trygor paced the floor of the shaft.

'A scent. One we would recognise?'

'Yes, my king. It was her scent.'

'And you didn't think to come and tell me. Instead you concerned yourself with rabbits.'

'I was going to come,' Iskard's voice was trembling, 'but she ordered the trapdoor to be closed. The boys must have jumped on it, making it shut quickly. It hit my head and shoulder making me topple from the ladder. I think I've broken my legs and both my arms. Help me please Trygor!'

To make sure that Iskard was telling the truth Trygor placed his foot onto the injured trogglebytes leg. His scream made Trygor and the others cover their ears.

'Are you sure it was Oyddiss?'

'Yes, my king. It was her scent.'

Trygor took the knife from his belt flicking the tip to his lips. 'So she lives. It has been a long time Iskard. A long wait.'

'Yes, my king. If it had not been for my injuries, I would have come and found you straight away.'

Trygor knelt down beside Iskard.

'You have done well. I can already feel her presence.'

Iskard was about to smile when the blade fell swiftly and plunged into his chest. Instantly the cloak of death fell over his eyes.

Trygor stood up.

'One of you climb the ladder and see if she is still there. The rest of you take this fool back to the old crones. Have them strip him of his clothes and prepare his body for the pot. He deserved to die.'

Trygor was annoyed. Instantly they did as ordered. Iskard should have easily fought off the children and taken the princess hostage. He kicked the lifeless body, his anger raging inside. Once again fate had favoured the princess. Soon however he felt the tide of change would favour him.

When the trogglebyte who had climbed the ladder returned to say that the trapdoors would not budge because something heavy had been placed upon them Trygor kicked Iskard again only harder.

'You ignorant fool, now we will have to find another way to obtain food. Your greed has cost the lives of many. Get him out of my sight. The next time I see Iskard I want it to be on my evening dinner plate!'

Sitting upon his stone throne Trygor's mood was black. He watched the three old crones stir the large cauldron.

'Tell me Marigold. How old are you?' he asked.

The old crone stopped stirring, her eyes full of concern and dread. Rubbing her chin with her knees knocking beneath her long dress she calculated how old.

'When we laid your dear father to rest I must have been about a hundred and perhaps a good bit more. It's hard to tell.' Her wispy tongue licked over what broken teeth she had left in her head. Looking at the other two women she wondered if Trygor would ask them the same question. Pushing out the side of her cheek with her tongue she was still trying to fathom out how old. 'With another five decades gone and nine before that and you being younger than me by at least twelve hands, I reckon I am a century and four decades, give or take a day here and there.'

Trygor rolled his eyes.

'How is it then that the three of you have survived so long? By my reckoning you should all be dead?'

'Berries from the finklespot bush.' Marigold replied.

Trygor studied each of them hard. Their craggy faces were lined, pitted with blemishes of ingrained coal dust. Their eyes as black as his own. They were thin and yet they filled their stomachs long before a lot of the others. He had never liked the taste of finklespot berries. His silence was worrying. He stood, restless and pondering over what to do next.

'When you've finished stirring, add more wood to the fire its cold in here today and I want a hot meal for once. Not the slurry you serve on my plate.'

Marigold replied cautiously. 'If we had fresh meat my king, we could provide a meal appropriate for your royal taste buds. Perhaps something young, fresh and tender, hopefully plump would be ideal.' She looked at Trygor's expanding waist.

'Soon, everything will change. We will fill our bellies with hot meat and fresh vegetables every day. Change is coming!'

The three old crones decided not to push Trygor as to how.

As they continued stirring the trogglebytes began emerging from their own hiding places, the smell of cooked flesh filling the air with the promise of food.

'Is that all you think about, filling your stomachs,' he growled angrily.

'The princess,' said a woman at the back with a young child clinging to her leg. 'Rumour was that Iskard saw her this morning?'

'Who is that speaks?' Trygor demanded.

Heads and eyes turned towards the back of the chamber where a young female trogglebyte stood stroking the hair of a young girl. Suddenly Trygor smiled. He remembered when she had been a girl, but she was no longer and now she was a woman. She was also attractive, more attractive than the others.

'I did my king. I have a plan.' She moved forward unafraid. 'A plan that I believe will work.'

Trygor sat back down on his throne.

'You are Selantra, if my memory serves me right.' He gestured for her to come forward.

Giving the young girl to another woman Selantra approached the steps of the throne stone.

'You have an excellent memory my king.'

Trygor admired her bravery. Few would dare to speak out of turn.

'The light is poor in the chamber today and yet your beauty shines in my weary eyes like that of a full moon.' Selantra blushed. Behind her there were hushed gasps from the older women, much wiser women.

'I know of a young girl who lives in the village of the outsiders who regularly goes to visit her grandmother. She takes with her a young goat. A plump and healthy young animal. We could take both girl and her goat, holding the girl for ransom in exchange for the princess. The goat we could cook.'

Trygor's face suddenly creased into a wide smile.

'You speak with confidence for one so young and yet your plan is devilishly simple as well. Come Selantra, come sit beside me and let us discuss the finer details of your brilliant plan.'

Selantra sat beside Trygor as the old crones filled empty plates from the cooking pot. Up close the young woman was even more striking and especially for a trogglebyte. Her eyes mirrored a keen and intelligent mind, not dissimilar to his own. Trygor saw a union coming.

'You have wisdom beyond your years Selantra.' Trygor watched a woman place two plates of food at his feet, bow then descend the throne steps. 'How would you like to benefit greatly from possessing such dexterity?' he asked.

'In what way my king?' Selantra replied. She fluttered eyelids playing a dangerous game that was not considered safe by the older woman who watched, who knew different. He tapped the arm of the throne that she occupied.

'It fits you well my young maiden. How would you like to make it a permanent feature?'

Selantra edged back although only slightly, not enough to alarm Trygor or annoy him. He smiled again, he liked the way that she thought through a proposal, not rushing in headfirst, but working through the options.

Selantra however, hadn't thought her plan would go this far. Suddenly her plan had taken on a different twist. She continued to smile seeking a way to wriggle her way out of the proposal.

'Surely my king there are much better-looking woman with more promise than I amongst your subjects. Women with more experience.'

It sounded weak and Selantra knew it. It had been a dangerous game to play and suddenly it had all backfired on her. She also recognised the look in Trygor's eyes knowing what he really wanted. Inside her chest her heart was beating fast, but for the wrong reasons. Suddenly Trygor stood up to address the chamber.

'A proposal of marriage has been discussed and I am proud to announce that Selantra will become my bride.' He turned to where the three old crones were standing around the cauldron their raspy tongues picking out the grizzle from their gums. 'Arrange for a bridal costume to be made as soon as possible.'

The older women amongst the crowd saw Selantra's head drop

'She played a dangerous game and lost,' whispered one.

Trygor stood with his arms raised triumphantly, the disappointment from Iskard momentarily forgotten. Selantra watched as he pulled up the cloth attempting to cover the bulbous stomach. He was unshaven and his hair was like a hedgehog caught out in the rain. Grabbing a hand he pulled her to her feet.

'Soon we will have change. You should all thank your new queen.'

The applause was enthusiastic and cheers echoed loudly around the chamber. Not necessarily for their new queen, but the prospect of change. Long had they lived like animals and eaten scraps. It was time that they lived like the *outsiders* did.

Trygor sat Selantra back down.

'Bear me children, girls preferably and you will be well rewarded.'

Selantra sat in silence, stunned at how quickly he was securing his future.

'Your father is the stone mason, is that right?'

'Yes,' she acknowledged nodding.

'I will see them and get their approval. It must be done the old-fashioned way.'

Selantra knew that neither her father nor mother would dare defy the king's wishes.

'I will give them a life of luxury. Your father can lay down his hammer and chisel, and your mother can sew instead of clean.'

Selantra knew that there was always an ulterior motive in his thinking. Nobody had ever been given nothing to do. Accepting her fate, she did have the fight left inside her to ask a question.

'And what of the princess my king. If the plan was to succeed. What would be my position then?'

Trygor wiped the grease away with the back of his hand from the sides of his mouth.

'Like her mother, Oyddiss would serve my chamber and become a slave. You should not trouble your pretty head with such trivial concerns my queen. Now eat what is on your plate and then go with the old crones. Let them measure you for your wedding gown.'

Trygor watched the young trogglebyte maiden descended the throne stone.

He grinned as he looked around at the empty plates. Little did they realise that their meal had been courtesy of the unfortunate Iskard. Soon with his belly full he decided it was time to take a nap and later decide who was to visit the village.

Taking a long hard look at his reflection in the polished stone mirror Trygor admired himself. He considered that he had aged well. As yet there was no blisters to mark his skin, unlike that of his father. He pushed a bone comb through his tangled web of hair finding the odd insect. None escaped as he popped them into his mouth. The one's that were too chewy he spat out and crushed underfoot.

'Soon father,' he muttered, 'I will avenge your death and the princess will live here in chains.'

Blowing the dust from the top of a dark green glass jar he anointed his mouth with the liquid. It was clear and cold, as crisp as the mountain stream from where it had been collected.

He was swilling the last of the bottle around his decaying teeth when there was a knock at his chamber door. He recognised Marigold's voice having agreed to her entrance.

'Has Selantra said anything whilst she was being measured?' he asked.

'No more than what the others before her have said my king.' Marigold grinned. 'There is always trepidation before a wedding. It's only nerves, nothing more!'

Marigold was glad of her age and that she was ugly too. Trygor only ever selected the young trogglebyte maidens to lay in his bed. Marriages never lasted long and some had died in childbirth. Other wives had just simply, mysteriously disappeared.

Her bony hands cast a shower of black dead flower petals over the top cover of the king's bed. Without uttering another word she bowed and retreated from his chamber leaving Trygor to his thoughts and nap.

She returned to where the other two crones had already began sewing together a wedding cloak embroidering into the black feathers a garland of ivy. Later that night Marigold would sneak out and pick berries from the finklespot bush.

Chapter Eleven

The question had often been raised by many in Finlostydd. Just where and when did the old woman in the cottage at the edge of the village appear. Nobody living seemed to know.

She kept herself to herself. She rarely ventured out and she had few friends. It was a mystery that had kept Behildwick Jones safe for years and the trogglebytes guessing.

But like all secrets, one way or another, eventually the whispers of truth blew in with the change in the wind and change was coming.

Centuries back Behildwick Jones without her knowing had escaped the mountain unwittingly leaving her mother behind. Since finding out the truth, the thought of her mother being at the mercy of Trygor had left her restless.

That night with *devils wolfbane petals* scattered on each of the window cills and door mats she lay on her bed knowing that the deadly pollen would kill anybody or anything who dare enter or touch it.

Dark nights were full of imaginary shadows, owls hooting to one another and the odd bat as it flew across the rooftops. Trogglebytes hated, could not abide the smell of *wolfbane* and to touch it was deadly. Long ago she had realised who it was, who was stealing the sheep, pigs, goats and chickens, but to have told anybody would have meant revealing her secret.

Lying her head gently on her pillow Behildwick Jones invited her mother into her thoughts. Sometimes it worked, other times it was a failure. The times that it did work she had an imaginary conversation, like when she had been a teenager and they wandered the castle garden arm in arm.

Without realising sleep had her drift into an unconscious slumber. It had been a long, eventful day and unexpected. With the curtains pulled she did not notice the shadows outside creeping past her window.

The next morning the sun was high in the sky and glowing brightly. The birds were singing in the branches of the trees outside and with an invigorating stretch Behildwick had no memory of her dream. Slipping into a dressing gown and slippers she was on her way to the kitchen to fill the kettle where there was a knock at the door. It was hardly likely to be a trogglebyte as they only went stealing under the cover of darkness. Pulling open the door Behildwick was surprised to see Amanda Brodrick and Daisy Gethall standing on her doorstep.

'Daisy slept over at mine last night,' Amanda said by way of greeting. 'Although neither of us could sleep. Yesterday started out terrifying, but ended exciting!'

She ushered them inside quickly.

'Your young minds should be thinking of other things.'

'We had to come, to make sure that you're alright.'

Behildwick laughed.

'That is very kind of you both, but girls I have survived for centuries and mostly alone. The older you become, the wiser you become.'

She had hardly time to complete the sentence when there was another knock at the door. This time it was Jonathon, Mostyn and Albert standing under her porch and on her doorstep.

'You might as well come in too,' she said. 'The other two are already in the parlour.'

The boys nodded to the girls.

'Where's Amy, Larissa and the others?' asked Albert, before taking a seat opposite.

Daisy used her fingers to count them down. 'Amy's got one of her migraines. Larissa had to go the Ashwestony to see her auntie. Annabelle thinks she has the mumps and Katelin has been grounded for visiting old Jonesy's farm.'

'Okay, but what about Abbie?'

'I think she got spooked.'

'And I don't blame her,' announced Behildwick. 'Who would like tea and toast?'

They each put up their hands.

Behildwick was relieved. Five from eleven was less to worry about. Ten minutes later she returned from the kitchen armed with hot tea, buttered toast and jam. She sat in her favourite chair beside the fireplace.

'I am grateful that you felt it necessary to check that I was alright, but I assure you that I have survived worse.'

Mostyn let forth a barely inaudible whistle. 'I don't know. Yesterday was spooky.'

She was pleased to see that it had affected the young teenage boy so. She had just picked up her teacup and saucer when there was another knock at the door. Taking the fire poker with her she went to see who.

Moments later she returned accompanied by an elderly woman.

'Grandma,' cried Amanda. 'What are you doing here?'

Eira Pryce scoffed. 'More to the point, what got you out of bed so early young girl?'

'We couldn't sleep grandma.'

'Then we have something in common my girl.' Eira Pryce replied.

Behildwick fetched another cup and saucer.

'You sleep like a log, what kept you awake?'

'The shadows outside.'

Behildwick felt herself sink in her chair. Eira Pryce sipped her tea.

'Something's happened... hasn't it? Trygor, he knows about you, doesn't he?'

Behildwick nodded.

'Then we need to hide you somewhere safe. He won't stop until he's found you.'

Amanda Brodrick sat open mouthed listening to her grandmother talk about the mountain king. 'You know about the trogglebytes grandma?'

Eira Pryce pushed her granddaughters jaw up.

'Behildwick and I have been friends for a very long time. Of course I know.'

'What you don't know Eira is that they went to Benjamin Jones farm yesterday where they opened the trapdoor to the deep shaft.'

They heard Eira Pryce's cup rattle on the saucer.

'No wonder I saw shadows creeping about the garden last night. It wasn't just my imagination.'

'We're going on a journey grandma,' Amanda suddenly broadcast. 'We going to make sure that the princess stays safe.'

Looking over the top of her cup Eira Pryce raised her eyebrows at her friend. 'Is this true?' she asked.

'Maybe you can tell them how dangerous such an adventure would be.'

Eira Pryce looked at her young, spirited granddaughter.

'And where precisely are you going?'

'We don't know yet…' Albert butted in, 'but we're ready for the fight ahead!'

Behildwick Jones raised both her hands in the air. 'Do you see what I mean?'

Eira Pryce looked around the room at the faces staring back at her. They were full of youth, confidence and would not be dissuaded. Most of all she looked at her granddaughter, as spirited as she had been at Amanda's age.

'Was it not you, who said to me, to conquer without fear, is to have won the battle before arriving.'

'That was different,' argued Behildwick. 'I was young and headstrong. I had soldiers guarding me.'

'You had Castilleon and yet they managed to sneak into the castle, render him unconscious and kidnap you. These children have the heart of a lion pride and the spirit of adventure to see them through anything thrown their way.'

Behildwick dropped her hands in despair.

'At times you can be so infuriating.' She finished the last of her tea. 'And infuriatingly right!'

'Does that mean that we can tag along?' asked Mostyn.

'I guess it does,' agreed Behildwick. 'What will your parents say?'

'That we should enjoy our camping trip.'

Eira Pryce shook her head. Her granddaughter was also sharp and quick witted.

'Leave your mother to me. I'll talk to her. As for the rest of you, you'll need to make it look like a camping adventure. Only just remember the element of dangerous will be forever present.' She looked specifically at Behildwick Jones. 'Perhaps a brief history lesson wouldn't go amiss!'

Reluctantly Behildwick agreed.

'*My mother, Queen Erikka was of royal patronage even before she married my father. During their era, my time, myths and legends were commonplace filling the darkest corners of a tavern where travellers of the road would regale fables full of mystery, of wizards and warlocks, even the odd dragon.*

'*No account was ever without a murder, torture or the horrors inflicted upon men, by men. Occasionally however and for the price of free jug of ale there would come a tale of extraordinary proportion, of magic and wonder. Such a story involved my mother and myself.*

'*Many believe Camelot to be only a legend, but I assure you that such a place did exist although to preserve its identity the land was then named Bywydhir. Nearby there was large lake although as we know visited by Arthur.*

'*He had a beautiful princess sister, Anna and she had her own daughter, Conwenna. Legend had it that the lake was guarded by a lady, a lake maiden who went by the name of Bleudele. She was there to make sure that only those entitled to visit did so.*

'The waters of the lake are said to be very blue and that in the centre of the water there is a magic staircase which descends below. Going down you find yourself in an underwater cavern where you are met by a queen. She is the spirit of longevity, everlasting life. I have heard it said that her spirit not only gives long life, it can take away life too where evil exists.'

Albert could not contain himself. 'But if Bywydhir is supposed to be such a guarded secret, how did the story get out?'

Behildwick gave a slight shake of her head. She wondered how conflicting the stories had been as told in the taverns.

'Children such as yourselves and from the castle would go to the lake and lay in the long grass. They came back with stories of seeing a lady rise from the water, sword in hand only to disappear, shrouded by a thick mist.'

She could see that Albert was satisfied as he rested his head on his hands, propped up by his knees. .

'One boy, more daring than that of the others stayed to watch. He saw Anna and Conwenna walk the path around the lake, stopping only when the mysterious mist appeared. In awe of what was taking place before his very eyes he saw Bleudele step onto the back of a swan where it glided across to the grass bank.'

She raised a hand to stop Albert interrupting.

'Having collected Conwenna, it took her to the middle of the blue water.'

'The magic,' said Albert enthusiastically. 'Did she the staircase and chamber below?'

Daisy dug Albert in the ribs and told him to stop interrupting, much to the amusement of Eira and Behildwick.

'*Quite possibly Albert.*' Behildwick replied. '*Only that part of the account I cannot say precisely what happened. You see the magic that lies within the mist and in the chamber below the surface is known only to Lady Bleudele.*'

Albert's head dropped faster than a falling stone. Behildwick went on.

'*When Conwenna stepped back onto the grass bank, Anna was neither curious nor questioning of her mother's visit knowing that one day she too would ride on the back of the swan.*'

Once more she raised her hand to prevent Albert interrupting.

'*What Conwenna did reveal was that she would soon be with child again.*'

'Is this the lake where Arthur got his sword?' Albert asked, keen to feed his own curiosity.

'No, that was given in another somewhere else, No doubt as equally special.'

'So the reason that we are going to this lake… Bywydhir, is so that you can get pregnant and have a prince or princess of your own?'

The girls in the group shook their heads at his incredibility. Behildwick smiled at Eira.

'Unfortunately Albert, I am too old to have children of my own now and if I were able, I would need a suitor to help.'

'Albert looked at Daisy. 'What's one of them?' he asked.

Daisy sighed. 'At times Albert Jones, you're impossible!'

The laughter helped remove the tension in the air. Behildwick didn't want to belittle Albert so she tried explaining only from a different perspective.

'The waters of the lake contain great magic Albert and stranger things have been rumoured to happen if you ride the back of the swan. What is apparent is that royal children, prophesized by the queen who dwells beneath the water live extraordinarily long lives. I am testament to that prophecy.'

Behildwick watched as Albert's jaw dropped low.

'And to answer your next question, Conwenna gave birth to a baby girl, a princess who was known as Morcaccia. This part of the legend is also true because I am related to Morcaccia through my mother's bloodline.'

'Wow… So you're a real living relative of King Arthur.'

Behildwick nodded. 'He was an uncle to my mother's great, great grandmother.'

'Wow, you are old!'

'Does Trygor know about the lake?' asked Jonathon.

The parlour fell into immediate silence.

'That is a very good question Jonathon,' replied Behildwick. 'To answer you honestly, I don't know. There is no telling what he did to my mother to have her reveal our family bloodline or secrets.'

'So is that why he is so keen to find you?' asked Amanda.

'Yes. His sole purpose is that I should give him a son or daughter, an heir to the throne, and of real royal blood. Trygor has somehow managed to find his own source of longevity. To introduce royal blood into his ancestry would be to destroy all memory of the quarter kingdom and my father.'

'Then we should get you away from here as soon as possible.' Announced Jonathon.

Mostyn balled his right hand into a fist and punched the open palm of his left hand. 'Don't worry princess. We will protect you at all costs.'

Like the original children from Mud Island, the ghosts, they were as determined, brave and loyal. Behildwick knew that whatever she said, they would not be deterred from making the journey ahead. Instead Eira Pryce said it for her.

'It seems that you've no choice, but to concede Behildwick. And just like the old days you have another guard to protect you.'

Albert punched the air. 'Bring it on,' he uttered, 'just like Arthur's knights.'

Sitting alongside Daisy Gethall shook her head at Behildwick and Eira. Albert was a dreamer, but in essence he'd said what they all felt.

'There is just one problem,' Behildwick suddenly revealed. 'If we reach the lake, I cannot swim and I don't want to end my life drowning.'

Albert puffed up his chest, making the cotton of his tee-shirt go taut.

'No worries princess, I've got my life-saving badge.'

Daisy nodded. 'Yes. He has. He'd like to think that one day he'll appear on Baywatch!'

Eira saved the moment.

'Don't ask because it's nothing important and you don't own a bikini.'

'Then indeed you are a knight, Albert. King Arthur would have been proud to have sit at his round table.'

Albert turned to face Daisy Gethall.

'A knight and by royal decree.'

'Sir Albert, it doesn't quite have that air of chivalry about it, does it!'

Once again, the room was filled with laughter and even Albert laughed.

'Tomorrow then…' Jonathon suggested. 'We should make an early before the village wakes. If what you say and the trogglebytes return to the mountain to avoid the sunshine, we'll travel by day and rest come the night. Hidden from sight.'

Begrudgingly Behildwick Jones agreed the plan and destiny had been written in her stars many, many moons ago. She could feel the wind changing outside, blowing in from the east.

Chapter Twelve

Later that afternoon Mostyn and Albert found themselves at the mud flats looking for adders. So far all they had found were frogs which persisted in croaking loudly warning of their approach.

'Do you think they were afraid?' asked Albert.

'Who were afraid?' replied Mostyn, lying on his back and staring up at the birds who were circling overhead.

'The lost children of Mud Island. The gang trapped inside the mountain?'

Mostyn sat up, drawing his knees in close to his chin.

'I know that I would have been, put in the same position. It is one thing going inside where it is dark and strange, but knowing that you can get back out is what helps keeps the fear in check. Why'd you ask?'

'I was just wondering that's all. I wondered what they did for a hundred years whilst they were trapped inside.'

'They're ghosts Albert. I don't know. I guess they ran through walls, played hide n' seek and spooked the hell out of the trogglebytes. How do I know what they did?'

Albert felt slightly embarrassed. 'I was just wondering that was all.'

Mostyn mellowed.

'I'm sorry, I didn't mean to snap at you. I find my mind wandering as well, wondering. Avoiding the trogglebytes must have been stressful. Ghost or not they just wanted to get clear of the mountain. I hope that when I die I don't end up somewhere as dark.'

Albert broke his chocolate bar in half handing over an equal share to Mostyn.

'Me neither. Seeing the teeth on that creature who peered up through the opening in the trapdoor reminded me of my dad's saw.' He took a bite of his chocolate. 'Are we right going with the princess on her quest?'

Mostyn remained staring ahead at the frogs gathered on the island opposite.

'I guess so. She needs out help. Even more now that the trogglebyte in the barn recognised her.'

They sensed somebody coming relieved to see that it was Larissa Joyce.

'I thought that you were at Ashwestony to see your aunt?'

Mostyn broke his half of the chocolate giving Larissa the portion without teeth marks. Albert grinned. He thought Mostyn liked Amanda Brodrick, but he'd been known to get it wrong before and both Daisy and Larissa liked Mostyn. Not that either would admit it.

'It was upsetting, so I came back with my dad. Have I missed anything?'

They both told her about the blue waters of Lake Bywydhir, Lady Bleudele and Eira Pryce turning up unexpectedly. They told her about their going on an adventure.

'I didn't miss a lot then,' Larissa replied cynically chewing on the sultanas in the chocolate.

'Is you aunt okay?' Albert asked.

'I think she's dying although I'm not sure as I've never seen anybody die.'

Albert felt his intake of breath suck his chest in. 'I'm sorry, I shouldn't have asked.'

Larissa shrugged.

'If we don't ask, we don't learn.' It was very philosophical. 'What do you think of the ghosts?' she asked.

Mostyn replied. 'It was spooky at first when they suddenly appeared because we'd opened the trapdoor. I thought they'd be wearing white sheets or something similar and that you could see through them, but they're quite ordinary really. They need a wash, but being inside the mountain for a hundred years I'd be dirty.'

I'm glad I was born now and not then,' Albert replied.

Larissa nodded. 'Me too!'

'Do you think that they'll join us, on our adventure I mean?'

Mostyn shook his head.

'No. Until Trygor is killed and the curse broken part of them remains inside the mountain.'

'What curse?' Larissa asked.

'I had a chat with Arwel Owens. He told me that when they realised they were never going to escape the mountain, they cursed the trogglebytes, especially Trygor. Arwel said they took a vow to see him dead before their spirits could be laid to rest.'

'Wow, that's some undertaking. No wonder they've hung around a hundred years.'

Mostyn and Larissa looked at Albert. For once he was right. He suddenly chuckled.

'What's funny?' asked Larissa.

'I was just thinking that if I was a ghost I could pass through a wall undetected. Can you imagine Daisy's face if I suddenly appeared.'

'Pervert!' announced Mostyn.

Albert flushed. 'No, I didn't mean when she was dressing. I meant any other time!'

'She'd kill you.' Replied Larissa.

They each jumped when the voice behind spoke.

'It doesn't quite work like that Albert.'

They turned to see the ghost of Tommy Jones standing behind.

Holding his chest where his heart felt it had missed a beat Albert grinned.

'I didn't think that I'd see you so soon.'

'This is a new experience for me too.' Tommy looked around. 'It has been a long time since I have been back to the mudflats of Mud Island.' Mostyn noticed that Tommy looked apprehensive. The ghost sat himself down between Albert and Larissa. 'I hear that you're embarking upon a journey tomorrow.'

Albert nodded. 'We're going to find a magic lake.'

Tommy smiled. 'Bywydhir. Yes I've heard of it.'

'Where?' asked Mostyn.

'A long time ago. I came to warn you that the trogglebytes are expecting the princess to show herself. They think that somebody, a friend maybe might help smuggle her out of the village only they don't know when. You need to be on your guard at all times!'

'And you overheard this…?'

Tommy nodded back at Mostyn.

'Yes. I went back inside using a secret passage that is naturally cut into the side of the mountain. I didn't want to go, but I drew the short straw.'

'We do that sometimes,' Albert implied. 'When we have to decide who commit a daring deed.'

The other two glared at him.

'Yes. I overheard Trygor talking. He's cunning and having waited so long for his opportunity to get back at the princess can wait a little while longer.'

'I thought that you'd be, maybe look older?' Albert said. Larissa sighed. Albert was so bad at keeping his thoughts together, orderly.

'Think of aging as your bike,' Tommy explained. 'When it was new, it was shiny and brightly painted. After use the paintwork got scratched and the rubber on the tyres began to perish, get thinner. I am a hundred and ten, but dying so young, we stayed young.'

'Oh, I understand.' Albert however was still curious. 'What did you do all day in the mountain?'

'We wandered most of the time, mostly looking for a way out.'

'But you knew about the secret entrance cut into the side of the mountain?'

'Yes, but for us to leave we had to be released by somebody living. Like when you opened the trapdoor.'

'But the trogglebytes, they're living?' Larissa seemed puzzled.

Tommy smiled. 'Yes they are. But unlike you, they have evil intentions. Our escape had to be through good.'

'Did you ever come across the dead miners?' she asked.

'Only the once. We crossed paths when they were out looking for one of their friends.'

Mostyn frowned. 'Looking… how could he be lost?'

'I know and it does sound stupid, but one of the dead miners went wandering late one night as the stars were coming out. He never returned.'

'How can a ghost get lost?' asked Albert mortified. 'Could he not just walked through the rock and find the group again?'

Tommy laughed. He noticed the frogs on the island opposite. He remembered as a chasing them with a stick and jar trying to catch one.

'There are some things like the mountain which are just too thick for us to pass through. You wouldn't believe but beneath that tall structure is a maze of passages, dig out by the trogglebytes. They had to live somewhere, so they dynamited and dug until they had their own cave. It can be like a labyrinth of tunnels inside and it's easy to get lost.'

'Can you see in the dark?'

'Not always. There is a lot of speculation and theorizing about what a ghost can do. Occasionally, we would hear the miners singing as they went wandering, but we could never find them. I think in a way they avoided us.'

'Why?' asked Larissa.

'Because they felt guilty. Having been trapped themselves, they should have paid more attention to Trygor and seen our plight.'

'Did you ever see Queen Erikka?'

'Yes, more than once. Although very kind she was always in a hurry, looking for her daughter. Of course none of us knew that Oyddiss had escaped the mountain.

'Why didn't she leave the mountain when you did, when the trapdoor was opened?'

Tommy shrugged.

'I don't know. It would have ended her suffering.'

'That is so sad.' Larissa lowered her head respectfully. 'One day they will be reunited. I feel it.'

Chapter Thirteen

Before the sun moved across the tops of the trees above Mud Island Albert, Larissa and Mostyn went off to find the others. Tommy went in search of the ghosts. He found them at the village church where many members of their own family were buried.

As Tommy had explained to Albert, time had no meaning once you were dead, but in the intervening years that had passed since their tragic disappearance the burden left behind with the living had been no less and ghosts too had feelings.

'Do you think that we'll see them ever again?' asked Scarlett as she tenderly touched the top of a headstone belonging to her mother.

Brianna placed her hand on Scarlett's shoulder. 'Almost for sure we will one day.'

Scarlett sighed. 'I still them Brianna. All of them.'

'Me too.'

Scarlett kissed the top of the headstone then moved away. Brianna went to where her parents were buried.

'I am really sorry. I should have told you where we were going that day. You would have said no, and we would perhaps be here lying beside you, instead of being tied to the evil inside the mountain.'

Coming alongside Dillan had already paid his respects.

'Maybe, if we'd been wiser, we would have seen the sense in not going.'

'Do you think we'll see them again?' she asked.

He slipped his hand into hers. 'Yes, and soon Brianna, I promise!'

'Good. Only I just told Scarlett the same.'

Together they watched the others pay homage to the members of their respective families.

'I never realised how nice it was here when the sun is shining.'

Dillan smiled. 'I never realised how nice the sun was when it was shining. There are so many things that we took for granted Brianna. I've a feeling that soon we'll come to appreciate them more.'

*****

Having watched Eira Pryce go Behildwick Jones had closed the door quickly. Suddenly she didn't feel safe. The latter children of Mud Island had unwittingly unleashed a monster and once again the dragon was awake.

Sitting beside the unlit fire she sat mulling over the events of the past twenty-four hours. Looking around her home she wondered if she would ever see it again. Behildwick closed her eyes, laying her head back on the cushion hoping that *Alstor the Winged Warrior* heard her trepidation. Maybe he would, she didn't know, but riding through the woods on her horse as a young girl she had felt his presence close. There was a presence close again only she didn't know to who it belonged.

Had she been swept along by the enthusiasm of the children eager for an adventure? It was another puzzle. She wished that she did have a black cat for company, but after the mysterious disappearance of the last cat ten years ago, she had lost heart in having another.

Reflecting on how much pain she had caused her mother and father centuries back Oyddiss wished to cause no more. She was still thinking of the good times spent in their company when her thoughts turned to sleep and a dream.

'*You must not ride so reckless,*' said her father, holding the reins of the horse steady.

'*I know father, but Alstor rides with me and I feel his presence as I race the wind gusting between the trees.*'

Felman laughed. '*Arthur would turn in his grave if he could see you know.*'

Oyddiss smiled, it was a nice thought. '*I would like to have been a knight sitting at his round table.*'

'*That is what concerns your mother. His spirit runs through your veins and you soul.*'

'*Just because I am girl father, it does not mean that I cannot have fun.*'

King Felman helped his daughter dismount the horse. He acknowledged that it was useless advising Oyddiss. She had the energy of two men, could sword fence as well as any of his personal guard and she would whisper in the ear of the horse when he was not around. Beast and princess had a pact that he had yet to discover.

'Have you fun Oyddiss because one day, when you are queen your responsibilities will be great and your days of fun short.'

Oyddiss was still dreaming, only she went elsewhere, somewhere that she didn't recognise when suddenly she heard a girl screaming. The closer that she went in the direction of the screams the louder they got. They were so bad that she had to cover her ears.

When Oyddiss next opened her eyes having shielded them from the approach of a large trogglebyte, not sure if it had been Trybulloc or Trygor, she saw Amanda Brodrick standing in the background. It had been her screams that had made her go back inside the mountain. She gestured for Amanda to join her where together they could run from the mountain and escape. A knock on the front door ended the dream. She instantly reached for the fire poker.

Behildwick Jones was surprised to see Amanda standing outside with the looped end of the dog's lead tried about her wrist to which the other end was attached to the neck of a young goat.

'I'm sorry to disturb you, but grandma asked me to come. She would like to invite you to her place for supper. She said you probably had bare cupboards having emptied them of cakes, biscuits and bread for toast.' She was surprised to see that the old lady was armed with the fire poker. She didn't ask if Behildwick had been expecting somebody else to call.

'Your grandmother is a very perceptive individual.' She invited the girl and goat inside. 'If you would wait a moment I'll get my key and diary.' Amanda frowned, a diary sounded like a strange thing to be taking along to supper. Behildwick laughed. 'I have never owned a handbag; I don't have use for one. Full of useless items, whereas my diary is essential. It contains within its pages my life. Losing it would be like losing part of my soul.'

Amanda nodded, now the diary made sense.

'We don't have a pet dog, we have Pippin instead.' The goat licked the back of her hand. 'Although he's like a dog. He needs to go for walks, gets into mischief and likes wide open spaces with fresh cut grass. That is why I generally end up visiting grandma as Pippin likes her back garden.'

'And the orchard with it many fallen fruit,' added Behildwick.

Amanda grinned. 'Yes, the apples as well.'

Behildwick stroked the goat's head. There had not been a goat in her dream. It could still have been an omen though as Celtic legend suggested that goats were the spirit walkers between good and bad.

'Pippin is very friendly.'

'Inquisitive more likely. Pippin is always to be found in next doors garden eating the neighbour's vegetables and fruit. The man goes mad and my dad is always having to apologise and repair the fence.'

On the way to Eira Pryce's cottage Amanda told Behildwick that she had been alone in her bedroom getting her things together for their journey when she had experienced a strange feeling. It had made Amanda sit on the bed where an hour later she had woken up from a bad dream.

'Was you inside the mountain?' Behildwick asked.

'Yes, and I was screaming although I had no idea why.'

'We have a connection, Amanda. At present I do not understand how or why, but it is strong.'

'When the trapdoor was open and the trogglebyte was looking, I got the impression that it was looking directly at me. Thinking about it made me shiver. It's like the boys had opened a portent, a gateway into hell.'

Behildwick shrugged.

'I feel stronger with you by my side.' She turned to look. 'I cannot explain why. Centuries ago when I would ride my horse through the wood weaving between the trees, I would feel the same. Back then I thought it was Alstor, a winged warrior. Now I am not so sure.' The lines on her brow creased deep.

'Ignore your dream it was probably just your mind playing tricks with your imagination.'

Amanda nodded, not exactly convinced, although she did want to alarm the old woman. 'You're probably right.'

'Have you known grandma long?'

'A very long time Amanda. Eira and I have been very good friends. My problem is that I outlive them all. It is so sad and unsettling...' the explanation seemed to trail away.

But Amanda was shrewd. 'Until they die...' she said.

Behildwick nodded solemnly.

'I've been lucky and my friends have been good to me. There are times when I forget what the quarter kingdom looked like. My little cottage is comfortable and has been my home, my salvation for a good many years, but it will never replace the high walls, the moat around the outside and the drawbridge of the castle.'

'Is it still there?' Amanda asked. She had never seen one in the valley.

'No. The trogglebytes set fire to it the night they killed my father. The rest crumbled over the years. Now there are no more than a few boulders left beside the river. The moat was filled in and the water diverted. That is why Mud Island is so boggy. The long grass hides the rest.'

Amanda pushed open the gate allowing Behildwick to pass through first holding Pippin back as the goat was eager to go around back and gnaw on the fresh grass down in the orchard.

'Supper's almost ready,' Eira Brodrick called out as they occupied the chairs in the parlour. 'I'll be through in a minute.' She watched the goat running to the end of the garden. It was a young and stupid creature, healthy and already plump. *'That goat eats too much,'* she thought to herself. Five minutes later she brought through a tray of food laying it down on the coffee table where they could help themselves.

'Pippin will get a stomach ache if he continues eating everything that he finds.' She told Amanda.

'What can I do grandma, he's a goat. He doesn't listen to reason.'

'Then he is so much like your grandmother,' laughed Behildwick.

They were eating when Eira Pryce suddenly announced.

'You've both had a vision, haven't you?'

Behildwick Jones went on eating. It was Amanda who seemed surprised.

'How did you know grandma?'

Behildwick looked up from her plate. 'Because your grandmother has the *sight* Amanda and she can occasionally see events before they happen.'

'Pandamorialius,' Eira Pryce corrected. 'Let's use the correct name.' She looked at Amanda. 'Your mother has the same gift, only she's never told your father.'

'Wow...' exclaimed Amanda, 'mum can see into the future, that's fantastic.' Amanda paused. 'Dad always said that you was a dark horse grandma.'

'I reckon he thinks a lot of things about me. And what about your sister? I know she's wary when I am around?'

Amanda grinned. 'Emma say's that you can be an old dragon at times.'

The two women laughed.

'So I am a cross between a dark horse and fire breathing dragon. I suppose it's better than being called an old bat or indeed a daffy old duck.' She took in a deep breath of air. 'Joking aside. The visions were dark, were they not?'

Behildwick answered for them both.

'Let's just say that there was a strong bond between Amanda and myself.'

Eira Pryce looked deep into their eyes reading their thoughts.

'The night Angharad Jones disappeared from the farm, my old bones rattled all night long preventing me from sleeping. The next day I went to see Benjamin Jones, but he refused to listen to me. He told me that I was mad and should be locked up.'

'What was it that you saw grandma?'

Eira Pryce shook her head. 'Something dark Amanda. An evil that had been awoken. I've had similar dreams lately.'

'Was it the trogglebytes?'

Eira Pryce looked at her young granddaughter. She had a wise head on such young shoulders. 'Never ignore their presence my girl. Most things that happen in and around Finlostydd, happen because of them.'

'Have you ever seen a trogglebyte grandma?'

Eira Pryce shook her head looking across at Behildwick Jones. 'Only in the shadows at night as they forage through the orchard picking up windfalls. I have never encountered one up close.'

Sat alongside Behildwick Jones, Amanda remembered the eyes of the trogglebyte looking up at her from the dark shaft in Jonesy's barn.

'Once seen grandma, you would never forget.'

Chapter Fourteen

The sound of clay flower pot falling from the window ledge and breaking on the hard ground below made them all jump to their feet. Mister Kinks, the tabby named because of the natural bend in his left ear arched its back hissing aggressively at the window.

Eira grabbed the poker from the log basket. She gave Behildwick the long-handled metal ash shovel.

'What was it grandma?'

'I don't know, but I'm not expecting visitors.'

The trio used the front door, going around the side of the cottage. Under the front window they had come across the broken pot.

'I only planted that up the other day. If it's that goat of yours Amanda it will have an ear like Mister Kinks.'

It was darker than usual and the sun had completely disappeared leaving shadows in dark corners, at the side of the shed, the compost heap and large oak tree.

Amanda was about to call out having seen three shadows move in the orchard, one holding the goat when Behildwick Jones clamped her hand over her mouth.

'Sccchh,' she whispered. 'This was probably what we saw in our vision.'

They stood alongside the side wall watching when suddenly Eira Pryce stepped away and with an almighty thwack of her poker hit out at a short bulky figure coming around the corner of the bungalow. The force of the blow sent the creature instantly down onto the paved slabs. Just to make sure she whacked him a second time.

Bradkar held his head which hurt. Short and stocky he somehow managed to roll onto his side and right himself. He produced a wicked looking knife, which he thrust out at Eira Pryce.

'Don't you come trespassing and threatening me,' she sat administering another thwack only connecting with the shoulder. '

'*Owwwww…*' cried the trogglebyte as it dropped the knife. Bradkar bent forward to pick it up but Behildwick Jones hit him with the shovel. This time he went down and lay unconscious. Standing under the cover of the apple trees the three trogglebytes watched in awe as Bradkar went down for a second time, only this time he didn't get back up.

'Come on…' said Stardd, 'there's only three of them and they only females. We can take easily take all three back to Trygor.'

A trogglebyte named Karlstad stepped in front of Stardd.

'No, we got what we came for, we have the goat now let's not push our luck!'

Stardd glared back angrily.

'Trygor will skin us alive if we don't take back at least the girl.'

'Is that the princess?' asked Oberran. The third trogglebyte hiding himself behind Stardd.

Karlstad had his knife held out menacingly at Stardd.

'They're too far away to tell and I ain't taking any chances. We'll tell Trygor that Oyddiss wasn't here, least not tonight.'

Stardd sucked in through his teeth pushing the outstretched knife aside.

'I say we take them and if the women are the girl's mother and grandmother then we kill them and leave them for the crows.'

Karlstad held Stardd's arm. He tapped the side of his own head.

'Think about it Stardd. Trygor trusts us. He will have us find the princess however long it takes. We would be free of the mountain. If we take the girl back tonight, he might send others instead. This way we can steal chickens, sheep and pigs for ourselves. We would eat like a king for a change and not survive on scraps.'

Oberran stepped around from the back of Stardd coming alongside.

'Karlstad is right Stardd. There's also a strong force here tonight. Something stronger than us three put together. Can't you feel it?'

Stardd sniffed the air, but he couldn't detect anything other than the strong odour of apples. 'What about Bradkar, we just can't leave him here to the mercy of the *outsiders*?'

The trogglebyte trio peered to the other end of the garden where the two women were standing guard over Bradkar.

Karlstad's mind was made up. 'Trygor will be more annoyed if we return with nothing. At least we have the goat and a few chickens will appease his hunger.

Remember, at present he has his wedding to think about. Bradkar could be lying there dead. Is it worth any of us ending up with the same fate? I say we go now, take the goat and steal some chickens from another garden. Bradkar should have been more alert. He was a fool.'

Holding onto her granddaughter's arm Eira Pryce watched as the shadows disappeared with the goat.

'Pippin,' Amanda whispered. She instinctively knew that it was the last time she would see the goat. She felt her grandmother's arm slip over her shoulder. Inside she was angry, seething.

'Let them try anything on the journey to Lake Bywydhir. I'll be ready for them!'

Eira Pryce looked down at the trogglebyte. It was the first one that she had ever seen close up. She thought it was an ugly looking brute, representing pictures that she had seen of Neanderthal cavemen. She watched as Amanda kicked the creature hard in the side.

'You would be wise to stay at your daughter's this night,' advised Behildwick Jones. 'Amanda will need to find a story to convince them that the goat ran off and couldn't be found. It would account for why she is late getting home.'

'What about you?' asked Amanda. 'Won't you be frightened that they'll come back?'

'No. Trogglebytes are fearsome on the outside, brutish, but they have little brain or indeed courage. They've failed this night and Trygor will be angry. They have more to fear than myself.'

*****

They stole half a dozen chickens from another garden near to the wood. Running from the owner who appeared at the back garden armed with his shotgun, but the shot in the dark hit the back fence instead. Walking through the safety of the trees in the wood the moon had decided to come out illuminating the mountain ahead.

Stardd looked up at the never-ending peak. 'I'm not sure that I want to go back up,' he stated. 'I can already feel Trygor's anger in my chest.'

Karlstad who had hold of the goat sniffed. 'He is always lying to us, so why do we not tell him one. We tell him that Bradkar got himself captured whilst chasing the goat. If we all stick to the same story, he will have no option but to believe us.'

Oberran however gave a shake of his head. 'I'm not so sure. Trygor is no fool when it comes to extracting the truth. And what about the princess?'

'What about the princess,' asked Karlstad.

'Did you not detect her scent in the garden?'

'No. all I could smell was the goat and apples.'

'Well I'm sure it was her holding the shovel.'

A bush rustled nearby, making them stop walking. Within a second it was silent again.

'It was probably a badger,' said Karlstad. 'Come on let's get back I'm getting hungry.'

'It's an omen,' Oberran said, looking in the direction of where the noise had originated.

'You're letting your imagination get the better of you. You know this wood is full of creatures which come out at night.'

They followed Karlstad back up the old stone track to the secret entrance and was almost there when a figure appeared. He was dressed in a long cloak made from dead bats wings.

'Well look what we have here. Maybe the dragon will save me the trouble of dealing with you.'

Seeing Trygor they instantly went down on one knee.

Stardd pointed. 'We did manage to bring you back the goat and some chickens my king. Its meat will help fill your plate at the wedding table. We thought it might impress your bride to be.'

Knelt alongside Karlstad kept his head low. Stardd was a fool to have opened his mouth before Trygor had vented his anger upon them.

Trygor felt the goat. It was young and plump. Succulent.

'I am glad that you think so Stardd.' Trygor dragged the nervous trogglebyte to his feet by tugging hard on Stardd's earlobe.

'And tell me, where is Bradkar?' he asked. 'I send out four and yet only three return.'

Oberran saw his chance to help redeem himself. Forgetting himself he stood without permission.

'It was the *outsider's* they killed him while we were chasing the goat. Being so young it wasn't an easy animal to trap.'

Trygor held onto Stardd's ear.

'And what say you Karlstad. You're not as dim-witted as these two. Is what Oberran says true? Did you see Bradkar killed?' Trygor came close, close enough for Karlstad to smell his king's rancid breath. He dared not back away.

'To be truthful my I could not really say either way. It was as Oberran described it and we had ourselves a chase to capture the goat. For some reason unknown to us Bradkar was lagging behind. He was overpowered and hit twice. He fell like a dead man.'

Trygor let go of the ear rubbing his chin he was thinking. 'How many *outsiders*?'

'Two initially, then more arrived. It was as though they knew that we would be coming.'

Stardd exhaled expressively. Trygor turned quickly.

'And what of you Stardd. Did you think to hide before checking on Bradkar? You have a yellow streak at times.'

Staring back at his king, Stardd wasn't happy to be undermined.

'We didn't have the chance to check my king. The *outsiders* kept coming from the bushes. It wasn't until we had reached the forked tongue of the woodland track that we managed to avoid capture ourselves.

'And the princess,' he turned again quickly facing Oberran. 'Was she there?'

Oberran stuttered looking for his reply. No... no my king. It was dark and I don't think she was one of the women. We didn't pick up her scent.'

'WOMEN... are you telling me that Bradkar was overpowered by women outsiders!' His anger was rising and the three of them could feel the mountain beneath their feet vibrate.

Karlstad inflated his lungs with night air.

'It was dark my king and difficult to see if the *outsiders* were men or women. We did not pick up the princesses scent and if we did not escape, we too would have been killed.'

Trygor stared at Karlstad but saw no flicker of shame in the trogglebytes eyes. Taking a knife from his waistband he stuck it under Stardd's chin.

'Amongst the outsider's my fat little friend, was there anybody there?'

Stardd gulped. 'Like who my king?'

'A certain princess or are you calling Iskard a liar. Should I kill him instead?'

Karlstad and Oberran observed hoping that Stardd kept to the story and that he didn't walk into one of Trygor's clever traps.

'We know that Iskard is no liar my king, but neither am I. it was dark and confusing in the old woman's garden. We found the goat wandering the orchard without the girl. When she did appear she was protected by the *outsiders*. We deserve your wrath for our failure.'

Trygor kept the tip of the knife under Stardd's chin. He looked up at the moon.

'We always made a sacrifice whenever there was a full moon. Do you remember my trusted warriors? Tonight however is my wedding night and I am in a genial mood. My bride would be disappointed if I lay on our marital bed with blood on my hands.' With that he thrust up hard killing Stardd. Trygor kicked the dead trogglebyte aside. He turned to look at Karlstad.

'Now go back down the mountain and visit the old woman's cottage. If Oyddiss is there, bring her to me. If anybody gets in your way kill them. Do not return unless you have the princess.'

Without looking at Oberran, Karlstad bolted down the old track as fast as he could. He knew that going back was futile and that by the time he reached the cottage the two old women and the young girl would already have disappeared. He wondered if he would ever see Oberran, his cousin again.

With his arms seized upon by two of Trygor's private guard Oberran was frog-marched into the mountain. Trygor ordered others to bring the dead Stardd. Walking behind the frightened trogglebyte Trygor spoke low with menace.

'I can smell fear. The same as I can tell when somebody is lying to me and you were all lying.'

As they neared the grand chamber that had been decorated for the wedding another trogglebyte stepped out of the shadows blocking their path. He whispered something in Trygor's ear then departed.

Oberran noticed the wry smile creasing Trygor's face.

'I had Schellian hide and wait your return in the woods. It was an interesting conversation that he heard. Your fate was sealed before you were even halfway up the mountain.'

Oberran felt his heart sink in his chest. He had known instinctively that it was too early for a badger to be about in the wood. Normally they only ever left the sett around midnight.

Inside the chamber eyes turned to see Oberran marched in.

Chapter Fifteen

For good measure Eira Pryce kicked the trogglebyte once again before she left.

'And that's for making me give up my home for a night. I have lived here for nigh on seventy-two years and never had to leave it ever before, that is until you turned up uninvited and interrupted the status quo.'

'Come on grandma,' Amanda encouraged, 'we had best get moving in case the trogglebyte does.'

Begrudgingly Eira Pryce agreed.

At Amanda's house Eira told her daughter that Amanda had a camping trip arranged and that she was staying with the family for the night as she had been sleeping badly of late. She wanted to see if a change of pillows helped. She had backed up Amanda's story that the goat had escaped the garden run off into the woods.

What Mary Brodrick did find strange although she didn't question why, was why Behildwick Jones was going camping as well. When she was alone with her mother later that night. She sat at the kitchen table opposite, gently drumming the table top.

'I've felt it too,' she said.

'I know you have, replied Eira Pryce. 'You were always able to read my mind.'

Mary smiled.

'She's spirited like you mum. I know that I should say no to this trip, but something at the back of my mind is telling me that I have to let her go.'

Eira Pryce looked at the kitchen chair where her shoulder bag had her overnight things inside.

'The weave of my bag is as complicated as our life Mary. Amanda has to find this out for herself. In time she will understand our *gift*. Behildwick is going along to make sure she does.'

Mary Brodrick sipped her coffee.

'I wonder why it skipped a generation and missed Emma.'

Eira Pryce studied the framed photograph of her eldest granddaughter hanging on the kitchen wall.

'Sometimes the choices are made for us Mary. Choices that have been made elsewhere. Places where only magic exists.'

*****

Returning from his unconsciousness Bradkar held his head in one hand and his ribs in the other. Both hurt although it was strange why his ribs did.

Overhead the moon was out and the sky was full of stars.

He remembered being hit with the metal poker and then the shovel, and then everything going black. It was also strange why Karlstad, Stardd and Oberran hadn't come to his rescue. Slowly he got to his feet. His knees felt weak and he thought he might fall again. Surprisingly the cottage was in darkness.

'That stupid old crone...' he swore. 'If we cross paths again I'll not be so slow the next time. Next time I'll gut her and leave her for the crows.'

He checked around but there were no signs of life anywhere. The beds were neat but unslept in. Forcing the kitchen door he made sure. From the larder he took a large round cake and some potatoes which were turning green.

'At least I'll not go hungry.'

He left making his way to the wood where he could bathe his head in the cool waters and make a fire to cook his potatoes.

*****

The experience with the trogglebyte in Eira Pryce's back garden had left Behildwick Jones feeling anxious. Sleeping in the attic with the fire poker by her side she had slept fitfully waking every hour and not helping was the cry of owl from the nearby wood. It was a different cry form that of its usual hoot to its mate. Tonight the calling was because there was a stranger in the wood.

She woke around three and using the flame of a candle she opened her diary. On the inside cover was an inscription.

'Watery steps of lost time

Mysterious, dark secrets
Where destiny meets legend
Unfolding with another and mine,
In the mist
Going below the blue watery grave
All will be revealed
Be brave, be bold
The quarter kingdom is yours to save.

Behildwick read through the inscription twice. She didn't remember writing it and it had been years before she had discovered it inside the front cover.

'Amanda,' she muttered. '*You must be the other.*'

She thought that she heard a voice speak. Sitting bolt upright she moved the candle left and right, but there was nobody there. She was alone.

When the voice spoke again, she replied.

'*Mother is that you?*'

'*The Lady Bleudele, she knows you are coming.*'

Oyddiss felt her head drop forward.

'*It is such a dangerous undertaking. I am fearful for the children coming with me.*'

'*Be brave, be bold Oyddiss. Be like the young girl that I remember. Was it not you who told me that nothing frightened you?*'

'*But the lake mother. It is so secret.*'

'*Maybe there is more than one destiny to be found by going.*'

There was suddenly silence telling her that the voice had disappeared. The princess found herself alone with her thoughts, the candle and her diary. Clutching the book to her chest she closed her eyes.

'One day mother, you will no longer be just a voice in the night, but real.

*****

In the bedroom at the end of the landing Amanda Brodrick lay on her bed looking up at the stars outside. She wasn't think about the encounter with the trogglebyte, but her grandmother. Why hadn't Emma come across Behildwick Jones she wondered and why was it that she had the gift and not her older sister.

She had been asleep, but had a nightmare, least she thought it was a nightmare.

Thrusting her arms up and out wildly Amanda had been swimming back up trying to save herself from drowning. She remembered the water was very blue, but something was holding onto her ankles and pulling her back down. She was still kicking and reaching up for the surface when she had woke with a start.

Blinking several times she thought that she had seen a small creature sitting on her window cill, not a trogglebyte, it was far too small, but something that wore a hat. She shook herself awake.

'A top hat, don't be ridiculous Amanda.'

She expected somebody or something to reply, but there was only silence. When she next looked the mystery vision had disappeared.

In the bedroom at the other end of the landing Mary Brodrick stood at the window looking out at the night which was very dark despite the moon and stars. She sensed that she was being watched, but with her husband gently snoring behind her in the bed, she felt safe.

Checking the time with the bedside clock it was almost three.

Powerful forces were at work and Amanda was about to enter a realm of magic that she should not have had thrust upon her, not until she was older. Mary Brodrick felt the forces of the quarter kingdom pulling at her from two sides, one good, one bad. Somewhere in the middle she saw her young daughter holding aloft a sword.

Chapter Sixteen

By the time Bradkar reached the stream his head was already throbbing and the wound swollen. He knelt and dipped his head in the cooling waters.

'*Ahhh, that's better,*' he muttered. In essence the cut felt like it was extensive, but in fact it was no bigger than from his last knuckle to his fingertip.

Pulling away a clump from the bank he wet it and held it against the swelling. Known locally as *devils porridge* the droplets ran down the back of his neck.

Gathering together broken branches and twigs he made a fire, caking the potatoes in mud. He had just placed the last amongst the burning embers when from behind a twig was snapped underfoot. Rolling over quickly he had his knife in his hand ready to greet the uninvited guest.

'Put your knife away Bradkar, you fool… it's me, Karlstad.'

Stabbing the knife into the ground the trogglebyte sighed, relieved that it had not been a group of *outsiders*.

'Where are the others?' he asked. 'Where's Oberran and Stardd?'

Karlstad could smell the potatoes cooking. He noticed the round cake wrapped in a cloth from the old woman's kitchen.

'Share the potatoes and cake and I'll tell you, but it's not good news that I bring!'

Bradkar agreed.

'We thought you were dead. Returning to the mountain Trygor was waiting for us at the secret entrance.' Using a small branch lying beside him Karlstad stoked the fire sending a flurry of sparks into the night air.

'Trygor was angry that we'd not returned with the princess. He killed Stardd as a warning and sent me back down the mountain to find the princess. He took Oberran as prisoner. There is no telling what will happen to my cousin.'

Bradkar watched the sparks disappear.

'The princess... she was one of the old women!'

Karlstad nodded turning over the mud-caked potatoes.

'I know and he knows too. Trygor had Schellian spy on us. He was waiting for us at the edge of the wood. Schellian heard us talking about the princess. Somehow, he got back to Trygor before we did. It must have been the goat that slowed us down.'

'I have never trusted Schellian,' said Bradkar, his eyes narrowing suspiciously. He was always hanging around Trygor and whispering in his ear. If we survive the night, I think I'll invite Schellian out on a night hunt and make an unfortunate accident happen.'

Karlstad saw the cut above Bradkar's ear which looked sore and angry. Karlstad didn't trust Bradkar or Schellian. Both had Trygor's ear.

'The old woman reacted fast,' he said, pointing to the injury. 'We should have thought she might.'

Bradkar plucked his knife from the earth.

'When I see her next time, she will go the same way as Schellian.'

They shared the hot potatoes, breaking the cake in half.

'Trygor has become more irritable of late. He is also much more unpredictable.' Bradkar picked at a potato skin that had got caught between his teeth. 'There was no good reason to kill Stardd, he was a skilled hunter.'

Karlstad swallowed what he was chewing.

'Trygor is suspicious of everybody and not just the *outsiders*, he doesn't trust us any longer. I think he's got a case of coal dust fever.'

Bradkar nodded. 'His obsession with the princess has turned his mind.'

They both nodded, agreeing.

'So what do you think we should do?' asked Bradkar. His headache was getting worse.

'Considering Trygor's current mood, I think we would be wise keeping out of the way.'

Bradkar agreed.

'The marriage to Selantra won't last long. None do.'

Bradkar suddenly had a thought despite his aching head. 'You say Trygor thinks that I am dead?'

'Yes. Although there's no telling that he hasn't sent Schellian to check. He could be lurking anywhere, even listening to us talk right now.'

Bradkar looked around in the light from the fire. There were shadows everywhere.

Karlstad was no fool. He had always wondered why Trygor had put so much faith in the stupid oaf sitting opposite him. Bradkar was no leader of men. He stumbled into situations and fell out the other side with lady luck watching over him. He was suspicious as to how Bradkar had been captured by the two old women so easily. As it, he wondered another plan of Trygor's?

'So do we go back to the cottage?' Bradkar asked.

'No not tonight.' Karlstad replied. 'We'll go when the sun comes up. They'll have gone into hiding tonight.'

'But the sunshine. It hurts my eyes.' Bradkar feigned.

Overhead the moon shone through the treetops down onto the campfire.

'You'll get used to it. Now I suggest we get some rest, we've a lot to do in the morning.'

Lying with his back against the trunk of a tree Bradkar watched the stars twinkle in the night sky.

'Did you feel it?' he asked.

Karlstad who was on the other side of the tree and watching the shadows replied.

'You mean the force, yes I did and the princess is still powerful. I think Trygor fails to accept or indeed recognises this.'

'He has never been the same since Queen Erikka escaped.'

Chapter Seventeen

Amanda sat bolt upright in bed with her mouth slightly open in awe of the presence in her room.

'Is there something wrong, why are you here?' she asked.

Brianna Roberts walked over to the bed and sat down beside Amanda. 'I am sorry that I startled you. We know that the trogglebytes took your goat.'

Amanda shrugged.

'Grandma was right. If I had chased after Pippin they would have taken me captive as well. It sends shivers down my spine thinking about what they would have done with me. I try not to think about Pippin.'

Brianna Roberts gently stroked the back of Amanda's hand. 'It's best you don't.'

Beyond the bedroom window the night stars were beginning to fade. Soon they would be replaced by the blue hue of a new day. Soon Amanda would be meeting the others and Behildwick Jones.

'Have you been in the room long?' she asked.

Brianna smiled. 'Long enough to know that you were dreaming. Perhaps having a nightmare!'

'It felt like I was drowning. As hard as I tried I couldn't get back up to the surface and something was holding onto my ankles.' She looked down at her bare legs expecting to see the indentation of finger marks.

'Night visions are not always bad Amanda. Some prophesize the future, others can be a warning, but your dream was about your undertaking today.'

Amanda looked surprised. 'You mean I'll drown?'

Brianna shook her head. 'No. it means you'll rise much wiser and different.'

Amanda frowned. 'Different, how come?'

'That is something that I cannot tell. You alone must feel it, experience it. You have the *gift* Amanda, use it wisely.'

'Did you have it?'

Brianna laughed. 'If I did, I never would have gone inside the mountain.'

'It was a surprise to find that mum and grandma have the *gift* and yet not Emma?'

Brianna nodded. 'There is always a reason. The same as why you are going to find Lake Bywydhir.'

'We're going because the princess needs to go. We're sort of like her royal guard.'

Amanda watched Brianna walk over to the bedroom window where she watched the dawn appear. 'I like it when the sun comes up. It energises the soul.'

She looked around at the house in the village. Many were new, some had been updated. The church was really the only place that had not altered in a hundred years.

'At the lake there will be other surprises Amanda. Go with your heart and not what your head tells you. I remember reading a quotation taken from a poem at school that read:

'To wander lonely upon the road is to see many things, but not see to them a blind man has to have a stick. And why does he have a stick, because made of wood the trees become his eyes.'

'So my going to the lake is important to me also?'

'Taking that road you will discover many things. That is all I can say.'

Brianna suddenly hugged her great niece.

'My time here with you has been cut short because I can hear the others calling.' She touched her chest. 'Remember, follow your heart, what comes next will satisfy the thoughts in your head.'

'Will you be with me on the journey?'

'Only in spirit, not physically and I cannot intervene. That is your destiny.'

'Or my fate.' Amanda replied.

'You will succeed where I did not.'

Brianna suddenly faded and vanished before her eyes. Almost instantly the bedroom door opened and in walked her mother.

'I thought that I heard you talking to someone?'

Amanda smiled. 'No, I was probably just dreaming mum.' She watched the sun rising throwing a yellow glow down either side of the mountain. 'I might as well get up.'

Mary Brodrick smiled. 'Okay, I'll put the kettle on.'

Chapter Eighteen

Somewhere between the third and fourth chime of the church bell before the hour they started to gather, coming together as a group. Six plus Behildwick Jones who was accompanied by Eira Pryce.

'Are you sure about this?' Behildwick asked. She checked for signs of hesitancy in their eyes, but there was none.

'Look upon us as your royal guard.' Announced Amanda.

Eira Pryce shrugged, grinning back at Behildwick Jones. 'I think you have your answer.'

'Alright,' agreed the older woman. 'But I warn you and the first sign of danger and you turn around and come back home. Is that understood?'

Mostyn who had been unusually quiet, responded with an adamant shake of his head.

'No deal princess. We start out together and we return together. We've a reputation to uphold, not just ours but that of our ancestors. The original gang.'

His reply made Eira Pryce laugh. 'I think you're outnumbered.'

'There will be many dangers, do you not understand that?'

Jonathon gently placed his hand on Behildwick Jones arm.

'The children of Mud Island have never shied away from a challenge. It's not in our blood.'

Behildwick sighed. She looked at Eira Pryce hoping for some support but knew it would be forthcoming.

'They remind me of me when I was their age. I was always so spirited. Not even my father's guard could keep up with me.'

'Give them the chance to prove themselves Oyddiss. I've a feeling you'll return a different woman.'

Behildwick nodded. Eira was right. 'I feel that I am already.'

Amanda gave her grandma a hug and with that they turned away from the church gate.

Eira Pryce waved watching them turn the corner at the end of the road. Some she thought would feel very different when they returned, not least her granddaughter. Seconds later she was joined by Mary Brodrick.

'I thought I saw you hiding up the road.'

'I didn't want Amanda to see me. She would lose street cred if the others thought her mum had come to see her off.'

Eira Pryce looped her arm through that of her daughters.

'Don't worry, she'll return. But when she does you'll notice the change.'

'I already did mum. I saw that when she turned thirteen. It's funny how the child in them suddenly disappears and almost overnight. It was not easy seeing the change in Emma, but with Amanda the pull is stronger. I guess I feel more connected.'

'People with the *gift* always do. Come on let's have a coffee.'

*****

Chatting amongst themselves in groups of two's and three's Mostyn and Jonathon made sure that they were at the rear. Any attack from behind would see the offenders having to deal with them first. Unbeknown to the others Mostyn had concealed in his rucksack his father's hunting knife. Honed sharp along the length of the blade with the back edge notched to help cut down small branches it was an impressive weapon.

'We had a funny dream last night,' announced Daisy who had her arm looped through Larissa's.

Walking alongside Behildwick smiled. 'I think we all suffered a restless night.' She looked behind to see that the two boys were okay. 'An adventure is like a hurricane passing through your unconscious thoughts. One minute you're walking across green fields and then suddenly you find yourself in a dark alley. The mind can play tricks on us as we sleep.'

'Do you think it has something to do with going to old Jonesy's farm?' asked Larissa.

'Quite possibly. Trogglebytes have haunted my dreams ever since I've known them.'

'In my dream,' began Daisy, 'I saw a lady calling out with her arms outstretched. I didn't know who she was, but I did think she might have been Angharad Jones and that she was calling out for Benjamin.'

'I've had similar dreams,' admitted Behildwick. 'Sometimes I see or hear my father or mother calling, other times Castilleon.'

'Was he really handsome?' asked Larissa grinning at Daisy.

Behildwick smiled remembering. 'Yes, he was.'

'Did you love him?'

'I'm still not sure. He was handsome and dashing. Spirited like myself, but we had never kissed so I'm not entirely sure what I really felt at the time.'

'Wow...' exclaimed Daisy. 'That's wicked. After hundreds of years you still don't know. I'm not sure that I want any boy kissing me. They're always wiping their nose on the back of their sleeves when they play football.'

The remark made them laugh making the others in the group wonder why.

'When we get there, to the lake I mean. What will we find?' asked Larissa.

'Hope, I hope.'

It was a strange reply and had both girls wondering about the different connotations. Behildwick dropped back to walk with Mostyn and Jonathon.

'Besides coming along for her protection, why are we going?' Daisy asked Larissa.

'I think because the princess needs to find something that she's lost.'

'Like what?'

Larissa shrugged. 'I don't know and I don't that think she does, not until she's found it.'

'Perhaps, if this lake has magic powers and a lady in the lake, she can tell me where my pet rabbit disappeared to, only *Bristles* never went further than the vegetable patch.'

'I never did understand why you called a rabbit *Bristles*?'

'Because when he was young he was hopping about the kitchen worktop when he jumped up and caught the top his head on a flytrap that was hanging down from the ceiling. My mum had to cut away his fur only when it grew back on his head it came back as bristles, a bit like a David Bowie haircut.'

'I doubt that the Lady Bleudele has time to worry about rabbits!' said Amanda joining them. She didn't tell them about Pippin.

The three at the back were joined by Albert.

'Do you know girls talk about the strangest things,' he said.

'Like what?' Behildwick asked.

'Anything…' Albert replied. 'They say something, giggle and then become serious. You never how to react without getting a rebuke.'

Behildwick grinned. The smaller of the other two boys Albert was forever inquisitive.

'One day Albert you will think differently and you'll catch up.'

Albert scoffed looking at Larissa and Daisy. 'My dad says he still doesn't understand my mum and I've a long way to go before I catch up with him.'

They laughed making the girls wonder why. Jonathon suddenly overtook the girls taking up the lead.

'Is he alright?' asked Behildwick.

'Yeah, he likes to lead.' Said Mostyn. 'He says it gives him time to think.'

Behildwick watched Jonathon striding ahead. She hoped that he'd not seen anything unusual and not told her.

'Sometimes the responsibility of being the leader can be a lonely place.'

They noticed the girls giggling.

'What's amused them now I wonder?' Albert asked.

'Same as usual I expect, nothing special, just them being girls!' replied Mostyn. Leaving Albert with Behildwick Jones he caught up with Jonathon.

'I thought that by now we would have noticed anybody following us?'

Jonathon looked both sides. 'Yeah, I guess.'

'Why'd you shoot ahead like that, did you spot something?'

'I wasn't sure,' Jonathon replied. 'I thought I did, but whatever it was, it was there one moment and gone the next.'

'Like what?'

'Don't laugh. It looked like an elf in a funny top hat!'

Mostyn laughed.

'At least you weren't daydreaming about Amanda.'

Jonathon looked sideways at Mostyn.

'Get away, I've more important things to be thinking about.'

Mostyn scoffed.

'Yeah right, like how to keep her safe if the trogglebytes do appear!'

Jonathon shrugged.

'That as well. I've a feeling that we'll come across them at some stage.'

Mostyn checked the group. They were all there. Albert talking with the princess. Amanda chatting to Larissa and Daisy.

'I'm not interested anymore.'

'In what?'

Mostyn laughed. 'In Amanda you fool.'

'Why?'

'Because she likes you more. I was thinking also, I'm not going to ask her out just to go walking a bloody goat around the village in the evenings. No... she's all yours.'

'You know Larissa Joyce really likes you.'

Mostyn looked back at the two girls.

'Getaway. We've been friends since nursery.' He checked again. 'We're always at one another's throats.'

'And who is it, who always defends your corner when things get tough. Larissa Joyce. You'd be a fool not to ask her out.'

Mostyn checked a third time.

'You're winding me up?'

'No honestly, I do most times, but not over something as serious as Larissa.'

'Maybe I will after we get back from visiting the lake.'

Walking alongside one another, both would admit that they were friends although fierce enemies in most things, knowledge, courage and sports. Girls had been a new thing. Mostyn turned again.

'She's laughing and joking now, but I thought Amanda was preoccupied when we started out?'

'What with?' asked Jonathon checking back.

'I'm not sure. Since the barn she's changed. She's always been a deep thinker, but since the other day something else has happened.'

Jonathon did agree with Mostyn.

'That's right. Whenever we talk about the ghosts, she's very guarded. She felt that the trogglebyte in the barn was looking at her until Behildwick turned up. I think it's unnerved her a little.'

Mostyn frowned. 'I wonder why she opted to come along then.'

'Loyalty and she's part of the gang.'

Mostyn was pensive. 'Yeah probably.' He wasn't convinced it was the reason and neither was Jonathon.

Behildwick Jones watched the girls happily sashay from side to side. It was a good thing that the group was in such high spirits although she knew it might be different when the sun went down.

'What do you think lies ahead?' Mostyn asked.

Jonathon continually checked the fields on either side.

'To tell the truth, I'm not quite sure. The princess believes that the trogglebyte in the barn detected her scent and she is convinced that they will try to kidnap her again. Late evening, tonight I think we need to organise lookouts, changing every two hours.'

'That's odd because I was thinking the same.'

They continued checking with the fields. Mostyn nudged Jonathon, although it was missed by the others. 'I'm not sure, but I think I saw something move in the tree line,' he nodded sideways, 'do you see it?'

Jonathon discretely looked.

'Yes. It could be a stag, there are some big ones in the valley.'

Slinging his rucksack forward Mostyn opened the top.

'Stag or trogglebyte, this'll deal with it.'

Jonathon felt his eyes open wide seeing the knife.

'Where did you get that?'

'It's my dad's. You want to see what he can do when he's butchering a pig. This knife will slice through to the bone as though the pig meat was made of butter.'

Mostyn closed the flap of the rucksack throwing it back over his shoulder.

Jonathon had noticed a change in Mostyn as well. A lot had changed since going to Jonesy's farm.

*****

Walking away from the church arm in arm with Mary Brodrick, Eira Pryce thought she had seen something move behind a gravestone on the far wall of the church, but with the sun in her eyes it was difficult to tell. Blinking and looking again whatever it was had gone.

'That was close,' exclaimed Karlstad as they lay behind a headstone each. *'She almost saw you Bradkar. Next time tuck you backside in as well.'*

When the second woman arrived, they knew that once again they had missed their opportunity.

Checking the back of his hands Bradkar was happy to see that the daylight was not burning away his skin.

'That's right,' whispered Karlstad. *'The daylight don't affect us none. Trygor has been lying to us for a long, long time.'*

'Why?' Bradkar whispered back.

'Trickery, power. Quick… duck back down. Somebody else is coming our way!'

Chapter Nineteen

With his face buried in the earth behind the headstone Bradkar dared not to look.

'*Who is it?*' he asked.

'*Shhhhh…*' Karlstad muttered pushing down on Bradkar's back. '*It's only the churchman.*'

Pushing up so that he could look Bradkar tutted.

'I've never trusted that man. He spouts off that we are all heathens and that his God will smite us down one day. I've still to see or meet this almighty God of his.'

Karlstad waited until the door of the church was closed again before standing.

'Come on, the *outsider's* will begin coming to life soon. We would be unwise to stay any longer.'

Bradkar looked at the church, the stained-glass windows and huge oak doors.

'Just what do they do inside there?' he asked.

'Mostly sing and chant. I think their lord's name is Amen.'

Bradkar picked up a heavy looking rounded stone with the intention of throwing it at one of the windows.

'Do you think he saw us?'

Karlstad scanned around. 'I'm not sure,' he looked at the stone that Bradkar was holding. 'You know Trygor forbids anybody to hurt this *outsider.*'

Bradkar dropped the stone. 'What's so special about him?' he asked.

Karlstad expected the vicar to appear at the door and look out. He must have seen Bradkar fat backside poking one side of the headstone.

'I don't know, but even Trygor is wary of what power lies within the walls of this church.'

Bradkar looked back at the church it was a funny looking building and he wondered what purpose the tall spire had sitting above the door and porch.

'We could kill him and then the power would be destroyed. Surely Trygor would thank us for that.'

A face suddenly appeared at one of the stained glassed windows.

'*Quick, get down,*' cried Karlstad, pushing Bradkar in the back. '*He's watching!*'

'*That settles it, I'm going inside and I'll gut him like a fish.*'

Karlstad held onto Bradkar's arm. 'Not without Trygor's say so. Touch this churchman and Trygor will gut us instead.'

Bradkar put his knife back in its sheath.

'What about the princess?'

'We follow them.'

Bradkar suddenly reached out and grabbed at something scurrying on by. A second later he had swung the mouse around by its tail, whacking its head against the top of the headstone. Opening his mouse he dropped it in.

'You really are an animal at times,' remarked Karlstad as Bradkar chewed then swallowed.

'I'd been watching that mouse flit between the headstones. It was begging to be caught. You should try then some time, they taste like chopped chicken.'

Karlstad grimaced. Although he was a trogglebyte he did have standards and eating mice was not one of them.

Keeping close to stone walls, hedgerows and running between trees they took the same route that the princess and the children had taken. Bradkar had manged to find more to eat, snatching at another unsuspecting mouse, a dozing vole and a cluster of fat juicy earth worms.

'Will you stop fooling around,' Karlstad scolded. 'This is important. If we don't return with the princess, Trygor will kill without taking another breath.'

'But I'm hungry...' Bradkar belched. 'It's been a long time since we had supper.'

They were tempted to steal milk from the delivery van, but when the woman at the door pointed there way they ran in the opposite direction. Without her glasses she thought it was teenagers returning from an all-night party.

When a cockerel stepped up onto the wall of a cottage near the edge of the village it didn't have time to crow as Bradkar grabbed it by the neck and with a quick twist made sure the bird would never crow again.

'At least we've something to cook later,' he said showing Karlstad the dead cockerel.

Karlstad nodded agreeing. For once Bradkar was right and they would need to eat.

'Maybe we can add a few rabbits as well.' He added. 'There are plenty about in the fields.'

Keeping to the tree line they could see the group walking ahead using the lane on the other side of the field. At one point Karlstad grabbed Bradkar's arm.

'*Stop…*' he whispered. '*I'm not sure if they spotted us?*'

'Don't be daft. She's sprightly for an old crone, but her eyesight must be failing after all this time.'

'Don't underestimate the princess. Only a fool would be so unwise. She proved how courageous and resourceful she is by killing Trybulloc.'

Feeling the frustration flow through his veins Bradkar was becoming irritated by Karlstad's constant disparaging remarks. Irked he squeezed the dead cockerel's neck.

'Soon I will kill the children and capture the princess. Trygor made me the leader of our hunting party. I'll prove he was right!'

'And what about what happened at the old woman's cottage?'

'That was lucky. She caught me off my guard.'

'That…' Karlstad added, 'was the princess. As I said she's resourceful. Unpredictable and not to be underestimated.'

Bradkar watched as Karlstad moved on again as the group took a turn in the lane. He would have to watch Karlstad. He didn't trust him. He wondered if Trygor had sent Karlstad back down the mountain to check on him. Trusting another trogglebyte was always difficult. This time he grabbed Karlstad's arm.

'Do you have any idea where we're going?'

'Back at the church it was difficult to hear everything that they said. I thought I heard one of them mention a place called *by-my-ear*. I've never heard of it, but we'll know when we get there.'

'I wonder why they're going there.' Bradkar mused.

'To meet some blue lady I think.'

Bradkar had never seen a blue lady. He seen some blue looking animals that had been frozen in winter, but never a blue *outsider*.

Karlstad suddenly grabbed Bradkar and pulled him down behind a large bush.

'Now what's wrong?' asked Bradkar.

Karlstad clamped his hand over the trogglebytes mouth.

'Not so loud. I've a feeling that we're being followed!'

They looked at one another coming up with the same name. 'Schellian.'

Bradkar laid the cockerel down taking out his knife.

'I'll gut the bastard!'

'No. Don't let him know, that we know.' Karlstad suggested. 'Let's crawl over to the trees and then keep on walking. We act natural as though we don't know he's there. When we reach the other side we'll decide then what action to take.'

'Okay, but I don't like being mistrusted. I especially don't like Schellian following me.'

'Me neither, but first we have to make sure that he's alone. Schellian we can deal with, but if he has others with him, we might be outnumbered.'

Bradkar agreed seeing the sense in Karlstad's reasoning.

'You're right. Trygor has changed and he is becoming unstable. I think his desire for vengeance has made him go mad.'

Karlstad didn't reply. Having witnessed Trygor kill Stardd there could be no denying that the mountain king was indeed insane.

The edge of the trees would be the ideal place to ambush the trogglebyte following.

*****

Having made sure that the heavy oak door of the church was shut and locked Owain James had run between the rows of pews to the window nearest the altar. Climbing the font stone he could see the two trogglebytes hiding behind the large headstone, but one was fatter than the other and his backside was sticking out. Inside his chest his anger was rising.

'Why would they be here?' he muttered to himself.

He watched the trogglebytes leave using the leafy lane walking towards the edge of the village, mysteriously taking them away from the mountain.

Kneeling down before the altar stone Owain James prayed for the lord in heaven to keep him safe. He prayed also that he be spared from making his own journey.

Chapter Twenty

I'm convinced that we're being followed.' Mostyn announced looking forward again. 'There was two, but now there's three.'

They slowed down letting the others catch up.

'Don't turnaround to look, but we've already got company.'

Behildwick Jones wasn't at all surprised.

'They've been following us for almost an hour Mostyn, but you did well to spot them. Trogglebytes are bulky cumbersome creatures and hiding isn't one of their strongest strengths.'

Mostyn grinned.

'I know what you mean. They've just both dropped behind a bush, but I could still see them and there's another about to join them.'

'They seem wary of one another which is good news for us.'

'Do they know that we know?' asked Daisy.

'Probably my dear, but don't let that worry you. They are very suspicious creatures and have to think something through before they act. It was how I gained enough time to escape before they realised what I had done.'

Behildwick pointed at the wood ahead.

'Hurry along now and we'll take shelter in there. As a teenager I'd spend a day riding through these woods, so I know them well, better than the trogglebytes. We'll shelter from the midday sun and our disappearing from sight will confuse them even more. We'll take a short cut through the field. They'll have to use the lane as the terrain is too difficult to climb over.

'What about the cows?' asked Albert.

'They won't hurt you,' replied Jonathon, 'as long as you don't annoy them.'

'Leave the gate open, 'Behildwick requested.

'But the cows, they'll wander out into the lane.'

'That's precisely what I am banking on.' Replied Behildwick.

They left the gate wide open and started to cross the field. It wasn't long before they had reached the safety of the trees.

'That was a neat trick,' Jonathon said to Mostyn as they watched the cows leaving the field and filling the lane, blocking the way.

'Cows are not as stupid as they appear,' Behildwick replied. Grazing all day they're always on the lookout for opportunities to find fresh grass. Cows don't like trogglebytes and will cause them some trouble. It'll give us the advantage to get ahead.'

Letting the girls go ahead with Behildwick the three boys held back where they could see anybody approaching and if needs be get in first with an attack.

'You know she's a wily old bird,' announced Albert. 'I would never have thought that she would be as interesting as this.'

Jonathon nodded. 'I guess when you've lived as long as she has, you see and learn a lot.'

*****

They struggled, as predicted by Behildwick Jones to keep the cows apart as Bradkar and Karlstad heaved and pushed, kicking out at the strong flanks of the disgruntled beasts. It was bad enough having Schellian following without the inconvenience of the cows.

'Move aside you useless creatures,' Bradkar called out receiving a swift kick in the shin from the nearest cow. He thumped the animals flank, but found himself being crushed between a pair of big mature cows.

'Help me Karlstad,' he cried.

In a moment's hesitation Karlstad saw his opportunity to get rid of Bradkar, but with Schellian hot on their heels it would need the two of them to deal with him.

Weaving their way between the agitated beasts they emerged battered and bruised all over.

'At least they'll slow Schellian down as well.'

'I need to sit down and rest,' complained Bradkar.

'When we reach the safety of the trees. We can hide and watch Schellian. We need to know where he is at all times.'

They reached the trees going in deeper where they could not be seen.

'That was clever letting the cows enter the lane. The princess is no fool.' Bradkar admitted.

Karlstad nodded, nut his interest was focused on a movement in the trees.

'Come on get up, quickly this way,' he whispered.

They hid amongst clump of dark green shrubs where they could not been seen.

'I'm fed up with this…' whispered Karlstad. *'I suggest we deal with this problem with Schellian here and now, otherwise it's going to slow us down. We can't be following the princess and watching our backs at the same time!'*

Bradkar put up his thumbs, signalling that he was in agreement.

They waited, listening for the sounds of Schellian's approach as he crushed the fallen leaves underfoot. When he was only a few feet away they pounced from their cover. Attacking from both sides Schellian didn't have time to get his dagger out of its sheath.

Karlstad plunged his dagger into Schellian's side and Bradkar the trogglebytes back. Schellian eyes opened wide as he fell to the ground mortally wounded. Holding the wound at his side he looked up.

'Trygor doesn't trust either of you… you're already dead men.'

Bradkar laughed out loud.

'That'll be twice that I've died. You were a fool Schellian believing you could outwit us.' He kicked Schellian hard as Karlstad drew the blade of the dagger across the dying trogglebytes throat.

'That's that problem sorted,' said Karlstad, 'now we had better catch up with the princess and the others, they've gained the advantage again!'

*****

Behildwick perceived that something had happened feeling the dead trogglebytes soul leaving the wood, floating through the air going to another place. Amanda sensed it too.

'Something's happened, hasn't it?' she asked.

Behildwick looked back.

'Yes. We should seek shelter before the sun goes down. There is a storm coming.'

Daisy looked up at the blue sky where there was hardly a cloud in the sky.

'It doesn't look stormy?'

Behildwick smiled. 'Nature tells us when a storm is coming dear. Look at the leaves and how they curl inward so that they capture the raindrops.'

All around leaves were curling.

Astonished by her wealth of knowledge Mostyn was in awe of the princess. 'Is there anything that you don't know?' he asked.

'There are many things that I do not understand.' She pointed. 'Over there would be a good place to rest. Its high ground and gives us a good vantage point.' She turned to face Mostyn. 'Had I known everything when I was younger. My reckless actions would not have seen my father killed nor his kingdom lost.'

Larissa Joyce came to her rescue.

'But it was Trybulloc's fault, not yours.'

'That is kind of you to think like that and say so. I've had many nights to think about my actions. Had I not gone riding alone Trybulloc might not have seen or seized the opportunity to attack the castle. We never listen to the wise advice given by our parents. My mother especially hated me going riding and she too paid a terrible price for my foolishness. I carry a lot of shame.'

None replied. They felt sorry for the princess carrying such a burden.

'And Castilleon. Do you ever think about him?' asked Daisy.

'Not as often as I should. We we're friends and I was very young.' She sighed. 'Being young can be confusing.'

'You can say that again,' Albert replied. He was looking mainly at the girls.

'That's really sad. I would feel lost if I lost my mum and dad.'

Albert raised his eyebrows at Daisy. 'Were there many knights?' he wanted to know.

'Yes,' replied Behildwick. 'They were brave, but they all died in the attck on the castle or going to the mountain with Castilleon.'

'*Did you feel that?*' Mostyn suddenly asked.

'The wind,' said Jonathon. 'It suddenly changed direction.'

'There is somebody or something else in the woods,' said Amanda. Behildwick Jones agreed. The girl's intuitive powers were growing stronger.

'Yes, I feel it too. We should stay alert.'

'Are the trogglebytes close?' asked Larissa.

'No, it not the trogglebytes. This force is friendly. Strong and yet suspicious!'

Amanda's explanation surprised even Behildwick.

Albert sniffed the air. 'I can smell salt in the air, we can't be that far from the sea.'

The girls went to the top of the ridge to look. When they returned, they said that they were only a couple of miles shy of the coast.

'I've never seen the sea.'

They all turned to look at Behildwick Jones, surprised by her admission. 'I could ride to the wood and although I ventured inside, I never went far. I would like to the see the seas and the beach.'

They had lunch and refreshments before taking on the challenge of the last two miles to the beach. Watching them eat, chat and laugh Behildwick sensed that they were being watched although it was a force she did not recognise. Destiny was approaching fast.

'Watch over them,' she whispered hoping that to whom or wherever it was heard.

After an hour of walking over and down hills, ploughed fields and through long grass the draw of salty sea air was ever the more inviting. Running ahead the girls left the boys to protect the princess.

When at last Behildwick saw the sea and the beach, she stood momentarily to look.

'It's beautiful, so big. I never imagined it could be so magnificent.'

'It's calm today,' said Jonathon standing alongside, 'you want to be here when it's wild.' He looked at the clouds coming in from the horizon. 'You were right about it being stormy soon.'

Stepping between the sand dunes the soft grains felt strange. Behildwick removed her shoes deciding to go barefoot. Amanda came back and took the older woman's shoulder bag.

'I like it here,' Behildwick said spreading her arms wide. 'My father should have built the castle here beside the sea.' She put her hand to cover her eyebrows protecting her eyes from the last of the sun. 'Does the sea fall over the edge?' she asked.

'No,' replied Jonathon. 'It stretches for hundred, thousands of miles to other lands.'

Behildwick smiled. 'We should find a cave to shelter the night. The storm will keep the trogglebytes away. They hate the rain.'

They walked the beach finding a small cave, but far enough that it wouldn't get flooded by the incoming tide and yet dry enough to keep them safe. The boys gathered wood for a fire as the girls collected shells to show Behildwick.

Standing at the entrance to the cave, Albert looked apprehensive. 'It's the first time that I've ever slept in a cave.

Coming alongside Daisy couldn't help herself. 'If you snore and keep me awake Jones, I'll have the mermaids kidnap you.'

Chapter Twenty-One

With the candle flame flickering in his eyes Owain James clasped his palms together thinking about his mother and sister. He asked God for his mercy and help.

It had seemed an eternity since he had seen either, in fact almost twenty years to be precise. The memories that he did have were patchy with bits missing. He continued to pray ignoring the parishioners who were arriving for his sermon. All that he did know was his sister had been given the name Selantra.

As the twin of Owain James she had arrived into the world two minutes after him. Born the first twins under the cover of the mountain, where their mother had been held captive by the king of the trogglebytes, their destiny cruelly cut without connection for so many years.

Separated from her birth mother and given over to the care of a childless trogglebyte couple named Alburus and Marianna, Selantra had grown knowing nothing about her brother.

Owain James and his mother had been cast out from the mountain to face the elements forging a life for themselves in the valley below amongst the *outsiders*. The sad memory of his grief, his prayer was reserved for their mother who had died from pneumonia shortly after finding peace away from the mountain. Not even Trygor knew she was dead.

Owain James as he had been named was raised under the roof of a kindly woman named Eira Pryce becoming the adoptive brother to his half-sister Mary. He had adopted his adoptive mother's maiden name to save embarrassment.

As the years went by eventually the truth had emerged regarding his twin sister. The vicar had vowed that one day he would overcome his lack of courage and go to the mountain to reclaim his sister. Kneeling before the altar he prayed hard.

With the service complete Owain James quickly discharged his parishioners from the church locking the door. Taking off his robes, he grabbed his bible and left locking the vestry door behind him. He knew the route through the mud flats, the path to take alongside Mud Islands and of the goat track on the side of the mountain. Today, at last he had the courage to face the terrible king of the mountain.

Standing at the bottom of the goat track he looked up at the imposing mountain. Despite the sunshine it looked grey and uninviting, devilishly mysterious and foreboding.

'*Courage…*' he muttered to himself. '*The lord is with you Owain.*'

Trampling down thorny brambles he began climbing the goat track clutching his bible in his hand. The loose stones made the going difficult, but Owain was determined that nothing would thwart his calling. The closer that he got to the secret entrance the stronger he could feel his sister's spirit.

Way back down in the valley he saw a shepherd counting his flock then scratch his head wondering where another had disappeared to overnight.

Nearing the entrance which resembled the gaping mouth of a mountain wolf Owain opened the bible at the page that he had marked. He began reciting the psalm of David:

'The lord is my shepherd; he makes me lie down in green pastures. He leads me besides still waters. He restores my soul. He leads me in paths of righteousness for his names sake. Even though I walk through the valley of the shadow of death, I will fear no evil...'

The trogglebytes watching from the entrance heard his approach.

'What's he say?' asked one holding a long pointed metal rod.

'I dunno,' he's mumbling on about somebody walking through the valley, he must mean the shepherd.'

The trogglebyte who had asked the question laughed. 'Several times already he's counted his sheep, but he still can't find the one we took early this morning.'

Owain James stopped reciting when he saw the trogglebytes watching him.

'And what business is it that you bring to the mountain vicar?' the biggest trogglebyte asked, his voice deep and menacing.

Owain looked down into the lush green valley below, but Richard Thomas, the shepherd was walking back to his farmhouse. It was too late to cry out for help. Taking a large intake of mountain air the vicar announced his intentions.

'I seek a private council with your king. What I have to say is for his ears only, not yours!'

The trogglebytes eyed Owain James suspiciously. Trygor had said that one day the man in black with the white collar would come to the mountain. It was synonymous that it was today with the king being married to Selantra.

'And what of he doesn't want to see you?'

Owain James eyes narrowed. He could feel his heart thumping in his chest.

'Just tell him that I am here. He will see me!'

They stood aside to let the vicar pass.

The one in charge told another, 'take him to the great chamber, but if he tries to trick you, maim him, but do not kill him not until Trygor has seen the man of the church!'

'I will not trick you.'

The trogglebyte in charge grabbed Owain by the sleeve.

'Know this man of the church, our king is in a foul mood today. I hope that what you have to say makes him smile. If you make him angry, be it on your head!'

Owain gulped clutching his bible. He took one more look at the sunshine then entered the dark passage following the trogglebyte leading the way with another walking behind.

Faces appeared from cracks in the passage, small hollowed doorways leading to an even bigger chamber inside. Some of the faces were old, others young and the ones hiding behind the legs of older brothers and sisters very young. Owain James kept his hands crossed over his chest resisting the urge to touch the foreheads of the very young. The escort read his thoughts advising that he might lose a finger if he did.

'They look half-starved, undernourished,' he exclaimed. He was clearly shocked.

The escort stopped walking and the trogglebyte leading turned around.

'Had you stayed, you might too have ended up like them. You should consider yourself lucky to have escaped the mountain. There are many here who wish they could.'

'Then why don't they?'

'Fear, man of the church. Our king is not to be messed with nor was his father before him.'

'How old are you?' asked Owain James.

'Older than you.'

They continued on their way. The vicar tried asking about his sister Selantra, but his questions were met with a wall of silence.

When at last they stepped beneath a stone archway Owain James was in awe of the size of the great chamber. Trygor still wearing his cloak of dead bats wings stood to greet his guest. He was bemused by the man who was clutching his bible.

'Does the book give you the courage to come visit at last?' he asked.

'Not the book, but what is contained within,' replied Owain James. He was surprised to see such a beautiful young queen sitting alongside such an ugly brutish trogglebyte. Trygor demanded that the hall be cleared, his voice echoing around the chamber walls.

'I must read this book in which you put so much of your faith in. I am need of something to humour me today. Tell me, what do we owe for the pleasure of this visit?'

Owain James could feel his knees knocking. If there was a chamber associated with hell this was it. In one corner near a bubbling cauldron he saw a pile of bones, some animal and possibly the others human. Staring back at him with the tips of their tongues protruding from thin lips were three very old women dressed in rags. He wondered why they had not left the chamber when ordered.

'I have come on a mission of mercy!'

Trygor responded with a scoff.

'Mercy, now there's a thing. Did your ancestor show us mercy so many years ago when there few inhabitants in the valley, when a castle stood along the bog.'

Owain James had heard of the stories of how the trogglebytes had been driven into the mountain to live.

'My church offers mercy to all. We try not to dwell upon the past.'

Trygor laughed loudly. He pointed at the three old hags.

'They tell our young children stories. Tales we do not want them to forget. We should see the sunshine every day and feel the warmth on our back, but instead we were forced to live here inside the mountain by your kind.'

'God protects all.'

Trygor dismissed the suggestion with a flick of his hand.

'State your business here?'

Owain James stepped closer, not that he wanted to get close to the king of the mountain, but to see the young queen. There was something familiar about her, something that he recognised. The shape of her face, nose, chin and eyes. Suddenly the recognition was like a light being switched on. The young woman was like his mother.

Again Trygor asked. 'Why have you dared to come here?'

'Like you, I have no luxury choosing a life serving others. I have come for what is rightly mine!'

Trygor leant closer to his queen. 'Did I not say that this day would end entertaining us.' The smile disappeared. 'Freedom is the most precious commodity Owain James. I have stopped others killing you as you have gone wandering the mud flats and stood staring up at the mountain. Freedom is a luxury we cannot have.'

Owain James continued to stare at the young queen.

'I offer you a trade.' He stopped fidgeting.

Trygor rubbed the bristles of his beard. He admired the *outsider's* courage. None in his chamber would dare make such a suggestion.

'Go on…' Trygor invited.

'I have important news that you would find attractive. News that interests you especially king of the mountain.'

'And what would I trade in return for such news?'

The three old hags stopped stirring the large pot.

'My sister,' he said.

Selantra suddenly stood and descended the stone throne. She stood in front of Owain James having seen the similarity. She looked deep into his eyes, soft eyes that told her they belonged to her as well. When she touched his cheek. Trygor snapped his fingers and the old hags immediately escorted Selantra from the chamber.

'What do you know that could so tempting as to allow me such an exchange?'

'An old woman left the village this morning accompanied by six children. She was heading in the direction of the coast. You know her as Princess Oyddiss.'

Trygor grinned. It was a good bargaining chip that the vicar had brought.

'To make the trade, I would need more than just a name.'

'She was followed out of the village by two trogglebytes. One excessively fat and the other half his size.'

Trygor ruminated tapping the stone arm of his throne. So Bradkar had survived and joined forces with Karlstad. He wondered why they hadn't just grabbed the princess outside the church. He wondered why Schellian hadn't dealt with the Bradkar and Karlstad and snatched the princess. He stopped drumming the arm of the throne.

'And how do you know that it was the princess?'

'I am a man of God and my flock tell me secrets. Long have I known of one such secret that has eluded you Trygor. Of all things you seek the one called Oyddiss.'

Owain James would tell of his association with Mary Brodrick or Eira Pryce.

Trygor wondered why he had never come forward before with this information. Had the man of the church heard about his marriage to Selantra, he couldn't tell. Maybe this was what forced Owain James to come to the mountain. Was Owain James toying with him? Again it was hard to tell.

'Give me the names of the *outsiders* who have been harbouring the princess and I will agree to your terms.'

Owain James shook his head from side to side.

'Names are not important now and not part of my bargain. Like you as king, I have a duty to protect the innocent.'

Trygor's eyes narrowed.

'Why take the coast road?' he asked.

Owain James shrugged. 'That I do not know about. I did hear them talking about going to a lake.'

Trygor had heard about Lake Bywydhir. His expression remained the same.

'So do we have a trade?' I have brought you something valuable, now let me leave with something that I hold dear.'

Trygor laughed.

'And what makes you think that your sister still lives here in the mountain?' he asked.

'Your queen is unlike any of the others. She has my mother's features.'

Trygor nodded.

'You are perceptive. Perhaps I should have kept you as well and your mother.'

'*She's dead.*' Owain James glared back at Trygor the fear having gone from his body.

Trygor's eyes suddenly grew darker with menace.

'Soon the princess will be returned to me. So your information carries little weight in the argument. However, I might consider your request if you can tell me something very important, something that has eluded me for many years. How has the princess kept herself hidden all these years without detection?'

'Apple and pear trees, along with lavender bushes to sweeten the air around her cottage.'

'You mean the one on the edge of the village?'

'Yes, that's the one.' He was eager to secure the release of his sister. Owain James was becoming increasingly impatient at the troggglebytes delaying tactics. 'She has been your prisoner for twenty years. Be merciful and let her live amongst her own kind. I beg of you, release Selantra.'

But Trygor was not about to give up his queen so easily. He wanted to see how far he could push the man of God, amusing nobody but himself.

'Truly I would let her go... if I could. Therein however lies the problem. You see your sister died ten years ago when the snow fell very deep in the valley. She could not withstand the cold and one dark night she was taken from us. Had she lived, I would have released her.'

Owain James gripped his bible feeling the anger rising in his chest.

'You lie. Your queen is my sister!'

'Enough,' cried Trygor becoming bored with the man of the church. 'Do you believe that you can simply come here and make unreasonable demands after all these years.' He pointed to the pile of bones.

'Leave now while you can. I am in no mood for your games. I warn you, stay and you will join the pile.'

Owain James looked over at the tangled mass of assorted bones. He dropped to his knees. Suddenly the hope of Selantra being released was vanishing before his very eyes. Balling his fists he charged at Trygor ascending the stone throne. He was within a foot of the mountain king when the arrow hit his side piercing both lungs. Owain James fell landing next to Trygor's large feet.

'You should have never come holy man. Here I am king, and my word is the law. Nobody leaves without my say so, including your sister.'

Owain James looked up knowing that he had been duped, tricked. Finding breathing difficult and knowing that he was going to die he gasped. 'You lied... she lives...'

Trygor grinned placing his foot on the dying man's shoulder.

'She is indeed my queen, and she will give me children.'

Owain James coughed trying to find the right words.

'When I've done with her, she will join the pile of bones.'

Suddenly Owain James realised why Behildwick Jones was going to the lake and what it meant to Trygor to have her recaptured. Despite his pain he laughed coughing up blood.

'You are the fool trogglebyte king. Mixing your kind with royal blood will never be successful. It is merely a myth, nothing more than a fairy tale.

'Look at your children Trygor to see that they are undernourished, underfed and need sunlit to make them healthy once again. You yourself are not the man that you used to be. You've just lost the right to be king.

'A great force is coming your way which will end your reign Trygor. Soon you will be no more, mark my word as God is my witness.'

Enraged by the prophecy Trygor grabbed the vicar by his hair and yanked his head up so that Owain James could look directly into his eyes. Taking the dagger from his belt he held it under the dying man's throat.

'Mark my words soothsayer. When you die I will be victorious. I will have the old crones strip you of your holy clothes. They will take great pleasure in cutting through your flesh and demonising your God before adding you to the cooking pot.

'Tonight I will invite your sister to a banquet. It will be held in your honour and I will make sure that she has on her plate your heart. One way or another you will be granted your last wish Owain James, and you be reunited with your sister.'

Like a madman possessed he laughed until the tears stopped rolling down his cheeks.

Trygor cut the vicar's throat and ended his life. He thought the death would make him feel happier, but instead he felt cheated. Angrily he tore the blood-stained dog collar from Owain James limp body throwing it into the fire beneath the cauldron.

Coming back into the chamber he told Marigold that she do her worst with the vicar. He told her to save the heart for his queen's plate.

Marigold rushed across to the throne stone dragging the body alongside the cauldron. She stripped Owain James of his clothes and began cutting. She kept some of the best bits for herself.

Watching from the shadows Selantra had seen Trygor kill her brother. She had clamped her mouth to prevent the scream knowing that she would join him if Trygor knew she had been a witness.

Turning away from the great chamber she went to find somewhere where she could cry and pray for her mother to come collect his soul.

Also witness to Trygor's savagery Queen Erikka waved goodbye as his spirit left the mountain. His death had been no more tragic than her own and Owain James had accepted death sensing that one day he would be reunited with his sister when her time came.

'One day Oyddiss, I too will be with you, but you've greater things to achieve before that day comes.'

Queen Erikka turned away. She had seen enough already.

Chapter Twenty-Two

Leaving the dead Schellian where he lay covered by a blanket of bushes and where the creatures of the wood could gnaw upon his carcass Karlstad and Bradkar continued their pursuit of the princess. Already she and the children were far ahead and they had lost time dealing with Schellian.

'He said that there'd be others!'

Karlstad looked back but saw nothing.

'It was only his ego talking. Schellian knew that he was about to die, so he issued one last idle threat. There's nobody else following us. I would know.'

The cloud overhead were becoming dark and menacing threatening rain.

'We should stay under the trees, Karlstad advised 'there's a storm approaching and the rain will wash away our tracks. If anybody is following, they'll have a hard job finding us.'

Bradkar also looked behind. He too saw nobody.

'I'll find some wood for the fire. I'm hungry.'

Karlstad shook his head in agreement.

'It'll be getting dark soon, we'll make camp and then leave at first light. We'll make up the ground that we've lost and catch them by surprise.'

He watched Bradkar lay down the pheasant and rabbits.

'You skin them while I'm searching for wood.'

Putting the pelts to one side Karlstad could hear Bradkar searching around. Stealth was not his best attributes.

*****

They were about to begin eating when suddenly there came a rumbling sound, followed by many others as both stone and fallen vegetation was crushed under the heavy wheels of a strange looking carriage pulled by a single horse. Kicking the loose earth into the fire Karlstad grabbed Bradkar diving for the safety of the undergrowth.

'The food,' cried Bradkar in a plaintive whisper, *'it's covered in earth.'*

'Better that we live and eat another time.' replied Karlstad.

They watched as the *outsider* riding up front of the carriage gently coaxed his horse through the trees.

'Not much further now,' said the man as he gave a flick of the reins.'

Bradkar took his knife from his belt, but felt Karlstad's hand resting on his arm. Karlstad shook his head.

'No, stay low and don't make a sound,' he warned, *'this outsider is armed. Look at this sword that he has behind his back.'*

'What is it?' asked Bradkar as the horse and carriage drew close.

'I've heard rumours that some of the outsiders live in a house pulled by a horse. They call it a caravan.'

The outside holding the reins was much bigger than them, stronger. He had long dark hair a beard and tanned skin. Humming merrily to himself he manoeuvred the horse past the bush where they could only watch and wait.

'I could easily surprise him and kill him,' Bradkar suggested.

'He would kill you first, then me. No, we wait. I've a feeling our paths will cross again soon.'

Bradkar watched the multi-coloured carriage, a mix of reds, yellows, greens and blues roll on by. The horse was strong and had good meaty flanks. Bradkar looked over at the ruined pheasant and rabbit lying burnt and caked in earth and ash on what had been their fire.

'When the time comes to kill him, we'll have cooked horse too.'

'Did you see the strange markings on the side of his horse drawn house?' Karlstad asked.

'No. Why are they significant?'

'I'm not sure. I think I recall seeing something like that somewhere before. Something that our ancestors handed down.'

A sudden movement to the side of the trees averted their attention away from the departing rider, horse and carriage. One by one the rabbits began to reappear.

'Get ready,' said Bradkar, *'supper might not be entirely lost.'*

Chapter Twenty-Three

Behildwick Jones prediction of a storm had been proven right as the rain lashed down hard on the sand outside the cave. The lightning way off on the horizon line was spectacular, but the thunderclaps that followed were loud and at times made the earth shake.

Crashing down on the beach the waves had grown in size and been consistently relentless keeping them awake all except Albert who seemed to be able to sleep through anything.

Around the five the next morning the storm had moved away and left in its wake a beautiful sunny day with a yellow hue in the sky. Only Amanda and Behildwick were left awake to keep watch. Adding more wood to the fire Amanda huddled in close.

'Are you alright?' she asked, concerned that the older woman sitting beside her had had little sleep.

Behildwick Jones opened her eyes wider.

'Yes dear, I'm fine although I've had better nights. All things considered though the cave saved us from getting soaked had we been out in the open.'

Amanda smiled back but it had been her second night without a lot of sleep. The older woman pulled her shawl about her neck and shoulders.

'It's really beautiful here, she said. 'I could stay here and watch the sea coming and going all day long.'

'I like the beach too,' Amanda admitted. She was going to say something else but Daisy turned restlessly in her sleep bashing Larissa across the arm. It woke them both. All three boys were still asleep.

'Is it morning already,' inquired Daisy stifling a yawn.

'Almost. Would you like some coffee?' Behildwick offered.

'Yes please.'

Once again Albert began snoring loudly like that of a lion.

Daisy gave a shake of her head. 'Cor… I'm glad that I don't have to sleep with him every night.'

Amanda and Larissa giggled.

Getting to her feet Daisy told them that she was going to splash water on her face in the rock pool outside. She was accompanied by Larissa who thought that black coffee first thing in the morning was too much her sensitive system. What Behildwick had forgot to tell was that she made her own coffee recipe consisting of blue chicory, diluted down with a clove of garlic, adding a pinch of spinach leaf and a spoonful of sugar for sweetness.

Beyond the entrance where she could not be heard by those inside Larissa cupped a handful of salty water into her mouth before spitting it out.

'Urgh… I don't think I could stomach that again, not first thing in the morning.'

'It wasn't that bad,' replied Daisy, who was scanning the deserted beach.

'What are you looking for?' asked Larissa.

'I'm not sure. I thought that I saw something move further up along there beach only it's not there now.'

Larissa also looked but saw nothing.

'The trogglebytes, where do you think they are right now?' Amanda asked.

Behildwick Jones sniffed.

'Somewhere nearby I don't doubt. I thought they might try checking the cave during the night, but the storm probably thwarted their plans. They don't like getting wet. That's not to say that we won't have an encounter with them at some time today.'

She rummaged through her shoulder producing a plastic container filled with meat pate, several packets of dried crackers and a jar of potted shrimps, none of which looked very appetising.

'I thought the boys could find some crab amongst the rocks. Sea food is good for you.'

'I'm not sure that I want it for breakfast,' Amanda confessed screwing up her nose. 'There has to be a tea room or café somewhere nearby.'

Behildwick laid out the cartons and packets using a flat stone for a table.

'Maybe they can catch some fish too.'

Sniffing the scent of the crab paste Albert began to wake.

'You look distracted?' she asked.

'I was just thinking what it would be like swapping places with Jonathon for a day?'

'Not a lot of fun I would imagine?'

'Why?'

'Well, just as you see the changes, both physically and mentally, so do they. They might appear strong and brash at times, but boys still have a lot to weigh up every day. Responsibility comes in different forms for girls and boys. Take Jonathon, he's protective of you, but he feels responsible for everybody younger and older, including myself. Would you want that moral obligation?'

'Probably not. But we do think differently.'

'Yes, that's true. Girls are generally calm, where boys can be more aggressive. It's in their biological make-up and the balance of chemicals. They think differently because of their male hormones. I'd rather be female that think and act like a boy.'

'But you told us that you went riding alone and into the wood. Wasn't that against your mother's wishes?'

Behildwick grinned.

'Yes, it was and often she would say that I should have been born a boy.'

'That's what I mean. I want to do the things that they can do.'

Behildwick stared beyond the cave entrance watching Daisy and Larissa forage amongst the rock pools.

'Castilleon had to prove himself to my father every day. That was the challenge that he accepted as part of the kings personal guard, but I would not have wanted such a demand to have been placed upon me. Life as a man is not always easy. My father had many troubles, as does your own father no doubt.'

Amanda grinned. 'I overheard him talking to my mother the other day. He told her that it had been no picnic with Emma, but what how he'd cope with me, he didn't know.'

Behildwick laughed waking the other two boys.

'Now he does sound like my father.' She noticed the boys stirring. 'Trust me, it's easier being a girl, even when you're grown up!'

'Have you any regrets?'

Behildwick kept her voice low.

'Many although perhaps one and that I wasn't honest with Castilleon.'

'Whether you loved him or not?'

'Yes, that. Even now I'm still not sure.' She watched Jonathon stretching. *'Tell me,'* she whispered. *'Do you ever dream about Jonathon?'*

'Sometimes. Mainly when I'm angry with him. At times he infuriates me, but other times he's funny and kind. He makes my insides get jumbled up.'

Behildwick chuckled. 'The art of growing. By the time you reach my age, you'll be an expert.'

Amanda opened the packet of crackers nibbling down on one corner.

She imagined Jonathon as a knight on a white charger coming down the beach to rescue her. Watching him rub the sleep from his eyes, then rotate his aching limbs having slept on cold stone she wondered if he would tell her how he felt about her. She was still daydreaming when he came and sat down next to her.

'Is this breakfast?'

'It's good for you,' announced Behildwick Jones.

'If you're a cat, yes, but I'd rather a slice of toast or a bacon sandwich.'

Amanda nudged him. 'Don't be ungrateful.'

'What's Daisy and Larissa doing?'

'Looking for crabs,' Behildwick replied. 'I thought you boys might like to try fishing for mackerel. The fire's still hot so we can cook them and have them on crackers.'

Jonathon pulled a funny face and so did Mostyn who had come to join him. Behildwick poured them both a coffee.

'It's my special brew.'

They both gulped down the coffee rather than upset her feelings.

'What are doing?' asked Mostyn.

'Looking for crabs,' replied Behildwick.

'I think I'll join them,' said Mostyn.

He was about to get up when Daisy yelled back their way and pointing at the headland on the beach. Immediately Jonathon, Mostyn and Amanda ran to see what had her all excited.

'Come on Albert,' said Behildwick gathering together her things, 'we might as well join them.'

Nestled in amongst the sand dunes was a brightly coloured gypsy caravan and nearby a horse was tethered munching the long grass. In front of the caravan was a large fire with a pot hanging above. Despite the distance Mostyn could smell the bacon.

'Cor... get a whiff of that, bacon sandwiches.'

He was off like a shot with the others following.

'Wait,' cried Behildwick, 'it could be a trap!'

The group stopped running and waited for her to catch up.

'You have to be on your guard at all times,' she warned. 'It looks harmless enough, but there's no telling what is on the other side of that yellow and red contraption.'

No sooner had she alerted them to the danger when a man appeared stepping down the short wooden steps to the sand below. He saw them and waved.

Pulling up a strong box covered in a blanket for Behildwick to sit upon the stranger introduced himself.

'I'm known as Gallius.'

Amanda swooned, feeling the rush of blood to her cheeks and chest. The tall, dark haired stranger was her knight in shining armour riding along the beach.

One by one they introduced themselves.

'We did not mean to interrupt your breakfast' she said thanking him for the box.

The gypsy smiled turning over the thick rashers of bacon.

'You might not have my lady, but they certainly did.' He pointed at Mostyn and the others. 'Would you accept my invitation to breakfast?'

'Not many,' replied Albert, his stomach grumbling to add emphasis to the invite.

Adding more wood to the fire the gypsy asked Amanda to fetch a container from inside the caravan. 'You'll find it on the left. It's full of bacon and you'd best bring the eggs too.' He asked Daisy to help bring the bread.'

Looking at Albert the man laughed.

'I'm glad that my horse is tethered, you sound hungry enough to eat him!'

Albert looked at the horse, it was one of the biggest that he had ever seen. Gallius was still staring when Behildwick turned his way. She added a smile to her face.

They were all surprised when he suddenly stood and bowed in her presence.

'Forgive me my lady, you must think my manners appalling. I am indeed honoured to be in your presence.'

Behildwick Jones stood and curtsied in return.

'The honour is reciprocated my lord. It has been a long time.'

'Do you two know one another?' Mostyn asked.

'Our families have known one another for year, centuries. Gallius is the Gypsy Prince from the Quarter kingdom of the North.'

'As are you Princess Oyddiss. There could be no mistaking.'

'Even though I am wrinkled and aged.'

Gallius smiled as he asked Larissa to fetch the basket of tomatoes from the caravan.

'Age does not mar your beauty princess.'

Amanda liked Gallius. He had a way with words that made her secretly sigh.

'We should eat a hearty breakfast to celebrate this union,' said the gypsy prince.

'Have you been outside all night?' Behildwick asked.

'Yes, but it was nothing to worry us, General and I have known worse weather and most of our days are under the sun and night the stars. Last night was an exception.'

'We slept in a cave,' interrupted Albert. 'It was a bit noisy and cold.'

Daisy sighed. 'How you know, you were snoring most of the time!'

They laughed including Gallius.

'You travel with a spirit escort princess.'

'They are both brave and foolish.'

'How is that?'

'Youth has courage, but not wisdom. They accompany me because they think I am incapable. There are undoubtedly dangers ahead, but they were foolhardy to come.'

Gallius scanned along the tops of the dunes.

'I take it that you mean the trogglebytes.'

'Yes, that right. Have you seen any?'

'I passed a couple travelling through the wood yesterday afternoon. Conspicuous creatures and especially as one had an oversized belly and a larger appendage to match.'

'They're the ones,' announced Mostyn. 'We saw them too.'

'They've been following us ever since we left the village,' exclaimed Behildwick. 'A herd of cows helped delay the way ahead.'

'There was three, but they killed one of their own. I found him lying hidden under a bush.'

The news pleased Behildwick although she wondered why there had been three having only seen two follow behind.

Gallius appeared puzzled. 'The young ones. They call you Behildwick and yet you are the princess. How is that?'

'It is the name given to me by the kind folk who took me in to protect me when my father was killed and his kingdom lost.'

'Word reached our castle that you had killed Trybulloc. That took great courage. Why some of our men would not enter that mountain and return alive.'

'It was necessary...' she lowered her head so that he could not see her eyes, 'in order that I survived. One day I will avenge my mother's death too. It is a long time since I have used the name Oyddiss.'

Gallius nodded. He had heard of her suffering, her father's death and mother's disappearance. 'I am very sorry. They were a good and kindly king and queen. My father was heartbroken to hear that you had all been lost.'

Behildwick passed around the plates as Gallius served up the breakfast and Amanda cut the bread into slices.

'Your caravan is great,' Albert said admiring the many strange patterns and colours. 'Do you live in it all year round?'

'Indeed young master, I do.' Gallius was pleased that the boy had taken an interest.

'And General...' Albert added, scooping up his egg with his fork, 'it's an unusual name for a horse?'

Gallius laughed, he agreed.

'And yet a noble name. Many years ago, a time when battles were fought in the fields and amongst the trees there was a bloody conflict that was known as *'the sunrise of the blooded knives'*. It was so called because early one morning many men, women and children were killed as they slept innocently in their beds. The attackers had come from the mountain, a vicious, marauding band of cut-throats.'

'Trogglebytes...' Jonathon added nodding.

'Indeed young master. Savages with hearts so cold that you would believe them chiselled from the mountain itself. The years have not been kind and still they are as evil.

'After the attack the remaining elders got together seeking revenge. One such elder, an old man who had once served in the king's guard owned a horse called General. The horse you see munching the dune grass is a descendant of the original horse, but he possesses all the spirit of his ancestors.

'Had the original General not led the men of the villages into battle, the battle might not have been won. My General has a more sedate life, although he is rightly wary of trogglebytes. He hates them as much as I do.'

Albert worked it out on one hand then used the other.

'All the same, General must be very old.'

'I never ask. There are some things that even a horse keeps secret.'

'General is legendary,' said Behildwick. 'Named by the villagers whom he saved during the battle, his courage was painted on the walls of castles in the other three kingdoms.'

On cue the horse sauntered over to the campfire to join them. Albert stood and stroked the horses head.

'He might be old, but I think he's magnificent.'

The horse accepted the compliment shaking its head up and down.

Daisy joined Albert in stroking the horses head.

'If you are a prince, why do you not live in a castle instead of travelling alone on the road and with only a horse for company?'

Gallius looked at Behildwick Jones and smiled.

'You pick strange companions for your journey my lady. So inquisitive.' He turned to Daisy. 'I did once live in a castle young miss, but things change and from your mistakes you learn about regret.

'My father was king Zarrion. Ruler of the quarter kingdom to the north. Together with my older four brothers we lived in a big castle where we eagerly awaited the arrival of a baby sister. However destiny offers a cruel hand in exchange and fate can never be undone. With the birth of a beautiful girl we lost our mother.

'King Zarrion was never the same ever again. He adored his only daughter, as we did our sister, but time can drag by so very slowly and the wound only heals over a scar going so deep. Eventually the zest for life diminishes and back then with my young sister growing I did something that I deeply regret now.' Gallius centred his attention on Behildwick Jones.

'Like yourself princess. It has been a long time since anybody has used my name or indeed called me a prince.'

Behildwick placed her hand on Gallius's arm.

'Being born into royalty does not protect us from the pain we endure as ordinary people. I too have many regrets, Gallius.'

Chapter Twenty-Four

Trygor was growing impatient and becoming ever suspicious of those around him, including Selantra, who for some reason had suddenly become distant and unresponsive to his demands.

If what Owain James had said was the truth, then Bradkar had survived the attack by the two old women. Trygor wondered why he had not returned to the mountain with the others.

Sitting on his throne with his chin in his hand the mountain king sensed the presence of deceit amongst his people. He believed that killing Stardd would have been a blunt enough message to have warned all trogglebytes that he would not be made to look the fool. Whispered mutterings in the great chamber were beginning to annoy him.

'*What…*' he cried out, when he was no longer to hear their whispers. '*What is it that you want from me?*'

Selantra sitting at his side, faced her king.

'They are wondering how Karlstad has managed to stay outside all day without being burnt by the sun.'

Trygor stared back. He detected a look of defiance in his queen. Standing he made those present in the chamber look his way.

'Karlstad is a coward. He hides where the shadows protect him.'

His address was met by a shaking of heads.

'No...' said a voice amongst the gathered. 'He lives because he is unaffected. Maybe the sun has lost its power to harm us. Maybe we should consider living outside with the *outsiders*.'

Trygor sensed the tension in the air as the rumblings of uncertainty filled the chamber. 'Oberran...' he called, 'come forward.'

Reluctantly the trogglebyte pushed his way through approaching the throne stone.

'My king,' he said bowing before Trygor, 'how may I be of service?'

'Take off your shirt. Show others what the power of the sun did to your back.'

There were astonished gasps especially from the women closest. Across Oberran's back were a dozen long raw looking welts where Trygor's personal guard had lashed his skin with the pelt of an old badger. Oberran had been sworn to secrecy under the threat of death if he ever revealed how he really received the injuries.

'That is what the power of the sun will do to you all, should you get caught outside during the day.'

Sitting on his throne Trygor grinned. Oberran had done well and he would be rewarded later.

The only one not fooled was Selantra. She had seen with her own eyes how ruthless her husband could be. She had wanted to tell her adoptive mother and father about the vicar's visit and demise, but she loved them and to have done so would have hurt them deeply. Keeping the truth inside was as painful and expressing her opinions.

Trygor descended down the steps and gently patted Oberran on the shoulder.

'This is a brave man. Look upon him differently from now on. If Karlstad returns, we shall see his back and how it bears the scars.'

Trygor asked Oberran to close closer so that he could whisper in his ear.

'Leave the mountain when it gets dark and head west where the land meets the water. When you find Karlstad and Bradkar. Give them a message from me and say that I know of their deceit. If however they bring back the princess alive their punishment will be forgotten.'

Oberran didn't waste time in leaving the chamber to gather together things that he might need for the journey. Trygor ascended the throne stone and rightfully took his place alongside his queen again.

'Your eyes display your contempt for my queen. It does not do to make me angry. Others before you have done similar and disappeared overnight.'

With his finger he discretely pointed at the bubbling cauldron.

'Come let us retire to the bedchamber where you can show me the loyalty you did on our wedding night.'

Changing her expression Selantra followed obediently, smiling at Alburus and Marianna as she went past. Trygor had been good to his promise and made their life easier, although Selantra wondered for how long. Her husband was always so unpredictable.

Jeffrey Brett

*****

As soon as he saw the first clouds of night appearing in the sky Oberran stepped clear of the secret entrance hastily descending the goat track to the green valley below. With his bag slung over his shoulder he was eager to get as far away from Trygor as he could.

Crossing the mud flats and passing by Mud Island he made his way to the edge of the village. He had heard of the old woman's cottage, but never been close. He approached warily knowing that if she had attacked Bradkar and rendered him unconscious she must be a witch as Bradkar was not easily beaten in a fight.

Going from window to window he checked although saw no sign of either the old woman or anybody else.

'The place is deserted.' He muttered rattling the handle of the kitchen door. Had he looked closer he might have noticed that the door of the wardrobe was slightly ajar and a single eye was watching him.

'*Not as deserted as you think troll,*' said Eira Pryce holding the iron from the fire in one hand and a large metal frying pan in the other.

Several minutes later she watched the trogglebyte leave and proceed down the lane to the edge of the village.

'You've a long walk ahead and my granddaughter, and the others are almost at their destination.'

Oberran came across the field where the cows were still munching on the moist grass. Having already encountered the previous two trolls they recognised his smell. The largest of the herd issued a warning moo. Oberran took the long way around to the wood opposite.

Walking with the assistance of the moon overhead he came across a fox that was busily gnawing at something under a bush. Pulling his knife from his belt the fox would make a good meal and the pelt would be ideal for winter shoes. He was almost upon the fox when he recognised a hand or what was left of it. The fox ran leaving Oberran with the corpse.

Seeing what was left of Schellian, Oberran jumped back in shock. He noticed that the trogglebytes throat had been cut, not by an animal, but sharp knife.

'I wonder which one killed him.'

Oberran knew that Karlstad didn't like Schellian, but that he had been wise enough not to have shared his opinions with Trygor. Oberran kicked the hand from sight walking on he wondered if he would come across Bradkar next.

*****

There wasn't a lot of heat in the early morning sun as Behildwick and Gallius sat beside the fire warming their hands, watching the children wash the breakfast utensils in the surf.

'I wish that my life had been as carefree as theirs.' Gallius remarked, the memory of his error still a plague on his conscience.

Behildwick watched as the children had fun in the surf trying to avoid from getting wet.

'They have days when they are not as free as we believe. Soo they will have to accept the challenge of becoming an adult. The transformation will be easy for some and hard for the others.'

'I miss my family.' Gallius waved at Amanda who had turned to catch their attention. 'She reminds me of my mother. She has a natural beauty plus a self-assured manner.'

'She has qualities that she is yet to understand.'

'Do you miss them?' he asked.

'More now than I ever have.' She replied. 'It was only recently that I learnt about the fate of my mother. I feel responsible for their deaths Gallius. Her spirit searches a dark kingdom of which I am no longer part of.'

'It is not the only tragedy that you have witnessed?'

Behildwick told Gallius about the lost miners and the children of Mud Island. She identified each one playing in the surf with a lost relative.

'They have their own sadness to deal with. Life is never fair.'

'Or in love and war.'

Behildwick agreed. She told him about the encounter with the trogglebytes in Eira Pryce's rear garden, the goat and the reason for her journey. She made no mention of Castilleon. It was good to be with somebody who had experienced heartache.

'I thought only born of a royal household could make that pilgrimage?'

Absently drawing patterns in the sand Behildwick watched Amanda.

'At first, I was reluctant to have them come on this adventure, but now I am glad that they did. Their youth makes me feel much younger Gallius and there is one among them who will benefit greatly from taking the risk.'

'I feel that there is something special about her too. She has wisdom beyond her years.'

'Destiny cannot be undone.'

Gallius watched the boys. 'They are young men, but without the skills of war. They have courage and tenacity, but you need more to outwit a troll. The road ahead will be criss-crossed with danger.'

Remembering what Eira Pryce had said, Behildwick reiterated the sentiment.

'We have to give them the opportunity to prove themselves Gallius. Did we not challenge the wisdom of our fathers?'

'Yes, but what a price we have paid for our actions princess. We are without a kingdom, castle or family. We have lost so much.'

Behildwick saw a sadness in his eyes.

'What ails you Gallius?'

He rubbed his brow hard the memory never far from his thoughts.

'I thought you would have heard.'

Behildwick gave a shake of her head.

'No. What I do know is that you are a long way from your own quarter kingdom and a prince never ventures far?'

She looked deep into his rich brown eyes sensing that there was a dark secret, never before told. Kicking the embers of the fire with his heel, they watched a flurry of sparks fly skyward quickly vanishing the higher they went.

'You I cannot deceive Oyddiss. Your heart is as pure as the day you were born a princess.'

Chapter Twenty-Five

G allius took in great gulps of salt air.
    He had always expected someone to ask the question one day and General had grown tired of listening to the endless excuses that had punctuated many a campfire discussion. The gypsy prince exhaled hard through the small gap in his lips.

'I am still searching for the reason, hoping that I would the answer in your quarter kingdom.'

'Maybe our coming together was as destiny expected?'

'Perhaps,' he smiled. He heaped the sand around the fire with the heel of his boot to stop it from spreading.

'Affairs of the heart can hurt more than we accept and love is reputed to be our strongest bond.' He looked into her eyes, she was still beautiful. 'Maybe our biggest enemy as well. It can strike harder than any sword I know and the memory that it leaves in its wake is at times unbearable. Long now, shame has been my constant companion. I thought travelling far away would lessen the burden, but that has not been the case.

'Like you Oyddiss I have seen more moons than I care to remember and General has guided me to places that I never knew existed. In each place that we visit I hope to find peace and forgiveness, but our dead ancestors are slow in handing out mercy.

'When death unkindly took my mother, my own grief was clouded by my father's bouts of rage. He became a stranger to us all including our baby sister. Fortunately, she was raised by a wet nurse until such a time when as brothers we could include her in our daily routines and adventures.

'One such day when the weather was unsettled, hinting at rain Aurora and I went exploring into the forest to look for wild flowers and to pick berries which she loved to do. The hours passed and we were happy until the dark clouds suddenly arrived overhead.

'There was a streak of lighting which spilt a large oak followed by a clap of thunder. It was only when the thunder ceased that I heard my sister's screams. Emerging from the thick undergrowth and approaching Aurora were a group of mountain trolls. Aurora was five at the time.

'I drew my sword and quickly stood between them and my sister, but when the rain came there was little shelter to be found. Seeing that the trolls were armed with crudely made cudgels, spiked spears and stone cut swords I told Aurora to run and make her way back to the castle. In the meantime I stood my ground blocking what space there was for the trolls to pass.

'Aurora had gone less than ten lengths of our drawbridge when I heard her scream once more. I tuned to see a trogglebyte scoop her up into his arms and disappear into the trees.

'I killed the three closest to me before I was struck from behind. When I regained consciousness, the rain had stopped and the forest was silent. I searched everywhere, but there was no sign of Aurora.

'When I told my brothers and my father what had happened, my father had to be restrained from attacking me. He cursed me, cursed the day that I had been born and he blamed me for taking Aurora to the forest. With my brothers looking Aurora I gathered together a few possessions and left the safety of the castle heading to the mountains where I believed the trolls had taken my sister.

'Days turned to weeks and weeks became months. Many moons later the years have come and gone as well. My heart is broken having lost my little sister. I loved Aurora more than any of my brothers. I failed to protect her that day and she faced a terrible fate alone. I've been wandering, looking ever since.'

Behildwick put her hand over the prince's hand.

'I too searched for ways to make amends for my shame, but we are destined to carry this burden until we ourselves are laid to rest.'

They heard the children giggling as they played.

'They are fortunate, their pain is not of their making.'

'Did you not get word that one of your brothers had found Aurora?'

Gallius shook his head.

'Long has there been bad blood between our people and the mountain trolls. They would surely have killed her, if only to cause my father even more pain.'

Behildwick surprised him by leaving her hand covering his.

'Sometimes in my dreams I hear Aurora calling out to me, oddly enough she is calling me back home to

Liatheclo. Every time I say that I am sorry the vision disappears.'

'Guilt interrupts my sleep,' admitted Behildwick. 'I try to say that I am sorry, but when I open my mouth nothing comes out.' She squeezed the back off his hand then let it slip away. 'Why don't you join us Gallius. Maybe accompanying us to the lake you will find the answer that you have sought for so long?'

'Go to Bywydhir…' he replied. 'I've heard the legend. I might not be welcome there!'

'Well you won't know, unless you go.'

A shrill scream from Daisy Gethall attracted their attention bringing to a halt their conversation. In an instant Gallius was up, sword in hand and running towards the dunes where the children had been playing. When he saw what had made Daisy scream, he yelled loudly.

'Get back to the campfire.'

Grabbing Mostyn who had been the closest Karlstad and Bradkar saw the occupant of the caravan coming their way.

'I hope you're ready, 'Karlstad warned, 'he's got his sword.'

Standing on top of the sand dune where they had the vantage point Bradkar held a dagger at Mostyn's throat.

'If you come any closer, the boy will die before your very eyes!'

Gallius stopped his approach and lowered his sword standing at the bottom of the sandy hill.

'Let the boy go and I will gladly his place.'

Karlstad shook his head derisively.

'That trade would not serve our purpose. We would much rather trade the old woman for the boy.'

Gallius looked back down the beach where the princess was surrounded by the children.

'And what use is an old woman to you?' he asked.

Karlstad laughed.

'Not just any old woman as you no doubt know minstrel of the woods.'

Gallius turned pointing to his friends.

'How would I know what or indeed who she is, we have only just met this morning? She's an old woman down on the beach with some children.' Gallius hoped that by stalling for time, it would give him the opportunity to think of a plan to protect the princess and help the boy escape.

Bradkar the less patient of the two was growing tired of the exchange.

'The boy for the princess… it's a simple trade.'

Gallius felt a presence by his side. He turned to see General standing there, the head of the horse head raised high so that he could clearly see the two trogglebytes. Gallius noticed the look in General's eyes.

'Of course,' he whispered. *'Like the time that we had to trade with the ruffians outside of the place called Maccaester. We need to equal the ground.'*

General nodded his head up and down.

'What's he saying to the horse?' asked Bradkar.

'How do I know?' replied Karlstad. 'Maybe he's as crazy as his singing.'

'He's not crazy, but you are. Gallius will easily deal with you.'

Bradkar moved the knife to cut Mostyn's throat, but Karlstad stopped him.

'Wait. I have heard of that name before, but I cannot think where?' he looked down at the beach. 'What is your reply minstrel? Do we kill the boy or have the woman in exchange?'

'I am willing to make the trade, only not here, not in front of the other children. Meet me in an hour at where the roads meet four ways and I will make sure that the old woman comes too.'

He saw the trogglebytes discuss the proposal. Then nod their approval.

'You have one hour. A minute over and we kill the boy and everybody else including you.'

They pulled Mostyn away kicking and yelling not to make the trade. A squawking seagull overhead veiled his cries. Larissa called out after Mostyn, but she was restrained from following by Behildwick and Amanda.

'He'll be safe, I promise,' said Gallius returning to where they stood waiting.

'You have a plan?' asked Jonathon.

'I said we'd exchange the princess for your friend in an hour.' He held up his hand preventing the instant opposition. 'Of course, I have no designs on making any such exchange except getting your friend back safe and sound.'

'I don't understand,' said Behildwick. 'For Mostyn's sake, I must be there?'

'Deception princess. General and I have used such a trick before.' He looked around the group at who was the same height as Behildwick. He chose Albert.

Chapter Twenty-Six

When they emerged from the caravan there was a chorus of laughter and pointing of hands, none louder than Daisy. Dressed in a long dress and shawl over his head Albert had been made to look like an old woman.

'You look like my nanny on a bad day,' hooted Daisy as she held her ribs.

Blushing as his cheeks turned pink Albert didn't like being dressed as a girl. 'My street cred has just slipped down the drain,' he complained.

'What do you think asked Gallius ignoring Albert's moans?'

Amanda who had stopped laughing was once again serious.

'It's good. Albert is about the same size and height. From a distance he could pass as the princess.'

'What about when the trogglebytes get close. They'll know it's not Behildwick?'

Gallius placed an encouraging hand on Albert's shoulder.

'By then the deceit will be long forgotten. I will have the advantage of surprise. Trogglebytes do not think as fast as us outsiders. I will rescue Mostyn and before they realise their folly we will have made good our escape.'

Somehow Behildwick felt confident that the plan would work.

'What about the rest of us?' she asked. 'Where will we be?'

'Jonathon can come with me. I have some spare swords in the caravan. Amanda can bring General and the caravan. If you wait for me in the lane beyond the junction we can meet up there.'

Amanda looked across at General.

'Are you okay with that?' she asked. The horse nodded his agreement.

'You make it sound so easy,' said Behildwick. 'Trogglebytes are not so easy fooled.'

'These two are,' replied Gallius. He pulled his sword from its scabbard. 'There's a broken oak next to the crossroads. I can hide my sword the other side and Albert can sit alongside me.' He laid the long edge of the sword over the crook of his arm. 'This sword has despatched both men and trogglebytes. It is made from toughened Arabian steel and can slice through the branch of an oak tree as though it were paper.'

Running her fingers along the steel of the blade Behildwick nodded.

'I will agree to this plan on one condition and that is, that you come with me to the lake.'

Gallius agreed.

They hitched General to the pulling bar and with Behildwick sitting alongside Amanda with Larissa and Daisy kneeling behind, Gallius gave Jonathon his sword.

'It belonged to one of my brother's. It is a good sword and has seen action in battle. It might feel light, but I assure you that it is swift as the wind.'

Gallius gave Albert one final check then the three of them made their way up the beach to where they would fine the crossroad beyond the sand dunes.

'When we get close, you crawl through the long grass. The trogglebytes will be distracted watching Albert and me to notice you.'

'I wish that I had a weapon.' Said Albert. Gallius pulled a curved dagger from his belt. It also originated from Arabia.

Flicking it left and right with his arm extended Albert felt happier.

'If you have to stab a trogglebyte, stick and twist.' Gallius advised.

'Stick and twist,' Albert repeated. 'No problem. Cool.'

Jonathon raised his eyebrows and Gallius laughed.

'This is like when I would go hunting with my brothers. You remind me of them. That is a good feeling. You are brave like them too.'

'Yeah, but I bet they never went into the woods dressed as a woman.'

'Do you think it'll work?' asked Larissa, concerned that if it didn't, both Gallius and Mostyn could end up dead. Maybe Jonathon as well.

'Trust in Gallius,' replied Behildwick. 'He descends from a long line of gallant warriors from the northern kingdom. I trust him.'

Behildwick crossed her fingers under the blanket over her legs. She hoped that the plan did work. Toom much blood had already been spilt on her behalf already.

*****

The time was almost upon the hour when Gallius and Albert dressed as Behildwick arrived at the fallen oak. With the handle of the sword where he could grab it they sat down and waited.

'I've got butterflies in my stomach,' Albert admitted.

'Me too,' replied Gallius.

Albert looked at the gypsy prince sitting beside him.

'Have you really killed many men and trogglebytes?'

'Enough. There's no glory in killing anybody or anything Albert, but at times it is necessary. The trick is to keep focused and not get distracted. Think of why we are here. Mostyn needs our help. Daisy will think you're a hero if you rescue Mostyn.'

'Really... wow. I could say that I was a real knight.'

Gallius nudged Albert and looked to where Jonathon was hidden down in the long grass. The two trogglebytes pushing Mostyn ahead of them were approaching.

'You made a wise move princess,' announced Bradkar, who had of Mostyn's arm. 'In a minute you'll be our prisoner and the boy can go free.'

It was Karlstad that sensed all was not right. He held out his hand putting it across Bradkar's chest.

'Wait, what's with the shawl Oyddiss. You didn't have that at the beach.'

'It's colder up here,' Gallius replied. 'The old woman is older than us menfolk.'

Bradkar was okay with the explanation. He pushed Mostyn forward, but the boy stumbled and fell to the ground. Gallius saw the opportunity which had presented itself.

'*Now,*' he yelled.

Instantly Jonathon was on his feet and coming for Bradkar that sword switching left and right.

'*What the...*' said Bradkar as he was in two minds whether to grab for Mostyn or defend himself.

Karlstad drew his dagger from his belt, but Gallius was quicker and cut the trogglebyte on the forearm. Karlstad cried out in pain.

'I knew this would be a trick, *outsiders* can never be trusted.' He held his injured arm. Suddenly Albert who had seen Mostyn fall and bang his head on a small boulder lying on the road, screamed like an agonised banshee. He kicked Bradkar on the inside of the knee sending the trogglebyte crashing to the floor.

'I saw you push Mostyn, if he dies, I'll gut you!'

Coming alongside Albert, who had the shawl down and flapping wildly over both shoulders, Jonathon held the tip of his sword at Bradkar's chest.

'Move and I'll run you through!'

He told Albert to check on Mostyn.

'He's alive, but banged his head badly. He's bleeding.'

They saw the other's waiting down the road. Gallius made Karlstad sit down beside Bradkar.

'You've gone to a lot trouble to kidnap the princess, but she rides with me now. If you come anywhere near us again, I'll not be so charitable.'

Gallius told Jonathon and Albert to carry Mostyn to the caravan.

'I suggest that you return to your mountain and tell your king that you failed. Lie if it saves your life and say that the princess drowned. But I warn you, come near us again and I'll leave you for the crows to feed upon.'

Albert was about to take Mostyn's feet when he noticed Bradkar reaching for a large stone.

'Watch out,' he cried at Gallius.

Rushing at Bradkar the trogglebyte was nimble getting to his feet. He launched the stone at Albert who ducked.

'You treacherous troll.'

Without thinking he stabbed Bradkar in the side just under his ribs. The trogglebyte staggered back the shock registered in his eyes. Bradkar stared at Albert and then Karlstad.

'A boy...' he mumbled, 'a mere boy has done for me Karlstad, help me!'

But Karlstad was nowhere to be seen. Having seized the opportunity he had rolled into the long grass alongside the crossroad and made good his escape.

'Do you want me to go after him?' asked Jonathon.

'No,' Gallius replied, 'your friend is injured we need to get him to somewhere safe where he can have his head healed. The trogglebyte won't bother us again, not on his own.'

Standing over the dying trogglebyte Bradkar looked back up.

'I recognise you know... you're the gypsy prince. I'd heard that you were dead.'

Gallius his sword back in its sheath. 'You should never believe all that you are told. I am very much alive troll, but you will join the others who have gone before you.'

He looked to check that Jonathon and Albert had Mostyn and that they were almost at the caravan. Kneeling down beside Bradkar he had a question to ask.

'Have you ever heard of a young girl named Aurora?'

Bradkar opened his mouth to talk, but no words came forth. Instead he died from his wound. Once again Gallius felt that the curse was upon him and that his search for his lost sister would continue.

When Larissa saw that Mostyn was unconscious and bleeding she jumped down from the footrest.

'*Is he dead?*' she cried.

'No, he's hurt,' replied Jonathon, 'but he'll live.'

They laid Mostyn across the footrest.

'Was it the trogglebytes?' asked Behildwick.

Albert responded first.

'One of them pushed him, Mostyn fell and banged his head on a large stone lying on the ground.'

Gallius joined them and immediately checked on Mostyn.

'He will need help and some rest,' he advised.

Larissa stroked aside the loose hair from Mostyn's forehead. Moments later he murmured and began opening his eyes. Larissa who was the closest wiped the tear from her eye.

Mostyn held his head where it hurt and was damp. Looking at how close Larissa was knelt over him Mostyn blinked then looked again.

'What you doing Joyce? Are you trying to get in a sneaky kiss while I lay incapacitated?'

Larissa Joyce ignored that he was injured, instead she thumped his left shoulder. Mostyn cried out feeling the pain sear through to his aching head.

'It was bad enough with the trogglebytes, but I'm not sure what's worse you or them?'

Looking at Behildwick, Gallius grinned.

'Young love is strange nowadays.'

'Young love anytime can be strange,' replied Behildwick.

Mostyn lay back down feeling dizzy.

'He needs a doctor,' said Amanda checking on the head wound.

Gallius inspected the head wound again and agreed. When he touched the boys arm Mostyn flinched.

'A needle and thread will sort his head, but I think he also has a broken bone in his arm. He can't go on.'

Mostyn shuffled until he could sit up, assisted by Larissa.

'Put a bandage on my head and my arm in a sling, I'll be right as rain in a couple of days. I ain't missing out on the fun, not having come this far.'

But Behildwick Jones had already decided that she had seen enough. Looking back up the lane she saw the trogglebyte lying motionless in the road.

'That's the one that came to the cottage the night that Amanda's goat was taken.

'He won't take any more live-stock. Albert killed him.'

Standing alongside Daisy's mouth fell open in both surprise and shock. Albert took out his Arabian knife to show them. It had been wiped clean of blood on the long grass.

'Each is as brave as any knight I have ever known,' said Gallius. The compliment pleased Behildwick.

'Why, I did nothing to help?' groaned Mostyn holding his injured arm.

Gallius disagreed.

'Being taken prisoner takes great courage young master and especially by mountain trolls. If you had not fallen, the element of surprise might not have presented itself to us.'

'*My hero...*' said Larissa Joyce. She instantly blushed realising what she had said. All the same it made Mostyn smile and wink at Jonathon. To everyone's surprise Daisy looped her arm through Albert's.

'I suppose I'd feel left out if I didn't say you were my hero.'

Puffing up his chest proudly Albert grinned at Daisy. 'I knew that one day I would surprise you Gethall. Perhaps now you'll show me some respect.'

Daisy scoffed. 'Don't get ahead of yourself Jones, you still drive me mad.'

'Right,' said Behildwick. 'My mind is made up.'

She turned to face Mostyn.

'I want no argument here. You are injured and need medical attention. We'll splint your arm and bandage your head, but if you don't get both looked at you could pick up a nasty infection. We just need to decide who takes you back and who goes on.'

Mostyn went to open his mouth to object, but Larissa placed her hand over his lips.

'No, not this time Mostyn. You do need real help. I'll go back with you.' Behildwick nodded, it was a good start. 'And I think Albert and Daisy should go too.' She held up her hand to demonstrate that she meant what she had said. 'The trogglebyte that escaped Albert knows that it was you who killed his companion. It is safer for us and you, if you went back to the valley.'

'But I'm not afraid,' protested Albert.

Gallius helped support Behildwick's decision. 'Nobody denies that you're not brave Albert, but Larissa,

Daisy and Mostyn will need somebody brave to protect them on the journey back, and who better than yourself.'

Albert thought about it seeing the others nod their approval.

Behildwick had another surprise.

'I suggest that Jonathon goes as well.'

Jonathon's head shot sideways to look at Behildwick Jones. 'Why?'

'You were all lucky today, but there could be others out searching for me. Albert is courageous, but alone he wouldn't stand a chance against two, maybe three trogglebytes. You're tall for your age Jonathon and together you would be a formidable challenge.'

'You can take the sword,' offered Gallius.

Jonathon felt Amanda's hand on his shoulder. 'Do this for me,' she asked.

Reluctantly Jonathon agreed. He could see the sense in what Behildwick had suggested and all of sudden the journey had taken on an unexpected twist of events.

'As long as you'll be my girlfriend, it's a deal.' Amanda smiled. It was as good as a yes.

When they were alone Behildwick had one question for Gallius.

'What about General, you and him have never been apart?'

'That's all the more reason that he takes them back. On foot the journey would be slow and Mostyn would not make it far before he collapses. General has an instinct for danger, he can smell it, sense it. At the first sign of a trogglebyte he'll gallop away until they are safe. When we've done what needs doing at the lake then we'll be together again. I've already spoken to the horse and he agrees.'

Behildwick Jones didn't dispute it. The old horse had seen a lot in his time and like Gallius, General was both wise and knowledgeable.

*****

They decided to eat before they left to make sure that didn't have to stop on the journey back. There were still grumblings and the others didn't understand why Amanda was going on with Behildwick and Gallius to the lake. Finding themselves alone Amanda too wondered why.

'You seem distant, distracted?' Amanda asked, watching Behildwick stare at the waterline where Gallius was talking with Jonathon and Albert.

'I am not so distracted Amanda, as I am concerned.'

'Is it going to the lake?'

'In some ways yes. You see I promised your grandmother that I would let nothing happen to you. Any of you. Already Mostyn has been hurt and still there is danger all around. I was foolish to have started any of this.'

'No.' Amanda disagreed. 'I think since the incident in the barn, going to the lake is a necessity. Although I cannot explain, I feel drawn to Bywydhir.'

Keeping her focus on Gallius and the others Behildwick nodded.

'Your destiny lies within the lake Amanda although you may not realise why. At least we will have Gallius to protect us.'

'Grandma told me that this journey would be important.'

'She says too much at times!'

Amanda giggled. 'She told me that in my dream.'

Behildwick turned to face her.

'Oh, I see. Even so, she shouldn't have said anything.'

'You were talking in your sleep, back in the cave.'

'Really, what did I say?'

Amanda shrugged. 'I'm not entirely sure, but it sounded like you were talking with somebody that you had not yet met. Does that make sense?'

'Perfect sense. I've had that dream many times. It what draws me to Bywydhir.'

'And Gallius, is there a reason that he is going to the lake?'

'Yes. Gallius has a nightmare that he needs to release. I feel that the lake can help. That is why I was insistent upon him joining us.'

'Not because he is tall, dark and mysteriously handsome.'

Behildwick grinned.

'For someone so young, you are very perceptive. I remember your grandmother being like you at that age, and in some ways your mother.'

It was Amanda's turn to smile.

Behildwick suddenly changed becoming very serious.

'When we arrive at Bywydhir you must do everything that I ask, everything. Is that clear? No argument, no reasons why, just comply with my wishes. Agreed?'

Amanda said that she would. 'Total compliance and no argument.'

'Good.' Behildwick was satisfied.

'They're disappointed not to be going with you.'

'One day, when they are older they will understand why. Things happen for a reason Amanda. I've come to understand this and stopped being a rebel. It's much easier to accept our fate than fight it. Larissa will nurse Mostyn and Daisy will make sure that Albert doesn't get into any more trouble. Jonathon will be Jonathon and look after them all. Their destiny in part has already been fulfilled.'

Finding Jonathon throwing pebbles into the sea Amanda joined him.

'What do we tell your mum when she finds out that you've not come back with us?'

'Don't worry about. She and grandma already know.'

Jonathon frowned, but had the good sense not to ask how.

'When you get back you'll find some other things have changed too.'

'Like what?'

'I don't know, just changes. I had a very restless sleep in the cave and many faces came, then went. One of them as the vicar, Owain James. I feel that something has happened to him.'

'You know, at times you can be a bit weird, almost spooky. Can you read my mind?'

'No, not yet.' She grinned laying her head on his shoulder. 'When I get back we'll go for a long walk, deal?'

'Deal...'

'What's Gallius saying to General?' Daisy asked Albert.

'No doubt to look after us and to get back as quick as possible.'

'Do you think it'll be dangerous?'

Showing her the curved dagger Albert expanded his chest. 'Nah, trogglebytes are not half as tough as they make themselves out to be.'

'What will your mum say when she hears you killed one?'

'She will probably call my dad from the shed and he'll say *'well best we celebrate then with meat and two veg, followed by pie n' custard.'*

Their laughter was lost in the wind coursing inland. Tethered and ready General could feel the time had come to begin the journey. His neigh told Gallius that he was ready. They waved until the caravan disappeared from sight whereupon Gallius kicked sand over the fire, leaving the beach clean and as he had found it.

'We should keep to the beach until we pass the headland. From there we'll go inland. The tide is on its way in so it will destroy our tracks should anybody else be following.'

Amanda walked on ahead kicking up the surf glad of the cold water on her feet. It helped keep her thoughts and her senses alert. She could not be sure, but she felt that they were being watched.

Lying low and hidden amongst the sand dunes and long grass, a pair of eyes keenly followed their progress along the beach. Soon they would reach the headland and because the water was much deeper, they would have to move inland. That is when he could introduce himself.

Chapter Twenty-Seven

To add to the fun Amanda amused herself by leaping over trapped pools of sea water that had been left behind by the previous outgoing tide.

Gingerly picking up a small crab between forefinger and thumb she had to avoid her nose from being nipped by the crustacean. What she had hoped to find was an unopened oyster shell with a pearl inside, something to take back for Emma.

Walking close behind Behildwick Jones and Gallius talked.

'Are you sure that you saw something?' Behildwick asked, casually looking at the dunes to her left.

'I'm almost certain there was something there,' Gallius replied. 'I think Amanda saw it too, only she doesn't want to concern us. It had on a strange looking hat.'

'Like a top hat?' asked Behildwick.

'Yes, how do you know?'

'Amanda told me about a dream she'd had before we left the village. In it was a funny creature wearing a top hat.'

'She's caught something.'

Joyfully Amanda was holding aloft a large crab, but there were no oyster shells anywhere.

'She is always so full of wonder.' Behildwick acknowledged.

They laughed as a wave caught her out splashing up her leg.

'This gift that she has. Can she foretell the future?'

'Perhaps her own, but maybe not others.' Behildwick replied. 'It's as though she has a predestined vision, a path upon which she has to tread to make it come true.'

'She tells me that she can hear the voices too.'

Behildwick nodded.

'She is young Gallius and at times her gift confuses her, but in time the voices will become recognisable. At present she hears what you and I hear.'

'And her mother, she is an oracle teller as well?'

'And her grandmother.'

Gallius grinned watching the sand dunes. 'So many in one family, that is unusual.'

'They're a nice family Gallius. Amanda's grandmother is my best friend and without her being there for me, I don't think that I would have lasted this long.'

Gallius suddenly looked down at the sand.

'There is definitely a small creature hiding in the long grass wearing a hat.'

'Yes, I saw him too. I don't sense that he means us any harm.'

They caught up with Amanda where she had come across another large rock pool. Watching warily were four good sized crabs besides the one that she had in her hand.

'Look what I've found,' she said, pointing at the crustaceans.

Gallius bent down and scooped the biggest from the rock pool, then another. The crabs started snapping, even at one another as they were lifted from the water.

'Well done...' said Gallius, congratulating Amanda on her find. 'At least that is supper taken care of.' He found a discarded container filling it with sea water to keep the crabs fresh.

'Do you remember my dream about the funny creature with the hat?'

'Yes. He's there amongst the long grass and watching us.' Replied Behildwick. 'I think he's been watching us since the others left.'

Suddenly there was an almighty kafuffle as Gallius ambushed their stalker.

'Gotcha...' he cried.

Hoisting the creature aloft it kicked out with both legs, but to no avail as the creatures legs were shorter than Gallius's reach. Hauling him down the sand dune by the scruff of his coat collar Gallius looked triumphant.

'Aye, that was most undignified. A simple hello as an introduction would have been more acceptable!'

'Had you not been spying on us, it would not have been necessary,' replied Behildwick Jones.

Eyeing the sword hanging down Gallius's side the creature casually adjusted the collar of his jacket and waistcoat. Amanda noticed the large belt buckle the helped keep up his trousers and his longish ears. Not as long as a rabbit, but like the fox terrier dog that lived three doors from her own house.

'What are you creature? Who are you and why have you been watching us?' Amanda asked as the creature had an interest in her more than the other two.

'Aye...' it replied. 'I've been watching you for sure. T'was a nasty involvement that you had with those ugly oafs at the crossroads. They both deserved to die, but one wanders the area still.'

Gallius looked down at the headland which they had not long passed. He saw no sign of the trogglebyte. The creature surprised them by suddenly bowing.

'Aye, Master Hobble's my name and a garblewart I am.'

Without any warning the creature produced a phlegmy fluid in its throat despatching it into the sand with a spit.

'That is a disgusting habit,' Amanda declared, repulsed by the creature's foul habit. 'I am not in favour of people or creatures who spit.'

Gargling again Master Hobble spat out the excess.

'Aye... it is missy, but it's what garblewarts do. We have a lot of phlegm.'

Behildwick Jones and Gallius watched the exchange, rather amused. Gallius relaxed his hold on the sword handle.

'And my name is Amanda, not missy.'

'Aye, I know missy.' The garblewart doffed his hat winking at Behildwick and Gallius.

'How do you know?' she pointed directly at his nose. *'And don't you dare spit!'*

The garblewart found it difficult rolling its tongue around inside its mouth as the phlegm started to gather momentum. With a swallow he almost chocked and she had to help slapping his back hard. With the calamity averted the garblewart had watery eyes.

'Aye...that was almost the end of me.' He spat quickly down at the sand and wiped his lips with the back of his jacket cuff. 'I knows because I was told you were coming this way.'

'Who by... who told you?' she demanded.

'Aye missy Amanda, by someone who knows.'

The garblewart shrugged at Behildwick and Gallius then spat at the sand again. Shaking her head disparagingly at the creature Amanda had her hands on her hips.

'Do you have a master or mistress?' asked Gallius.

'Aye, a mistress, my prince.'

Amanda held up a finger and the garblewart swallowed only he didn't choke this time. Gallius looked at Behildwick.

'I've a feeling who,' he said.

Master Hobble couldn't hold in the next collection. He spat it out. Coming close almost nose to nose although Amanda had to bend a little, she looked into the creatures eyes.

'I am not sure what school you went to garblewart, but it didn't teach you any manners.'

'Aye, school... what's that?' he asked. 'We all do it. My brothers, my sister and my old grandad.'

Amanda shrugged realising that to remonstrate would only make it worse.

'How comes you didn't show yourself at the crossroad?' asked Gallius.

'Aye, my instruction was for only three. I had to wait until the others had left.'

'You sound as though we are expected?' asked Behildwick. 'Are you a guide?'

'Aye princess, that who I am.' He bowed. 'At your service.''

'Then you know the reason for our going to the lake?'

'Aye... my lady. It is why I am here.'

'You seem like a funny guide to me,' Amanda said.

'Aye...' agreed Master Hobble. 'I've been told that before, but it's me position and guiding I do.' He gargled and spat it out. 'I was doing it long before you was born missy.'

Amanda handed over her handkerchief.

'If you must partake of that revolting habit, take the handkerchief and don't think about giving it back.'

Master Hobble promptly wiped clean his lips, scrunched up the handkerchief and placed it in his jacket pocket.

'Aye... thank you missy, that'll help. Sometimes I gets chapped lips. I am honoured to receive a gift and we've only just met. I should give you something in return.'

Amanda told him that it wasn't necessary, wondering what he would keep in his jacket pockets or under his hat.

Craning his neck to look in the container Master Hobble noticed the crabs.

'Aye, they'll be fine specimens and there's four. We should get off the beach and eat. I know a good place to make a fire. I don't usually do breakfast, but today I'll make an exception!'

Amanda pointed to where the sun was sat high in the afternoon sky.

'It's not breakfast time, nor lunchtime... and pretty soon we'll be having supper.'

Master Hobble rolled his tongue around the inside of his mouth.

'Don't…' she warned.

The garblewart eyed her warily believing that he had met his match.

'Aye… well whatever the time, suppers is as good. Do you need help dressing the crabs? I've been nipped before and I knows how to deal with these blighters.'

Gallius handed over the container as they followed the garblewart to a field where they used a disused barn to collect wood and dry hay.

Gallius watched Master Hobble dress the crabs.

'I've been to many places and all three-quarter kingdoms. How come I have never heard of a garblewart before?' he asked.

'Aye… that you probably haven't my lord. I've watched you on your journeys and the sadness that has you hang your head low. I have to remain unseen and only friends can see me normally.'

'But I saw you on the beach?'

'That's because I knew that we would be friends.'

'Who sent you… was it the Lady Bleudele?'

'Aye… that's who it was. I was told to find you and guide you to the lake. Taking supper first won't make us late.'

'And what do you know of the dead?' asked Gallius.

'Aye, the dead. I knows that they don't come back. You can hear them talk, but at times not see them.'

'Do you know of my sister, Aurora?'

Master Hobble gave a shale of his head making his hat wobble.

'Aye… I know of her my lord. However my powers are limited. I cannot say more as my mistress would be angry if I did.'

Gallius saw another opportunity go begging. He wondered if he would ever find Aurora.

Master Hobble sensed his new friend's disappointment. He didn't want to leave the prince disenchanted and without hope.

'Aye my lord. It was a worthy question. Worthy of being asked again, but next time with my mistress. She sees and knows all. Be strong of heart my prince.'

Master Hobble continued cleaning the crabs leaving Gallius to find Behildwick and Amanda.

'He's a strange creature.' Said Gallius.

'Disgusting, if you ask me.' Replied Amanda.

'Maybe,' exclaimed Behildwick, 'although I sense that there is more beneath his rough exterior and that Master Hobble came to help.'

'He told me that he's seen me on my journeys through all four quarter kingdoms. I wonder why he has never introduced himself before.'

'Maybe,' Behildwick pondered, 'he had to wait until you agreed to visit the lake.'

'Everything seems to hinge on us going there.' Said Amanda as she added a log to the fire. 'Has he seen any more trogglebytes?'

'No, only the one we left in the ditch at the crossroad. I don't think we will not until after we've to the lake.'

'At least that's a relief.'

They saw Master Hobble coming with the prepared crabs. He sniffed catching a whiff of fresh coffee. After consuming supper they rested with the garblewart resting his head against a bale of hay.

'Tell me Master Hobble,' asked Behildwick Jones, 'furthest south of my quarter kingdom, does the land of

Camulyddium still exist? Legend has it that King Arthur was laid to rest there along with his beloved Guinevere.'

'Aye... it does my lady, only many cannot see the castle nor indeed the lake Bywydhir. Myth and legend exists so that children believe in fairy tales. As adults they become suspicious of what they cannot see, but the magic never leaves.' He looked specifically at Gallius. 'All I can tell is that you are all linked and will be after you visit my lady. Now I dare not say anything more otherwise my hat will be stripped from my head and not returned.'

'What is so important about your hat?' asked Amanda.

'Aye missy, it is important. It keeps my head warm and my brains from falling out of my ears.'

Amanda wondered why the garblewart wore the hat so low over his ears.

'So is there a boat that takes one to the middle of the lake?'

'Aye missy there is, only maybe not quite a boat.'

Amanda frowned not understanding. She saw Behildwick nodding and wondered if she knew.

Master Hobble put his hand over his mouth and stopped himself from talking.

'Aye, I've said too much already.' He held on tight to his hat.

Beyond the door of the barn the blue sky had changed to a hue of grey, red and yellow as the sun began dropping. Closing his eyes Gallius heard a soft, infant like voice calling his name. When he next opened them Behildwick and Amanda were both resting, only Master Hubble was left awake. The garblewart noticed the tear that escaped the corner of the prince's eye. He smiled at

Gallius, then pulled the brim of his hat down to cover his eyes.

Chapter Twenty-Eight

Sitting alongside Gallius, Behildwick had noticed a difference.

'So it would seem that when we die, we at least get to go across the lake rather than under it.'

He watched to make sure that Master Hobble who was chatting with Amanda was distracting her attention.

'I would rather they set fire to the boat,' he added. 'That's an honourable way to go, although going to the lake isn't the end for us.'

'You seem very optimistic. Has something happened?'

Gallius shrugged. 'A voice in my dream told me things. I feel different.'

'You are different, calmer.'

'The wind is blowing in changes princess. Changes we could never have imagined. Don't ask what because I don't know. I just know that they're coming.'

'Romany myths,' she grinned to have him know that it was meant to be light-hearted.

Gallius grinned back. 'Maybe.'

A voice from behind interrupted their conversation

'Aye… I too have heard about the sacred writings of the Romany Kings.' Master Hobble pointed to the sheathed dagger tied to Gallius's belt. 'And the inscription on the handle my lord is both interesting and intriguing. It bears the mark of Delva the Romany God.'

Gallius took out the dagger and handed it to the garblewart. 'What else can you tell me about Delva?'

Master Hobble scrutinised the dagger and handle carefully showing particular interest to the inscription along the length of the blade.

'Aye, indeed this a knife crafted by a master. A man from far away where the land is not so green, but covered in sand, much like the beach, only a man can become lost amongst the grains as easily as when the wind changes direction.'

Amanda run her finger along the inscription.

'It was made in Egypt...'

Master Hobble nodded.

'Aye young missy, that's the place. I've only ever seen this writing once before and that was when my cousin went to help a man who had lost his way looking for dead kings and queens.'

'So what does it mean?' Amanda asked.

'Follow the stars to your destiny.' Replied Gallius.

'I like that,' said Amanda. She looked up where there were many. 'I hope they never leave.'

Master Hobble closed his eyes rubbing the handle of the knife. When he opened them again he knew to whom the knife had originally belonged.

'Aye, a worthy weapon and it once belonged to a Prince Aramakah, a man whose kingdom was full of magic and charm, and sand. A man of vision, a gypsy of the dessert. One night, believing that Aramakah was wealthy and that he took his riches with him on every trip an evil-minded merchant entered the tent where the prince was sleeping. He found no jewels, but instead he kidnapped the princess, Aramakah's wife.

'A ransom was made, but it could not be paid as Aramakah and his wife only took from the desert what they needed to survive. I remember this knife because I was sent by my mistress to help. The stars helped guide us to where she was being held captive. Prince Aramakah killed the merchant and rescued his princess.'

Master Hobble handed back the knife.

'Aye, if we had not followed the stars that evening we might never have found the Princess Attizi. It is indeed a special knife and worthy of its present owner.'

Gallius nodded accepting the compliment for which it was given.

'You have travelled far with your quests Master Hobble.'

'Aye, the *nulleum* helps.'

'*Nulleum*, what's that?' asked Amanda.

Master Hobble had to think for a few seconds before he could answer.

'Aye missy, think of it as a portal between two places. I thinks it and then I arrive.'

'You don't have to touch something magical to have it transport you there?'

'Aye... no.'

Behildwick and Gallius laughed when the expression on Amanda's face changed.

'You are impossible,' she remonstrated. 'I try to have an intelligent conversation with you and you say *'aye and no'* in the same sentence.'

'Aye, I agree and no it doesn't work that way.' He tapped the side of his hat and head. 'This is my portal.'

Amanda sighed. 'It's a wonder you go anywhere. I doubt that there is little inside between those ears.'

'Aye missy, but I hear everything!' he replied.

'Then why can't you tap that portal of yours and transport us to the lake?'

Behildwick and Gallius were keen to hear the garblewarts answer. They too had wondered why not.

'Aye, that could be possible, but I try to reserve my energy for more important times and where there is danger. Where there is not, it is better that we arrive by using our feet.'

Amanda gave a shake of her head, her disappointment evident.

'It is good to hear that we are not walking into danger Master Hobble.'

'Aye, indeed my lady.' He winked at them both. 'And this way, I can get better acquainted with young missy.'

'Young missy has a boyfriend,' replied Amanda, the indignation glaring back at the garblewart.

'Aye missy, I know.'

Amanda took a step closer so that she was almost nose to nose. 'And what else do you know?'

Aye, now that would be telling and I would like to keep my hat on top of my head. Maybe when you've been to the lake I will tell you.'

Amanda stepped back. She wondered if the funny little man in the top hat, jacket and waistcoat was leading them into a trap.

'And when exactly are we going to the lake?'

The garblewart went to the door of the barn to spit.

'Aye, it's a good night. Full of stars. Now would be as good a time to set out.'

Passing deer, rabbits, badgers and the odd fox, the owl in the tree watched them make their way through the trees, crushing the undergrowth underfoot. The closer that they got to Bywydhir the thicker the mist seemed to descend. Amanda kept close to Gallius.

When they did emerge the other side of the wood there before them was the most magical of lakes. Blue in colour it was shrouded in a veil of mist, a lot less haunting than that of the trees, and much brighter.

'It's wonderful,' announced Amanda with Behildwick and Gallius standing either side.

'Aye missy,' agreed Master Hobble, 'it's where special invited people come to find their destiny.'

Amanda wanted to say that she hadn't been invited to the lake and that she had volunteered to come because of Behildwick Jones, but something about the lake and the blue water told her to keep silent. The trees and the bushes that surrounded the lake were dotted with firefly which gave the blue water a shimmering luminosity. Despite the mist Amanda could see the stars in the waters reflection.

'We've arrived,' said Behildwick sensing a calm sweep through her whole body.

Unable to contain herself Amanda needed to ask. 'Is she here Master Hobble... is the Lady Bleudele here?'

For once the garblewart did not clear his throat nor did he spit. He did however use the cuff of his jacket to wipe his nose dry before replying.

'Aye missy, she's here. You have to be patient though and when the time is right she will appear.'

Gallius who'd had his hand on the hilt of the sword, let go when he felt the princess gently pull it away.

'*You won't need that,*' she whispered, '*look...*'

Approaching them from out of the mist came a large cob swan with a lady sat on its back.

'It's like it's gliding across the water,' gasped Amanda as the cob came closer.

When the swan reached the bank, the lady held out her hand for Behildwick to join her. 'I will return,' said the Lady Bleudele.

Fascinated by both swan and the lady of the lake Amanda watched as they, along with Behildwick Jones disappeared into the mist.

'Where have they gone?' she asked sitting down on the grass bank.

'Into the middle of the water,' replied Gallius, peering as hard as he could.

A few minutes later the swan returned and this time the gypsy prince was invited to join the Lady Bleudele.

'I'll wait for you,' Amanda promised kneeling on the grass as she waved at Gallius.

'Aye missy, you do that. You stay calm now because your turn comes next!'

Amanda's head shot sideways at the garblewart.

'But I can't go, I am not of royal blood. By rights I shouldn't be here.'

Master Hobble smiled and his eyes seemed to twinkle.

'Aye missy, that's an interesting way of looking at it, but see for yourself the swan returns with the Lady Bleudele.

Amanda watched as the cob glided gently through the water coming to rest alongside the grass bank. Lady Bleudele held out her hand.

'But I am not a princess?' Amanda explained.

The lady of the lake smiled and looked at the garblewart. 'You have done well Master Hobble. She is pleased with you.'

Master Hobble let go the rim of his hat and bowed at the Lady Bleudele. 'Aye, thank you m'lady. It was a pleasure.'

Lady Bleudele held out her hand for Amanda to take.

'Do not question what you do not know child, instead accept what you will come to learn.

Confused, but excited Amanda took her place beside Lady Bleudele. She waved at the garblewart and he waved back. He sat himself down on the grass bank.

'Can I touch the water?' asked Amanda as the cob continued to glide towards the middle.

'Would it stop you, if I was to say no?'

'It would. Although I feel it wants me to touch it. To absorb its energy, its magic.'

'Then please be my guest.'

Amanda let her fingers drop below the surface of the blue water, it wasn't cold nor warm, but felt just right. In her wake she had created a small ripple. Closing her eyes and breathing in deep she could already sense the energy, the magic and surprisingly the presence of others flowing up through her fingertips. She turned to tell the Lady Bleudele, but the lady of the lake was already heedful of Amanda's surprise.

'The water feels your presence too Amanda. Accept what it gives you and soon you will come to realise why it was essential that you accompanied the princess and the prince here to the blue lake.'

Reaching the centre of the lake Amanda was surprised to find that there was no island upon which she would find Behildwick and Gallius waiting.

'Where are my friends?' she asked.

'They have already gone on down. They will await your arrival before approaching the chamber.'

Amanda looked at the water beside the cob where there was stone staircase spiralling down.

'But I'll drown,' she exclaimed remembering her dream.

'Do you believe in magic?' asked Lady Bleudele.

'Yes, but I had a dream and in it I was…'

Lady Bleudele stopped her. 'No. I must never be party to your dreams. Who I am, and what I am cannot influence your destiny. That is for you alone to overcome. Trust me Amanda and stepped from the boat onto the top step. Go down, where you will meet the prince and princess.'

Stepping from the cob she placed her foot tentatively upon the first then the second step, then a third and fourth until her head dipped below the surface of the water. Surprisingly she found that she could breathe. When she looked back up both the swan and Lady Bleudele had disappeared. Going down deep she could see the blue water swirling around and yet she was not getting wet.

The deeper that she went the more wondrous the experience and the water became, changing colour. Nearing the bottom of the spiral staircase she could see two figures waiting surrounded by glowing translucent stones, from which gold and yellow rays of light exploded.

Stepping away from the staircase Amanda hugged them both.

'Boy, am I glad to see you both. That's not an experience I would want to trust too often.'

Behildwick smiled.

'I think it's an experience that we will only ever do the once. Come, we think the chamber is this way.'

They walked through an illuminated passage lit by brightly coloured stones emerging into a chamber which was surrounded on all sides by water. Sat on a throne make from seashells was a beautiful woman with long gold hair and a long dress the colour of the blue water above. In the water Amanda could see fish swimming and what looked like small mermaids. The woman invited them to come closer.

'Welcome to my palace. My name is Queen Avallana.'

She pointed to where positioned around her throne were twelve carved rounded stones.

'Please sit yourselves down.'

Seeing that they were settled and comfortable, Avallana explained why they had been invited to the chamber. Amanda noticed that her dress was made entirely of blue seashells.

'This is my kingdom and I protect the destiny of kings and queens and their family. You have been invited to the lake because there are things you need to know. Long have I watched and felt your suffering. The time has come for me to grant you an audience.'

Amanda stood up curtsied.

'My name is Amanda Brodrick your majesty, but I must point out that I am not of royal birth. My father is a carpenter and my mother a housewife. My sister Emma thinks she's a princess, but that's only because she acts like one.'

Queen Avallana stood and walked over to where Amanda was stood. She gently invited her to sit again.

'Only royalty sit upon Arthur's stones. He had once a large round table with twelve chairs fashioned from the trees in the forest, but in exchange for the sword he had his craftsmen carve me twelve seats for my chamber.'

She stood between Amanda and Behildwick.

'I am a guide in your destiny. Where fate has altered your path, I try to return the balance. This includes you Amanda.'

Amanda was surprised that she knew her name.

'I've heard you, heard your voice. It came to me in my dreams.'

Avallana nodded at the prince and princess.

'I have spoken to you all from time to time. I will come back to you Amanda, but first I must speak with Prince Gallius.'

She went and stood in front of Gallius taking his hands in her own. She spoke to him through his thoughts.

'For so long your heart has been grieving over the loss of your young sister, but prince of Liatheclo has your heart not cried enough tears. Have you not heard your sister calling you back home?'

'But she is dead.' Replied Gallius. 'The mountain trolls killed her when they took her from the forest.'

Queen Avallana asked Gallius to close his eyes.

'Do you not see the woman standing beside me?' she asked.

Gallius gulped the surprise caught in his throat. Stood next to Avallana was his mother. For the first time in centuries he heard her speak.

'Gallius my son, you should have no shame to burden such a caring, gentle heart. My death was a sadness that cause great

pain, especially for your father and his sons. Aurora was too little to know why. But death is just another journey on the path of our destiny.

'There is no right, nor indeed any wrong the day that you and your sister went to the forest. What took place you could not have prevented.'

'But she was so little mother, Aurora was my responsibility.'

His mother smiled which Gallius found strange.

'And she still is your responsibility my son. A group of hunters from another village hunting deer heard Aurora's screams. They fought with the mountain trolls and rescued your sister. The next day they returned Aurora to the castle and her father, and brothers, but by this time your grief had taken hold of your heart and head, and you have gone looking for your sister. Your brothers tried to get word to you, but you were nowhere to be found. You have tortured yourself endlessly my son. Every night your sister prays for your safe return.'

'I occupy one of Arthur's stones and very soon your father will too, as will you. But not for a long time yet to come. You still have a future Gallius and a castle that awaits your return. Queen Avallana has watched over you all these years and kept you safe, but now it is time to repay her kindness by looking after Oyddiss and Amanda Brodrick.

'My time with you my son is almost at an end, but know this Gallius. I love you and want for you to be happy again. No longer must you carry a burden that saddens your heart and soul. Rejoice that your sister lives and that soon you will be reunited. When you go back to Liatheclo, pay homage to your father's grave. He died with your name on his lips Gallius.'

The vision of his mother faded and vanished. Gallius opened his eyes to see Avallana standing before Oyddiss. She held out her hands for the princess to take.

Behildwick Jones saw Gallius wipe the tears from his eyes, but didn't have time to ask why. Holding both hands Queen Avallana had another message to pass on.

'And what of you Princess Oyddiss, the treasured, beloved daughter of Felman and Erikka. You have lived alone for too long and seen the lives of your friends, wither into bone, then dust. Childless and without love, you wander the lost kingdom blaming yourself for the deaths of your mother and father. What took place that fated evening in the castle garden was as written in the cold stone granite of time. We cannot interfere. No more than you can foresee the future.

'Taken in by the residents of Finlostydd they did so because you were a princess. It was wise to change your name, but in your heart you will always be Oyddiss. After the death of your father the villagers were left confused. They searched for you Oyddiss. They needed comfort and guidance, like when you had given them bread and grain. When they could not find you, many perished. But even now you will find your name spoken in some quarters of the kingdom.

'You were invited here today because one of the stones in my chamber is occupied by somebody you loved dearly. Now close your eyes and see who.'

Oyddiss felt the tears welling fast in her eyes when her father stood and walked towards her. Taking her in his arms he cuddled her as only a father can.

'The king of the mountain was a very wicked man Oyddiss and he destroyed everything that you held dear, but the time of tyranny will soon come to an end. You must not blame yourself for what happened, but blame me. I was king and should have acted rationally. When they kidnapped you, it is I who should have defeated the trogglebyte warriors. Castilleon was too young and inexperienced, and love is a poor friend in battle.

'You still have a future my beautiful daughter and soon your troubles will come to an end. Queen Avallana will watch over you until that time comes. Forget the past Oyddiss, it was not your burden to bear, but mine. Now go and be happy. Your mother and father love you dearly. Go and hold your head high. Remember, you are a royal princess.'

Oyddiss felt her father kiss her cheek then begin to fade taking his place on one of the stones. Within seconds he had disappeared. When she opened her eyes her heart felt much lighter, not as heavy and she felt different, very different. When she looked across at Gallius he was a handsome young man again.

'You are really beautiful,' he said changing stones to sit beside her.

'And you, you're so young and very handsome.'

Oyddiss caught sight of her reflection in the water pools on the chamber floor. Gone was her wrinkles and wispy hair, in its place was a beauty that she remembered from when she went riding her horse in the nearby wood and down her back and covering her shoulders was long silky fair hair.

Gallius and Oyddiss both looked at Avallana who was stood in front of Amanda.

'A life without children is magic lost. Now you are both young again, you should think about a family.'

Reaching out for Amanda's hands she was quick to oblige.

'Now close your eyes and we shall talk, said Avallana.

'And what of you Amanda Eira Brodrick. A young girl full of strong character, adventure and wisdom beyond her years. You wonder why Lady Bleudele invited you to the centre of my

blue waters. Surely, you must have had dreams even as a young girl where you thought that you were a princess?'

'They were only fairy tales like the books that I read before I went to sleep.'

'Really. And where do you think fairy tales originate? You tell me that you were not born into a royal household and yet here you find yourself sitting on one of King Arthur's stones. Destiny does not make mistakes, people do. Perhaps after today you will believe in yourself more and how the gift of dreams is more than just premonition.

'Neither your mother nor grandmother, or indeed some before them know that your family descends from a royal house. Lost in translation down the centuries your surname was Heden and you would have been called a Brudyr, a name well known and respected throughout the Nordic wastelands of Europe, a name associated with the royal house of Heden. Your being here Amanda is not by chance, but because it is your right to be here and occupying a royal stone.

'You are very young and yet your path has already been chosen. Since your birth I have watched over your progress and growth. You have a purpose to fulfil Amanda that will be revealed in time, when the time is right. Do not be so impatient to dismiss nor cast aside your youthful years. Instead gain wisdom and use it wisely. Show others the way forward.

'When you leave this chamber, you cannot tell of your ancestry. And neither can you use it to gain advantage over others. Long has the Heden household been lost, but a royal you are. One day, a long way off in the future you will take your rightful place in the chamber. One day, you will occupy my throne.'

When Avallana removed her hands, Amanda immediately slumped forward. She was caught by Gallius who had seen her start to fall.

'Fear not...' said Queen Avallana. 'She only sleeps. The news that she has received is a lot for a young mind to absorb. When next she wakes, she will be on the grass bank beside the lake. She won't remember this visit.'

'Will we?' asked Behildwick.

'Why yes, and your destiny is different to Amanda's. In some ways both your burden has been conquered, whereas this young lady's is just beginning. Master Hobble will escort you back.'

'I take it that we will never return to the lake?' asked Gallius.

'No. You only come here the once my prince. The next occasion is a permanent visit to occupy one of the stones and be with your ancestors. Now follow the passage back to the spiral stairs. Lady Bleudele is waiting. I am tired and need to sleep. Such visits are exhausting.'

Gallius picked up Amanda and carried her in his arms. Taking one last look before the passage took a bend before the stairs, they saw that Queen Avallana was already asleep under a blanket of shells. Slowly the light in the chamber didn't seem as bright as the stones stopped changing colour.

Master Hobble helped lay Amanda on the grass bank before he doffed his hat at the Lady Bleudele.

'Aye, Lady Bleudele, the young missy, she is going to be alright?' he asked, running the back of his jacket sleeve along the underside of his nose.

'Isn't everybody who comes to visit here Master Hobble.'

The cob pushed away from the bank watched by Gallius and Behildwick. Soon both lady and swan were lost in the mist once again.

Chapter Twenty-Nine

O pening her eyes Amanda immediately noticed the stars above which were punctuated by the odd shaped hat belonging to Master Hobble. His ears which had fallen from under the brim of the hat appeared longer than before and they were hanging close to her nose.

'Aye, she's alive...' he exclaimed, the relief creasing his lips into a smile.

Pushing the garblewart away she sat herself up.

'Don't you dare spit while I am sat this close,' she warned wagging her finger before the tip of his nose.

'What happened and why was I asleep?' she asked looking at Behildwick and Gallius. 'Have you been gone long?'

Behildwick Jones came and sat down beside Amanda.

'Don't you remember anything?'

Amanda tried to think through the mist inside her head.

'No. I remember the swan coming back to the bank after it had taken you. Gallius waved and then...' she banged the side of her head, 'then nothing. I must have fallen asleep.'

She looked at Behildwick then Gallius, there was something different about them.

'Goodness, you're much younger. You're beautiful Behildwick.' She looked at Gallius. 'And you, you're even more handsome.'

Gallius grinned.

'And you're a princess Amanda.'

Amanda blew out between her lips. 'A princess, yeah right. The only princess in the family is my older sister and the way that she prances about the house.'

Master Hobble was about to say something, but Behildwick stopped him.

Amanda stroked the side of Behildwick's face, the skin was soft and without wrinkles. The hair was silky and had body.

'Was it magical?' she asked.

'Wondrous things happened here Amanda,' she looked to Gallius, 'magic that neither Gallius nor I expected. In time you will become part of that magic.'

Amanda frowned, confused she couldn't see how.

'I feel no different than when we arrived.'

The mist covering the middle of the lake appeared slightly thicker, she could not see the swan nor indeed the Lady Bleudele.

'I wish that I could have seen what was in the centre of the blue water?'

Behildwick once again stopped Master Hobble from talking. Instead he gargled and spat out his frustration.

'Maybe one day you will make this journey again,' Gallius responded, 'perhaps when you are older.'

'Aye missy and I'll bring you.' From his jacket Master Hobble took out a funny twisted green bottle. He uncorked the stopper. 'Drink this it will help unfuddle your head.'

Without hesitating Amanda drank the solution and immediately the fog cleared. Moments later her stomach started to echo noisily with a bubbling and her mouth belching.

'What was in that bottle, I feel like I'm going to explode?'

The garblewart laughed. 'Aye missy, it has that effect on me too sometimes. It's a special brew of frogs tongue, lizard blood and the trail of a snail, mixed with the juice of a few berries found locally.'

Amanda thought she was going to vomit, but with one final belch the sensation ebbed.

'Don't ever offer me anything ever again!'

Despite his horrible habit of spitting there was something about the garblewart that she found endearing, although she would never tell.

'So what happens now?' she asked.

'Now we go back, said Behildwick. 'There are things to do and some that need out attention. Some from the past.'

Feeling much better Amanda stood up. 'Do they include me?'

'I've a feeling that anything we do will include you,' replied Gallius. 'I don't think we would be able to get rid of you that easily.'

Amanda offered a determined nod in respond. She surprised them both by turning towards the garblewart. 'Does this mean you can come too?'

'Aye missy, I'll be around. Perhaps not always seen, but I'll be there to watch over you.'

Amanda grinned.

'Good, only don't appear when I'm saying goodnight to Jonathon.'

The garblewart adjusted his hat upon his head pushing back up his ears. He looked at Gallius for an explanation.

'In time you'll understand why,' said the gypsy prince.

Behildwick Jones nodded. She agreed.

'Now we should make our way back to the beach. We'll follow you Master Hobble.'

They followed the funny little creature as he retraced his steps through the trees, across the ploughed fields and to the sand dunes where they had first met. Unusually the garblewart was quieter than the previous journey. Gallius was wary and had his hand on the hilt of his sword the whole time.

'Do you sense it?' whispered Behildwick.

'Yes and even Master Hobble is quiet. He hasn't spat phlegm in the last hour.'

'Is there something wrong?' Amanda asked coming alongside the garblewart.

'Aye missy, there is something wrong only I don't know what.' He took the handkerchief that she had given him from his jacket pocket and offered it back. 'It'll need washing.'

There was no way that Amanda wanted it back. 'No Master Hobble you keep it. It will be a reminder of our friendship.'

'Aye… that I will missy,' he wiped the tear from his eye, blew his nose then stuffed the handkerchief back in his pocket.

Standing on top of the sand dunes they looked out at the sea which appeared calm.

'Do you know, I do believe that those two are going to miss one another,' said Gallius to Behildwick Jones.

'That would account for him being quiet. He desperately wants to tell her that she is a real princess, but he's frightened that he'll lose his hat if he does.'

'I wonder what he keeps under that hat?' asked Gallius.

'A multitude of memories I wouldn't wonder.'

They watched as Amanda put her hand around the garblewarts shoulder pulling him in close.

'If I come back here for a holiday next year, would you appear again?'

'Aye, more than likely missy, unless I was elsewhere.'

She bent down and kissed the garblewarts cheek.

'Aye, what was that for?' he asked his eyes. 'I've never been licked before?'

Gallius laughed.

'Just accept it Master Hobble. It was a kiss, a sign of affection between friends.'

The garblewart swallowed the phlegm rather than spit it out.

'Aye friends, that's what we are missy.' He kissed the back of her hand before bowing. 'I am honoured to have met you, Amanda Brodrick. Our time together has been an experience that I will never forget, but I hear my mistress calling. I will see you again soon.'

In a flash the garblewart disappeared. The only sound left was the gentle lapping of the waves down on the beach.

'I think you made quite an impression,' said Gallius as he scanned the beach looking for signs of movement.

Behildwick inhaled hard filling her lungs with the salty air.

'This is just the beginning Amanda. There will be many times ahead when you will call upon Master Hobble. Now we should find somewhere to sleep.'

For the rest of the night they each had dreams. Good dreams unlike the recent disturbing nightmares. In her subconscious visions Amanda saw Nordic kings and Queens. She even saw Emma wearing a crown. It was when she saw a mirrored reflection of herself wearing a crown that she woke.

Chapter Thirty

General cantered along the lanes avoiding the potholes and loose stones as best as he could knowing that in the caravan lay the injured boy.

So far he had not seen any sign of the trogglebyte who had made good his escape at the crossroads. Trotting along he had sensed his presence the once then not again. Keeping his stride even General did as Jonathon asked holding the rein.

Lying low behind a clump of bushes Oberran had watched the brightly coloured caravan go hurtling past surprised to see that two young boys had hold of the reins. He did think about jumping on the back and seeing what was inside, but instinct told him that he should keep walking towards the coast instead.

Making his way across heathland and lane he was almost at the coast road when he saw a shadow move between the trees ahead. Ducking behind a large oak he drew his dagger ready. A herd of deer nearby had also stopped moving seeing the shadow. Oberran waited until the last second before he leapt, his dagger thrust out defensively. It was cast aside by the stranger.

'*Oberran you bloody fool…*' shrieked Karlstad. '*You could have killed me.*' He gave his cousin a whack to the side of his head to show how displeased he was.

'I'm sorry Karlstad. I didn't know it was you.' Oberran noticed his cousin holding his arm. 'What's wrong?'

'There was a fight and I got cut.'

'Was it the princess?'

'No, she wasn't there. It was an outsider and some others.'

Karlstad was not about to reveal that a boy had caused the injury. Cousin or not Oberran would make the situation worse.

'Where's Bradkar, I thought that was with you?'

Karlstad wondered how his cousin knew. 'Bradkar was overweight. He was slow. He didn't survive the ambush. How did you know about Bradkar anyway?'

'Trygor sent me to find you.'

Karlstad snarled. 'I our king grows more suspicious every day. I thought he would kill you!'

Oberran showed Karlstad his scars.

'His temper and punishment grows worse. Trygor had me flogged with the badger pelt because I had let the princess escape at the old woman's cottage.'

Karlstad wondered if Oberran had the chance, would he kill him.

Oberran sensed the apprehension.

'I found Schellian's body in the wood. Was it you who killed him?'

Karlstad gave a disinterested shrug of his shoulders.

'I never trusted Schellian. He was always hanging around Trygor, whispering in his ear and telling untruths. He deserved to die.'

The admission had Oberran think that Karlstad had changed. A warrior yes, but his cousin was not a cold-hearted killer. He would have to watch his back.

'Besides trying to scare me half to death, have you seen anybody on your travels?'

'Only a herd of cows, deer and a brightly painted caravan, that's all.'

Karlstad checked the stars which were beginning to fade.

'It'll be light soon. We should hunt for our breakfast, then decide what to do next.'

'Do you know where the princess is?'

'Yes. She and the gypsy prince are accompanied by a girl from the village. They're near the beach.'

Picking up a broken branch Oberran threw it at the tree nearest. A dead pigeon fell to the ground. 'That'll do for a start.'

They killed other birds and even some rabbit. Soon their stomachs stopped groaning.

Laying back and resting after eating Oberran was patting his stomach grateful of the cooked food.

'You said gypsy prince?'

Karlstad who also had his head resting against the truck of an oak tree watched the sun rising over the treetops.

'Do you remember the story about the missing prince from the quarter kingdom of the north? Trybulloc's brother, King Stelfor tried to have his sister kidnapped, but the hunting party failed and all were killed. Stelfor would welcome the news that the gypsy prince is still alive. The news would bring about an alliance between Stelfor and Trygor once again. If we could deliver the princess as well,

Trygor would forgive our past misdemeanours. He would reward us handsomely.'

Oberran looked north in the direction that the caravan had been heading.

'Does he have the sword with him?'

Karlstad nodded. 'Yes, and the dagger.'

'They say that both sword and dagger possesses magical powers and that no man can defeat the owner.'

'That is a myth, nothing else. Come we should make our way to the beach. They will be waking soon.'

Oberran helped apply the sap of beaver leaf palm to Karlstad's injured arm. Its healing power was well known for reducing any swelling and risk of infection.

Taking the lane down to the coast Karlstad considered bashing his cousins skull with a stone or log and going on alone. Oberran had a loose tongue and if they got the princess, it would be his cousin who told Trygor about the gypsy prince. Checking both sides of the hedgerow Karlstad scanned around looking for a moderately sized boulder.

Chapter Thirty-One

Sensing the tension between them Oberran was also looking for something to hit Karlstad with. If he killed his cousin and took back the princess, he could claim all the glory. Neither had found anything suitable when they were aware of three figures coming towards them, making their way between the trees. Pushing Oberran to the ground Karlstad rolled himself under a bush.

'There... just as I said. You see, the gypsy prince, the princess and the girl.'

Oberran peered ahead.

'I see three *outsiders*. A young woman and a man walking beside a girl, but that's not the princess. She was a lot older.'

Karlstad looked as well. Oberran was right. They wore the same clothes, but the two older *outsiders* looked different, much younger except the girl.

Instead of springing a surprise attack they stayed hidden, watching until the trio had gone past.

'That woman is the princess, only she's much younger and so is the gypsy.' Said Karlstad. 'How can that be?'

'She is nothing like the old woman that was in the cottage garden where we took the goat. The princess is beautiful again, not some old crone.' Oberran sniffed, but could not detect any scent. 'She does not possess the trace anymore.'

'There's been a magic happening,' said Karlstad. 'He wondered if they grabbed her how he would explain the change to Trygor.

'We should go after them and kill the prince and girl, then take the princess back to the mountain.'

'Sccchh, don't be a fool Oberran. Look at the gypsy prince. He is young again and much stronger than before. Do you want to fight him whilst I attack the girl, remembering that he has the sword?'

Oberran shook his head. 'No. Maybe we can catch them when they're apart.'

Karlstad nodded. 'That is what I was thinking. See, they are heading for the river. There are places there where an ambush gives us the advantage.'

They followed keeping a good distance behind so that the gypsy didn't pick up their scent. As expected, the trio stopped at the river to take breakfast and to wash.

'Amanda is unusually tired.' Said Behildwick Jones as Amanda lay down resting her head on the moss laden bank.

'She has a lot to think about and much of it must be confusing. Would it not be better if we told her what happened back at the lake?'

'No, it's best that she finds out for herself and when the time is right. At present she is too young to comprehend what responsibility lies ahead.'

'We were both young when the burden of responsibility was thrust upon us.' Gallius argued back.

'That was different. Times were different. Amanda doesn't know that she has royal heritage. The shock or surprise could be too much for her at present. She could lose her friends or perhaps have to move away from the valley.'

Gallius considered the years that he had spent alone and, on the road, looking for his little sister. He agreed it was best not to say anything.

'I'll look for firewood so that we can brew coffee. I think we all feel rather tired. Seeing Queen Avallana was a lot to absorb.'

Behildwick held onto his arm.

'Did your parents come through for you?'

'My mother did. My sister lives Oyddiss. She was rescued by a hunting party and returned to the castle. My heart is no longer heavy.'

Behildwick smiled, it was good news.

'And you,' he asked, 'did you receive good news?'

'My vision told me that I was not responsible for the loss of my father's kingdom. I know that I cannot get it back as there is a queen over all the kingdoms now, but I still feel a great loss. Many died because of me Gallius. I will never be able to forgive myself, whatever anybody says.'

Gallius left Behildwick and Amanda by the river as he went looking for broken branches and dried moss.

'Are you unwell?' Behildwick asked, as she checked on Amanda.

'I feel fine, but for some reason my head still feels like it's fallen down a deep gorge and is struggling on the climb back up. I remember dipping my fingers in the water, but then everything else goes hazy. In my dream last night I saw kings and queens, and Emma was wearing a crown too.' She stopped momentarily. 'Towards the end of the dream I was also wearing a crown, but I am just an ordinary girl from the valleys.'

'Maybe you'll be the prom queen, isn't that what they have at the dance?'

Amanda smiled. 'Maybe that's it.' Her frown said otherwise. 'Where's Gallius?'

'He's gone to fetch wood for the fire.'

'He's very handsome.'

Behildwick Jones grinned. 'Yes, he is Amanda.'

'Are you related?'

'Not really. Not by blood as far as I know.'

She pulled her shoulder bag over so that Amanda could rest her head properly. 'Lay here while I fill the kettle. There is a shallow bend in the river just along the bank where filling the kettle would be easier. I'll be back in a minute.'

Closing her eyes Amanda started climbing back up the gorge. Slowly she began to remember more of being beside the lake.

Watching the princess's movement Karlstad nudged Oberran.

'Wait until she is crouched over the water then we can snatch her when she least expects anybody to be around.' He pointed to the trees. 'The gypsy prince went that way and the girl sleeps on the bank. When we get the princess, we go that way.' He pointed in the opposite direction. If we have to silence the princess, do so, but do not hurt her. Trygor would kill us instantly if she is returned injured.'

When Karlstad's strong hand clamped itself over Behildwick's mouth, pulling her back sharply from where she had almost filled the kettle she instantly kicked and scratched, but the hands that propelled her backwards and onto the grass bank were too powerful for her to break free. Thrusting the tip of his knife under her chin Oberran was in no mood to fail a second time.

'If you so much as make a sound like a mouse, I will kill you here and leave you for the woodland creatures to feed upon.'

Glaring back at the trogglebyte, her eyes blazing wildly Behildwick stopped wriggling. She could see Amanda sleeping and wondered why Gallius was taking so long to collect firewood. Biting down hard on Karlstad's finger he managed to stifle the cry of pain. Instead he lashed out and catching her on the chin knocked her unconscious. In one swift movement he threw the princess over his shoulder. They left the river unheard and unnoticed.

Walking behind Oberran lifted up the unconscious woman's' head. He saw the bruise on her chin. 'You should have not hit her so hard. Trygor will flay you alive.'

Karlstad turned about sharply.

'And you should not have angered her by putting the knife under her chin. I had the situation under control. We have a long way to go back to the mountain. At some point she will wake. It is best if she is co-operative.' He licked his tongue along the finger that she bitten. It was sore and the skin was dented. 'She has the bite of an angry fox.'

Retuning with firewood and moss Gallius looked for Oyddiss. He dropped the firewood and moss when he saw the kettle lying on its side. The falling wood woke Amanda from her slumber.

'What's wrong?' she inquired, rubbing her eyes.

'The princess, where is she?'

Amanda looked in either direction.

'She was going to fill the kettle. I must have dozed off.'

Gallius pointed to where the kettle had been dropped and lay on its side.

'Something's wrong. I sense it.'

Gallius ran to where the grass beside the shallow bank had been scuffed by heavy feet.

'The trogglebyte, he has her.' He checked back coming away from the bank. 'Quick, grab her bag, they went this way.'

Amanda retrieved the shoulder bag and ran after Gallius who was cutting through the undergrowth like a stag.

'I'm sorry,' Amanda apologised, 'I should not have fallen asleep.'

Gallius kept on running.

'No, if it is anybody's fault it is mine. I should not have been so long collecting wood for the fire. Avallana will never forgive me if anything happens to the princess.'

Amanda threw the bag over her shoulder so that she could run easier.

'Avallana... I've heard of that name. Where will the trogglebyte take her?'

'Back to the mountain.'

After half an hour of continuous running Gallius stopped. So did Amanda.

'I didn't think that they could run this fast.'

Gallius breathed in hard. 'Neither did I.' He scanned the trees, the fields and the lanes, but saw nothing. 'They're hiding up somewhere, only I don't know where?'

He checked the ground, but had lost their tracks in the shorter grass.

'When the sun goes down it'll be harder for us to follow. If they get to the mountain, we'll never find a way in.'

Amanda suddenly clicked her fingers together.

'You have an idea?' he asked.

'I know a way that we could use. I'd go alone, but with you I'd feel safe.'

Gallius nodded. 'We could do with Master Hobble, do you think he's around?'

'I hope so. Ever since the riverbank, I've been trying to get him in my thoughts, but something seems to be blocking them.'

'Think of the handkerchief that you gave him. It'll link you together.'

'That's a good idea.'

They walked to conserve energy with the sun on their backs.

'Where exactly are we going?' asked Gallius.

'To a place called old Jonesy's farm. There's a barn with a trapdoor. It leads down to a secret passage which I believe leads inside the mountain.'

'Well done Amanda,' Gallius gently patted her back. 'One day I'll introduce you to my sister. You two will get on famously.'

Undoing the chain and pushing back the gate to the track leading up to the farmhouse and barn nothing had changed since her last visit.

'I remember passing through here a long time back,' said Gallius taking out his sword from the scabbard, 'they were a nice, friendly couple as I recall. They gave me fresh milk and eggs, and hay for General.'

'Unfortunately, they're both dead Gallius,' replied Amanda. 'They were nice, especially the wife.'

Are the mountain trolls any different in Liatheclo?' asked Amanda, only metres from the disused barn.

Gallius remembered the encounter back in the forest where they had snatched his sister.

'Whatever the quarter kingdom Amanda, mountain trolls or trogglebytes as they like to be called can never be trusted. Trygor is as wicked as his father Trybulloc and the dead king has a brother who still lives in the mountain at Liatheclo. King Stelfor is much worse than the others put together. I have always thought the best kind of troll was a dead one.'

Amanda didn't push with another question. It was clearly apparent that he hated each and every one of the mountain people with a passion. She wondered what the children of the mountain were like. Did they have different opinions like the teenagers of today? Did they want to live outside?

Gallius searched around the inside of the barn for something that he could use as a torches. Bundling straw over the end of a piece of wood he dipped them both in a bag of Flaxbuam the flicked water from a bucket over the ends. Instantly the torches burst into life.

'Wow, that's amazing!' exclaimed Amanda.

Pushing aside the cart left over the trap door by Jonathon, Mostyn and the others Gallius managed to raise one side. Amanda gave him back his torch.

'A traveller from a place where the stars gather at night came by the castle one day. He showed me the trick of the magic fire. Flaxbuam is used by farmers to burn off the stalks leftover by the harvest.'

Amanda watched as the hay continued to burn. 'It's so bright.'

Gallius nodded. 'Yes, it is, although unscrupulous purveyors of evil have used it for magic much darker than what is meant to be used.'

Halfway down the ladder Amanda whispered that the air was turning foul. Gallius thought something had died recently at the bottom of the shaft.

Stepping away from the last rung Amanda was happy to have her feet on firm ground again albeit they had climbed down a long way. Waving the torch about she found the torn remnants of a woman's dress. Bring the torch close she saw the initials 'AJ' sewn into the collar. Amanda gasped making Gallius turn her way.

'What's wrong?'

'This dress, it belonged to Angharad Jones, the farmer's wife. She disappeared and we all thought that he had killed her and buried her in the wood nearby. Now I'm not so sure.'

Gallius guessed what had really happened.

'Come on,' he muttered, 'you're right and the air here is foul.'

Having pegged the last of the laundry to the line Angharad had been snatched by two trogglebytes and taken to the barn where they had forced her to descend the metal ladder. A fierce struggle had ensued and, in the fight, to get free her dress had been torn from her body. After that a clenched fist had knocked her unconscious.

'We should move swiftly,' Gallius advised, 'there are pockets of gas down here that could explode if we linger.'

Amanda followed vert closely. On both sides and overhead the passage had been roughly cut and she already had scratches on her forearms. Here and there large patches of damp moss hung from cracks in the rock like the mucus belonging to a dragon.

'*I wouldn't want to live in the mountain,*' whispered Amanda.

The air was suddenly infused with a cool draught, coming from the direction in which they were walking.

'*That was unexpected...*' Gallius watched as the flame of his torch danced erratically. '*We're close to where they have a great chamber.*'

'*How do you know?*'

'*I was told by a traveller who escaped from the mountain at Liatheclo.*'

Gallius put his finger to his lips.

'*Did you hear that?*' he asked.

'*It's a sort of hammering. What do you think that they're doing?*'

'*They're either tunnelling or digging out a burial chamber.*'

Amanda noticed small tufts of sheep wool snagged in the rock where ewes had been taken during the night to boil in the pot. The closer they walked the louder the hammering got.

'We can use the noise to our advantage,' said Gallius taking the turn in the passage. Once again, a sudden gust of fresh air blew through the passage mixing with the faint pungent smell of methane.

Amanda rubbed the eruption of small pimples on her arms.

From seemingly nowhere a woman walked towards them followed by a man. He was in battledress. Gallius thrust the tip of his sword forward.

'Who are you?' he asked. Amanda stood at his side her hand holding his free arm.

Surprisingly the woman smiled at Amanda.

'For someone so young, you are brave to come here. We mean you no harm, but instead we have come to help.'

Amanda suddenly realised who the woman was.

'You're Queen Erikka.' She looked at the soldier standing alongside. 'And you must be Castilleon.'

The woman nodded looking at Gallius.

'My daughter did well to choose you as friends,' she stepped nearer coming close to Gallius. 'And if my eyes do not deceive me you are the son of Zarrion and Laventra from the quarter kingdom to the north.'

Gallius put his sword back in its sheath. He bowed low out of respect for the queen.

'And you my lady are as beautiful as your daughter.'

'Wow,' said Amanda. 'I have never been this close to a real queen.'

Suddenly other faces began to appear, faces that Amanda instantly recognised. Brianna Roberts came and stood alongside her great niece.

'You crossed paths again,' said Amanda.

'We did,' replied Brianna. 'We thought you might need help.'

'Queen Avallana or indeed Master Hobble cannot help, not instead the mountain.'

'You know the garblewart?' Amanda seemed surprised.

'Some of us have had that privilege.'

Amanda didn't see his revolting habit of spitting as being a recognisable privilege.

'And did he help you?'

Queen Erikka smiled sensing Amanda's apprehension.

'He did when I was about your age.'

'Wow, he's older than what I thought.'

Gallius intervened.

'Oyddiss is in trouble, it's why we are here.'

Queen Erikka nodded.

'Trygor intends to make her his own. He wants her children hoping that our royal blood will change his own bloodline. What he does not know, is that it doesn't work like that.'

Castilleon stepped forward. He acknowledged Gallius.

'With your permission my prince, I would like to help. Princess Oyddiss once had my love, although I am not sure that it was reciprocated. I know that she is in love with another, but it is my duty to protect. Please allow me this one opportunity to put right the errors that I made before.'

Queen Erikka put her hand on Castilleon's shoulder.

'You were not to blame for the troll's actions. Fate decides our destiny Castilleon.'

Gallius was glad of the lieutenant's help.

'We both have a debt to pay. It would be my honour to fight alongside you.'

'Remember Castilleon,' warned Queen Erikka, 'your physical presence will suck the energy from your spirit. You might be lost forever.'

'Then I will gladly die once again my queen in order to save Oyddiss.'

Amanda saw the look of surprise on some of the ghosts faces as they stared at something approaching from behind where she was stood. She turned to see Master Hobble standing behind her.

'What in heavens are you doing down here?' she asked. Disguising her surprise although she was pleased to see him. 'I didn't think you could enter the mountain and isn't this an extremely dangerous place for a garblewart to be?'

Master Hobble bowed before Queen Erikka.

'Aye, it is, but there are some chances that I must take to protect those that I serve.'

Amanda thought he meant the queen.

'It's been a long time Master Hobble,' said Queen Erikka, 'but your presence is both gratifying and most welcome.'

The garblewart gargled and spat at the floor making some of the ghosts giggle. He wiped his mouth with his handkerchief. 'Aye my queen, although it's not very nice down here, is it?'

'Oyddiss is in trouble,' her mother replied.

'Aye, then is it my duty to help.'

He rearranged his hat removing a spider from behind his ear before producing a long-knurled stick from the inside of his trouser leg. Amanda watched as he withdrew the stick which appeared longer than the cloth of his leg. He saw her looking.

'Aye missy, it's a magic stick.'

Amanda felt a lot safer now that Master Hobble had appeared.

'We should get to the chamber now,' Gallius advised, 'before the evil cannot be undone.'

Gallius and Castilleon lead the way with Master Hobble immediately behind, and behind him Amanda. When she looked back there was nothing but darkness.

'They gone ahead,' advised Castilleon. 'They'll help with our arrival. You'll see.'

'We're going to need all the help we can get,' said Gallius his sword drawn. 'Trygor will not be pleased to see us.'

Amanda ran after them not wanting to be left behind. The mountain was a cold, uninviting place and she wondered how the ghosts of the children felt, even now being inside the mountain. Before this was over, she had to find a way to release their spirit from the mountain. They and others trapped inside.

'Wait for me,' she cried, 'I'm coming.'

The torch casting long eerie shadows on the coal face on either side, like dancing goblins.

Chapter Thirty-Three

The great chamber fell silent with the arrival of Karlstad and Oberran. They had with them a female captive.

Belligerently Behildwick Jones looked up at the ugly fat troll that now stood atop of the throne stone. The last time that she had seen Trygor, he had been looking up at her as she stabbed his father to death. Trygor stood, pleased to greet his visitor.

'I knew that one day you would return princess.' He ran the tip of his tongue along the underside of his upper lip. 'Although not as young or indeed beautiful.'

'I am not here by choice you odious toad.' She sniffed the air. 'Your ugliness is matched only with the foul smell that emanates from your kingdom.'

Trygor laughter was both loud and tinged with mockery as he spread his hands and arms wide.

'My kingdom is of your making princess. You, your father and your mother's. Had she scrubbed the floors better it would have smelt more to your liking.'

Behildwick Jones tried to break free of the trogglebytes hold, but they held on firm.

'Soon king of the mountain trolls you will meet with a death befitting your evil.'

Again Trygor laughed.

'And who precisely is coming to rescue you. The ghost of your dead parents. A gypsy prince and a young girl.'

All about the chamber there were gasps of surprise.

'Oh, I know that they are coming.'

Oberran looked at Karlstad, who was looking back. Just how did Trygor know? It worried them both. They scanned the faces of those close to them, but they saw no sign of deceit amongst the crowd.

Sitting on her throne Selantra looked down at the beautiful young princess. She recognised the determined look in the eyes of the woman who had been brought to the chamber and before her husband. Trygor was as she had described, odious, a toad and repulsive. The only reason she continued to endure his demands had been to save her mother and father from a cruel fate worse than death

'Times have changed,' Behildwick announced finally breaking free so that she could address the trogglebytes. 'Your king lives inside the mountain because he chooses too. He keeps you in darkness to satisfy his own need, but outside the mountain is a new world. The sunshine will not strip the flesh from your back, nor will it kill you. Your children should be free to run wherever they want. You could once again live amongst the people you call the *outsiders*. It is only your king who prevents you from having a better life.'

They were powerful words, words of hope and of freedom. Trygor recognised the dangerous mutterings and uncertainty amongst his people.

'*You lie,*' he screamed back. '*I do my best to protect my people. If it was not for me they would starve before they perish.*'

'If it was not for and your father before you they would have left the mountain years ago.' She pointed at two children nearest to where she stood, looking at the mother she asked. 'Would you not want fresh vegetables and meat, fish and fruit for your children to eat? Would you not want them to be educated and play in the sunshine?'

The mother looked up at Trygor waiting for his response.

He could feel the unrest, the tension rising in the chamber. Angrily he replied sensing that if he didn't act swiftly, they would turn on him.

'Oyddiss talks nonsense. She plays for time hoping for an opportunity to escape. Going beyond the safety of the mountain will endanger anybody who tries.'

Sitting alongside Selantra knew that what her husband really meant was that anybody who did try to leave would be killed by his personal guard.

With an aggressive flick of both hands he ordered everybody to leave the chamber except the three old hags, Karlstad and Oberran. When nobody moved Trygor felt the shock sweep through his body.

'We want to know the fate of the princess?' demanded and unknown voice, backed up by others dotted about the chamber. 'And what of Queen Selantra?' cried another.

Trygor's voice trembled as he spoke.

'Do you not remember seeing what the sun did to Oberran's back? Do you not remember that Stardd did not return?' He was grasping at straws in the hope that his words would make them see sense.

'His back was lashed with the beaver tail,' came another cry again hidden amongst so many. There were further cries and shouts of *'let her go'* and *'she will bring about bad luck once again if she is not released'*.

But defiant as his heart was black Trygor refused to give in. He raised his hand high making the gesture shake as though fighting the thunder that roared outside on extremely bad nights. *'Silence.'* He demanded.

'One day soon we will all be able to leave the mountain. Tytanius, the dark lord has promised that it will be so. But to make that promise valid a new a new breed of mountain troll is essential. A baby must be born of trogglebyte and royal blood. A baby that will grow to be your ruler long after I am gone.'

Trygor pointed at the children in the audience.

'Think how they will benefit from one so sovereign. An equal to match the outsiders. A new era would be born and no longer would we need to teal food, hide in the shadows or cower from the sun. That is why I had the princess brought back, so that she sire such a child. It is not bad luck, but our good fortune.'

'It's just another promise full of empty air!'

Trygor searched amongst the faces wondering who dared to challenge him, but even the three old hags had their heads down low.

'The bellies of our children grow large not with food, but malnutrition. Are we to stand by and watch them die, whilst you grow fat and give us false hope?'

This time Trygor did spot the speaker. A woman with two children at her side. He ran down the steps of his throne stone and fell at her feet. Kneeling he kissed the back of her hand.

'Good maiden would I be so evil as to see our future die. I beg only that you give me the chance to mate with the princess whereupon a royal baby will come forth. You and I, we should not think of ourselves, but of our children. The future belongs to them.'

He watched as the mother looked first left, then right, seeking support from those around her.

'Trygor is right and the children are our future,' she replied meekly.

On either side heads started to nod, then eventually more joined in.

With his head bowed low Trygor was grinning. Once again, he had won them over. Pulling himself back up he gently caressed the cheeks of the two young children and thanked the mother.

On his way back to the stone throne he spoke to Dwyain, the captain of his personal guard.

'Have your men mingle amongst the crowd. If they spot any troublemakers intent of causing any further unrest, have them take their names. We will deal with the offenders later.'

Passing by the princess, she grabbed his wrist.

'Perhaps you should consider letting me go. Look at the faces of your people Trygor. They are unhappy with your rule. Maybe I do bring you bad luck.'

But this time Trygor was ready with his reply. With members of his personal guard dotted about the chamber, he spoke confidently. 'There will be a union this night and fight if you want. I will put you in chains if need be, but you will give me a son or daughter as my heir.'

It was as Behildwick had feared. Trygor wanted nothing else than to breed with her. Once it was done and she gave him the first born she would be killed and dumped in the cooking pot. This time he grabbed her wrist only harder.

'Lord Tytanius prophesised to me that you were coming Oyddiss. My wife satisfies my physical needs, but you will satisfy my dreams.'

He flicked his hand summoning the three old hags.

'Now you will be taken from this chamber and dressed in readiness for our union.'

Behildwick looked up at Selantra, her eyes pleading for the young queen to help.

'Does your queen mean so little to you?' she asked stalling for time.

Trygor grinned as he looked at Selantra then Oyddiss.

'Why of course she does, but there are always others ready to take her seat on the throne next to mine.'

Behildwick ascended the first few steps of the throne stone coming close to Selantra where she could address the queen more directly.

'Your position will not protect you young queen. If you had any sense in that pretty head of yours, you would leave this chamber now before you forfeit the opportunity with your life.' She pointed at Trygor. 'This foul abominable creature will replace you as quick as he dare look at you.'

From the back of the chamber came a sudden loud howl.

'Noooooooooooo...'

Selantra saw her father Alburus holding on her mother Marianna as she tried to forge a path through the trogglebytes who were blocking her way to the throne stone. She saw the fear in her father's eyes. Fear he could only express for his daughter.

Trygor bent in close to Selantra.

'The princess speaks wise words that you should heed. Now remove yourself from the throne and leave this chamber. This throne has only been kept warm by you until the princess was retuned. She will sit here so that I can see her belly swell, until, such day that I tire of her too.'

Selantra ran down the steps of the throne heading in the direction of her parents who had been surrounded by Trygor personal guard. Calling Dwyain to his side, he told the captain of the guard to take the former mason, his wife and their daughter to the entrance where they were to be cast outside and left to the mercy of the *outsiders*. 'Let the sun burn out their eyes and scorch the flesh from their backs.'

Waiting at the base of the throne stone the three old hags watched Selantra being escorted from the chamber.

'Do not concern yourselves with Selantra any longer,' said Trygor. 'The marriage is hereby dissolved by mutual consent. Your priority now is to get ready my bride. Take Oyddiss away and watch her like a hawk. If she escapes, I will leave you naked on the side of the mountain where the wolves can tear you limb from limb.'

Behildwick Jones was being dragged from the chamber by the three old crones when the chamber fell silent to the cry from Selantra, who was stood at the far back with her parents.

'I heard all when the man from the church, Owain Jones was here. You killed a sacred man, my brother. His God is all powerful and even Tytanius kneels before him. Your treachery will be your undoing Trygor.'

Selantra left quickly with Alburus and Marianna.

Trygor who was sat on his throne slowly got to his feet. He needed to prepare himself for his wedding, but before he went he had one last thing to say.

'Let a warning echo throughout the mountain that if any person here gives Selantra, Alburus or Marianna any assistance, then they along with every man, woman and child of that family will find themselves cast beyond the mountain. Tytanius watches, he listens, and he tells me everything. Now be gone from the chamber and ready yourselves for a celebration to the future.'

Trygor watched as they fled from the chamber, some disgruntled, others afraid, but most confused. Another moment of discord had been averted, but he was concerned that they were becoming too frequent. He looked up to see only three left in the chamber, Dwyain who was stood behind Karlstad and Oberran. Descending the throne stone Trygor had a smile for the pair.

'You did well, and I should reward you both.' He looked over Karlstad's shoulder at Dwyain. 'Do you not agree captain?'

'Indeed my king. They deserve something for their efforts.'

Trygor let his hands rest on his waist. 'Such devotion and loyalty is rare.' The mountain king paced back and forth his forefinger tapping his upper lip. 'However, before I applaud your skill in tracking down the princess and bringing her back to the mountain there are one or two things that first I need to ask to satisfy my curiosity. Where did you find the princess?'

'By the river my king, where the woods meet the meadow.'

Trygor continued pacing.

'And was she alone?'

Oberran reply was hesitant and Karlstad closed his eyes not wanting to look.

'Why no, my king. She was when we took her, but she had been accompanied by a girl and a man.'

Trygor noticed Karlstad's injured arm.

'Did she do that to you?'

No my king. That was as a result of a skirmish with some unrelated *outsiders*.'

Trygor stopped pacing.

'In total there were four of you and yet only two returned. Where is Bradkar and Schellian?'

Karlstad opened his eyes.

'He was stabbed in the skirmish my king. He didn't survive the day. We never saw Schellian.'

Trygor looked at Dwyain, but it was impossible for Karlstad and Oberran to know what gesture the captain responded with.

'And when you snatched the princess, did she resist?'

'Like a wild fox,' replied Oberran, eager to please.

Karlstad wanted Oberran to shut up, to stop talking.

'She was kicking and gouging, and biting.' He grabbed Karlstad's finger where the teeth marks were still visible.

'And the mark on her face was because of her resistance?'

'She had that before we caught up with her.' Again it was Oberran who answered.

Trygor came in close.

'Which one of you hit her?'

Inhaling hard Karlstad owned up.

'I did my king. She was struggling and as I tried to stop her, she bit my finger. As I went to hold my injured finger my elbow accidently collided with her jaw. She was only unconscious for about two minutes. It gave us the opportunity to escape undetected.'

Oberran expected to be asked if it was true, but Trygor seemed satisfied with Karlstad's explanation.

'In the circumstances, I would have done exactly the same. The princess is wild and untamed like most outsiders.' He patted Karlstad's upper arm. 'You did well my friend.'

Sensing that it was going well Oberran relaxed.

'And what of you Oberran,' asked Trygor. 'What part did you play in this brave capture?'

'I found Schellian.'

The words left his lips before Oberran could stop himself. Karlstad felt his heart sink.

'Was he alive?' asked Trygor.

'No my king.'

'Did you kill Schellian?'

'No my king. He was already dead.'

'Let me see your knife. We'll see if it has the trace of blood on the blade.'

Oberran did as requested.

'I did kill rabbits. The blood belongs to them!'

Trygor noticed that Karlstad's knife was missing. He asked why.

'I lost it during the fight with the *outsiders* my king.'

Trygor nodded accepting the explanation. He turned back to face Oberran.

'Rabbit blood is not so rich. This is Schellian's blood on the blade. You killed him, didn't you?'

Oberran's jaw started to quiver nervously. He felt the back of his throat going dry and constricting as he tried to find the right words. Trygor took his silence as meaning guilt.

'You came across Schellian and you murdered him, didn't you!'

Oberran could only shake his head as he stared back at Trygor, the fear running down his spine and making his knees knock together. Stood alongside Karlstad realised that he should have killed Oberran when he'd had the opportunity.

When the knife embedded itself in the underside of Oberran's ribcage he felt his knees give way first, then his whole body as the ground rushed up to meet him. Leaving the dying trogglebyte writing in the dust of the chamber floor Trygor surprisingly put an encouraging hand upon Karlstad's shoulder.

'And what of you Karlstad. Without your ingenuity and quick thinking Oyddiss would have escaped capture once again. Oberran got what he deserved, but how can I reward you?'

'I would like to a member of your personal guard my king, where I could serve you best.'

'And nothing for yourself?' he asked.

'No, nothing my king. Serving you would be ample reward.'

Trygor liked the reply. As unexpected as it had been, it did sound genuine.

'And what say you Dwyain, do you think our fine hunter here would make a good member of your guard?'

'Indeed he would,' beamed Dwyain.

'Then it's settled.' Said Trygor. 'Go with the captain and he'll show you your duties Karlstad.'

As they walked from the chamber the spear thrown by Trygor hit Karlstad dead centre of his back. Dying amongst the dust just like his cousin, Trygor knelt low so that Karlstad could see him.

'The tracks that were found near Schellian's body belonged to you Karlstad. Without being there I cannot tell which of you killed Schellian, but now by killing you both I can say that I got the right one.'

Trygor stood and walked towards his bedchamber. He had to get himself ready for his new queen. Before he left the chamber, he had one more task for Dwyain.

'Make sure that nobody enters the chamber after I've gone and when the old crones have finished with Oyddiss, have them strip these two and add them to the cooking pot. At least there will be enough meat for the feast. That should stop the other's moaning.'

Chapter Thirty-Four

Mostyn Owens walked out of the surgery door with his arm wrapped in plaster and a new bandage around his head looking every inch a wounded Arabian prince.

'Why the head wrap?' asked Jonathon Evans.

Mostyn shrugged, 'I know it looks ridiculous doesn't it, but Nurse Dawson insisted on me wearing one or it was complete bed rest. I opted for the bandage as a compromise.' He touched the side of his head where it still ached. 'It hides the bald patch where she stitched the wound.'

'Well I think it's sensible,' said Larissa. 'And coming back was a good idea too, although I have this funny feeling that something's happened.'

'Like what?' asked Daisy glad to be back in the village.

'Like they've had another encounter with the trogglebytes.'

Albert wasn't going to be left out. 'You and your funny feelings. If we listened to every funny feeling you had, we'd never do anything interesting.'

'No, this is more.' Explained Larissa. 'Even General's restless.'

To show that he understood the horse raised, then lowered his head.

'Now that we are back, what are we going to do with General?'

Jonathon was about to suggest letting him go when they saw Eira Pryce coming towards them. She was breathless as though she had been running. She looked at Mostyn's bandages and asked if he was okay.

'I'll live, least that's what Nurse Dawson said.'

'I had a feeling that you were back. Where's Amanda?'

'She insisted on staying behind with Behildwick,' replied Jonathon.

Eira pointed towards the mountain, inhaling hard to regain the oxygen lost in racing through the village to find them.

'The mountain trolls have recaptured Behildwick.'

They each looked at each other, then back to Eira.

'Then that's where we're going,' said Mostyn. We're the gang from Mud Island and we don't let our friends down. That's our motto.'

'You can't possibly go, not in your present state.'

They looked at Eira wondering what she could suggest.

'Perhaps you could wait at old Jonesy's farm. I've a feeling that they'll come out there if anywhere, once they escape.'

'The hay cart, somebody must have moved it.' Said Albert tapping the handle of the knife that Gallius had given him.

'That looks deadly,' remarked Eira seeing the knife.

'It is…' replied Daisy. 'But Albert knows how to use it.'

'Okay the barn it is,' said Jonathon accepting that once free of the deep shaft they could once again seal the entrance.

Larissa put her hand on Eira's arm.

'If Amanda is with Gallius, then I lay odds that she'll be safe.'

Eira looked surprised.

'Do you mean Gallius, the gypsy prince from Liatheclo?'

'Yes, that's him!'

'Do you know I thought I caught sight of him passing through the village a couple of days back, maybe more. He was in my dream too.'

'He's handsome,' said Daisy. Larissa nodded to confirm that we was.

'Don't worry Mrs Pryce, we will get them all back safe and sound.' Jonathon gave a slight tug on the rein turning General as they made for the farm.

Eira Pryce felt a hand slip through her arm knowing that it was her daughters.

'Amanda's inside the mountain, isn't she? Asked Mary Brodrick.

Eira Pryce looked at her daughter, her eyes full of optimism.

'Yes, but she's with a prince and from what I've heard, he's a good fighter.'

'I know, he was in my dreams last night.'

Eira Pryce smiled. 'He's a very popular man.'

'Where are the others going?'

'To old Jonesy's farm. That's where I believe they'll emerge, eventually.'

'Then   that   is   where   we're   going.'

Chapter Thirty-Five

Where is everybody?' Amanda whispered, standing in the shadows where they peered under the arch at the vast chamber.

'*I'm not sure.*' Replied Gallius. He could see the bodies of the two dead trogglebytes, one with a spear sticking out of his back and by the far arch there were two guards. '*Something's happened here, there is a restless air in the chamber.*'

Unseen by the guards Queen Erikka appeared before them.

'*The three old hags have Oyddiss. They are getting her prepared for the wedding ceremony.*'

'*I thought that Trygor had a Queen?*' said Castilleon.

'*She has and her family have been banished from the mountain.*'

'*They've had a lucky escape,*' added Castilleon. '*Do you know where we will find Trygor? If I kill him there can be no ceremony.*'

Queen Erikka raised a hand to stop Castilleon from advancing.

'*Be patient Castilleon, the opportunity will present itself soon. First we must wait until we see that Oyddiss is safe and unharmed.*'

'I assumed my queen that if I dealt with Trygor there would be no need of a ceremony.'

Amanda saw the pile of bones next to the large cauldron which was bubbling away. Standing alongside Brianna Roberts she asked. *'Is that what I think it is?'*

Brianna Roberts nodded slowly. *'Nothing goes to waste in this dreadful kingdom. Unless it is a king.'*

Master Hobble gargled before spitting out his contempt at the evil that lived beneath the mountain.

'Aye... you're right young missy. This chamber has long harboured a trail of death and destruction.'

For once Amanda agreed with him spitting. She felt like doing the same. It was a horrible place. In fact there wasn't anything that she liked about the inside of the mountain.

'It won't always be like this Master Hobble,' she whispered, *'one day even the trolls will want peace.'*

'Aye missy, one day maybe.'

Suddenly one of the old hags appeared making her way over to the cauldron where she gave the contents a stir.

'Is she ready?' asked Dwyain growing restless just waiting around.

'Almost,' replied the toothless old hag. She took a spoonful, tasted it then spat it back in the pot. She was satisfied that it had tasted edible. 'What about those two?' she asked pointing at Oberran and Karlstad.

'Trygor says you're to strip them, keep their clothes, but add them to the pot.'

The old hag looked into the cauldron. 'There's not a lot of room!'

'Well then cut them up small.' Dwyain suggested.

'Do this, do that. That's all we ever do,' grumbled the old hag as she gave the contents another stir hoping that the liquid would solidify.

I hope that you washed that ladle,' remarked the other guard having seen her spit back the contents.

The old hag turned with the ladle in her hand, from the end dripped a globule of sticky brown liquid. 'When your time comes Hagabard, you'll not be worrying whether the ladle is clean or not. You only wish will be whether you are dead or still alive to be boiled alive.' The toothless old hag let out a long cackling chortle that seemed to fill every crack in the chamber. Her cackle brought forth Trygor from his bedchamber. He was already dressed in his cloak of dead bats wings and on top of his head sat a crown of braided ivy.

'What amuses you, you old crone?' he asked.

The gummy, bent over hag pointed at the guard who had made the comment.

'I was just saying your majesty, how Hagabard would one day fill the pot and thicken the gravy.'

Amanda felt the bile churning in her stomach. A hand rested over hers.

'Try not to think of anything, but getting out of here when this is done.' Brianna Roberts advised. 'This is how the trogglebytes live.'

'They're savages,' said Amanda. 'Cannibals.'

Amanda looked away as the old hag dealt with the two dead trogglebytes. When she next looked all around the cauldron the floor was awash with blood and bits of body. One by one the old hag added them to the cauldron stirring with her free hand.

'How do they get everything in?' she whispered.

'Somehow they manage.' Brianna replied. She looked at the pile of bones, wondering if her own were amongst the heap.

Suddenly the chamber began to fill with trogglebytes. The mood was subdued and much different to when Trygor had married Selantra. Many still believed that Oyddiss would bring them bad luck. To ensure that there was no more dissent Trygor ordered Dwyain to have his guard mingle.

'We've lost the element of surprise,' said Castilleon as he watched the mountain trolls take their place at the roughly made tables and chairs.

'Not necessarily,' replied Gallius. *'We should let the ceremony go ahead then surprise Trygor later.'*

'Where?'

'The bedchamber.'

Castilleon was about to suggest that Gallius was mad, but Queen Erikka saw the sense in what Gallius had recommended.

'Of course. The ceremony would not be recognised outside the mountain and Trygor's bedchamber would be occupied by only him and Oyddiss. It's a good plan Gallius.'

Using the shadows they slipped successfully across to the next passage from where Trygor had emerged.

'I will stay and watch,' said Queen Erikka. *'The rest of you go with Gallius.'*

Walking between the two old hags was Behildwick Jones. She struggled to break free, but the strength in the old women's grip amazed her as they dragged her towards where Trygor was waiting.

'Come my beautiful bride. Come forth,' he gestured. 'Let us rejoice this union and that today history will be made later!'

Behildwick looked around for a place to escape, but Trygor had guards posted at each entrance.

'Don't even think about it,' he warned, 'and today there will be no cutting of the palms, no knives, no blood mixing. The only mixing will happen in my bedchamber.'

'You contemptible oaf. I will never yield to your plan. You are a fool mountain king and tonight will be your undoing.'

Standing near although unseen Queen Erikka was pleased to see that he daughter was still as spirited.

Trygor laughed, he too liked his bride spirited. It would make the coming night more fun.

'Now...' he ordered. *'Let the ceremony commence. I am hungry and I need to eat. I will need a lot of energy for later.'*

Marigold draped the wedding garland over each of their wrists. She was about to begin the chant when Trygor thought that he heard a noise coming from his bedchamber, but such was his insistence that the ceremony begin that he let it pass unheeded.

The guard blocking the passage went to investigate, but he never returned to his post having been swiftly dealt with by Castilleon. They dragged and left the dead trogglebyte under Trygor's bed.

Queen Erikka appeared as they kicked the dead troll's feet under the bed.

'Problems?' she asked.

'Not now,' said Gallius with a smile. 'Castilleon is still quick with the sword.'

A loud cheer suggested that the ceremony was complete and now the chamber could eat and drink. Victorious at last Trygor held Oyddiss's hand up high with his own.

Dejectedly Behildwick looked at the passage from which she had escaped before.

'You can look and wish my queen,' said Trygor as he gloated in triumph, 'but I guarantee that none of your friends will ever come to rescue you in time. My captain has every passage covered. You would do well to accept your position now. You need to please your king and your subjects.'

Behildwick watched the juices run down the sides of his beard and he gorged himself on the food on his plate. When he was done, Trygor wiped the spills with a rag then dragging his bride from the throne stone demanded that the chamber enjoy themselves.

'Make as much noise as you like this night. Let the dragon roar loud,' he invited.

Trygor dragged Oyddiss into the passage. He wondered why there was no guard in the passage, but he had other things on his mind. He would find out why later.

'Listen to them rejoicing,' said Trygor, 'they are happy!'

'That is only because they fear you.'

Trygor turned sharply pinning Oyddiss against the passage wall.

'And you would do well to be the same. I am not to be messed with my queen. Please me and I will give you everything. Anger me and I will have you put in chains.'

Behildwick Jones glared back her eyes full of hate, venom. Somehow, she would find a way to kill Trygor. Pulling her away from the wall he dragged her to the bedchamber   door.

Chapter Thirty-Six

Behildwick Jones held back the anger rising inside of her until they reached the inside of the bed chamber and then like the bubbling cauldron back in the great chamber it burst.

She physically attacked Trygor with every ounce of her strength hitting him, kicking him and biting anything that came back her way. At one point she grabbed his metal chamber pot and smashed it down over his head which made him stagger over to the bed. He landed on the bed, but chuckling to himself, her aggression was no more than he had expected, and it only fuelled his desire for her.

She stood over him, chamber pot in hand ready to launch another attack. 'I did not reclaim my youth so that you could besmirch my body, your foul loathsome toad.'

Trygor rubbed his head where she had hit him. Slipping from his wedding cloak and crown, he launched himself at her, but Behildwick swung the chamber pot back and forth menacingly keeping him at bay.

'Did you learn nothing from the death of your father?' she asked. 'I told him that the man I marry, will be of my choosing. This marriage here in the mountain is not legal and never will be!'

She lashed out to strike the side of his head again, but Trygor was swift, much faster than she had anticipated. He caught her by the wrist, cast aside the chamber pot and flipped her onto the bed. Tearing at her wedding cloak he was waiting no longer. He did the same with her dress, but got no further as a pair of strong hands yanked him from the bed and clear of the princess.

Trygor landed heavily on the stone floor banging his head against the side of the bed leg. Down low he saw the face of the dead guard looking back at him.

'What...' he cried before looking up at the man standing over him. The anger in his eyes blazing like that of a stricken wolf.

'What trickery is this?' he yelled, but the noise from the festivities beyond his passage drowned out his cries.

Castilleon held down the king of the trogglebytes for as long as he could, but very soon his energy was almost spent and he had to relent. Gallius moved to take over, but Trygor was surprisingly agile as he sprang to his feet. Pushing his bride aside he grabbed a dagger from under his pillow. He grinned at Gallius and the young girl standing beside the door.

'So prince of the gypsy's, you dare to enter my bedchamber and on my wedding night. I will deal with you then keep the girl. She will serve me well as my personal slave. I have need of a new maid servant and somebody to look after my queen.'

'*I am not afraid of you...*' said Amanda taking a step forward. 'Other than the foul smell in here, you're nothing but a fat loathsome overgrown slime ball toad.'

Trygor responded with a laugh as he tried to grab Oyddiss, but she too was slippery and managed to flick aside his reaching hand. From seemingly nowhere he felt the hard cold hand slap his face. It stopped his laughing.

'Who's there?' he asked, but saw only the gypsy prince and the girl.

Slowly the ghost took on a shape.

'Well... well,' said Trygor mockingly. It has been a long time Erikka. I wondered if you were still here in the mountain. Have you come to congratulate us on our wedding?'

There was no smile on the queen's face, only loathing.

'Time is irrelevant from where I come from Trygor, but time has not improved you. Look at you. You have grown fat and become repulsive. You rule through fear. Even the children despise you. I chose this moment to appear to have you know that you will not harm my daughter. Oyddiss will leave this leave this mountain this day and be free once again.'

Standing alongside Master Hobble held onto Amanda's hand, not that Trygor could see him. Master Hobble had his funny stick outstretched just in case. Dillan Evans and Brock Platt helped the exhausted Castilleon to his feet. They took him outside the bedchamber which was now becoming overcrowded. Queen Erikka stood herself between Oyddiss and Trygor with Gallius at her side.

'Sorcery and magic has no place here Erikka and what took place today is binding by our mountain law. Oyddiss is my bride and she will serve me as I see fit.'

Suddenly from the great chamber came a howling and hooting of confusion as tables and chairs were upturned, plates and cutlery tossed into the air as the terrified trogglebytes took shelter not knowing what was happening. Dwyain ordered the guards to stand fast and kill anybody causing the commotion, but even he didn't know. Queen Erikka knew.

'It is not sorcery Trygor, but the creation of your own evil. Hark, listen to what takes place outside your bedchamber. Your subjects are scared of the things that they cannot see.'

Master Hobble whispered in Amanda's ear. *'Aye missy, do not be alarmed, it's just the children having some fun.'*

Realising that he was outnumbered and trapped Trygor launched himself at Queen Erikka, but Gallius was ready. He pushed the trogglebyte king back hard against the chamber wall. Trygor however was not going to be taken without putting up a fight.

Sword and dagger clashed as the pair battled one another. For several minutes they fought until Trygor staggered backwards. Stumbling awkwardly he fell back onto the bed clutching his stomach. The king of the mountain lay on the bed amongst the dead flower petals staring across at Oyddiss. He saw his vision of a new generation of trolls disappearing as the blanket of death began to descend.

'We will meet again, in the afterlife,' he said, but his words were difficult as the blood filled his lungs.

Behildwick turned to congratulate and hug Gallius, but she stopped herself short seeing the dagger sticking out beneath his ribcage. With a look of concern Gallius muttered something then slumped into her arms as his knees began to buckle.

Behildwick turned to Amanda.

'Gallius, he's hurt badly. We need to get him away from here as soon as possible. Eira will know what to do.'

Spitting out the phlegm from his throat Master Hubble helped.

'Aye, this is my moment. Hold tight onto Gallius, I know where your grandmother is waiting.'

Amanda and Behildwick did as requested as Master Hobble struck the ground hard with his stick. Moments later they were transported to the floor of the barn with the others following.

There waiting were Eira Pryce, Mary Brodrick and the gang of Mud Island.

'Quick, close the trapdoor,' ordered Behildwick looking at Jonathon and Albert, 'and cover both doors with the hay cart again.

Eira and Mary immediately attended to Gallius.

'Are you okay?' asked Mary as she helped remove Gallius's waistcoat.

'I'm fine mum, but please look after Gallius. He's badly hurt.'

'We'll take him back to my cottage,' said Eira. 'I can look after. If we take him to Nurse Dawson it'll take too much explaining and she'll only involve the police.'

They gently placed Gallius in the back of caravan and when they were all aboard Jonathon flicked the reins not that General needed any encouragement.

'Hurry Jonathon,' cried Amanda, *'Gallius has blacked out.'*

The horse galloped down the track and through the lanes to Eira Pryce's cottage.

Sitting opposite Eira Pryce was Queen Erikka.

'You can see me?' she asked.

'Indeed I can your majesty. This is indeed a great honour. Your daughter and I have been friends for a very long time.'

'Then the honour is mine,' replied Queen Erikka, 'and you have a very brave granddaughter.'

There came the sound of an explosion back at the barn. Amanda looked through the rear window of the caravan where she saw Mostyn and Albert standing outside of the barn.

'Wow, they've blown up old Jonesy's barn.'

Behildwick Jones smiled.

'Not the entire barn. Only the shaft leading down to the mountain passage below. There was a box of the miner's dynamite leftover in the corner of the barn. I suggested that they block the entrance forever. Anybody could move the hay cart and we might never know. This way is safer.'

'My guess is that the guards would have found the body of their dead king, they won't be happy.'

Behildwick smiled at Amanda as she held Gallius's hand.

'Many will. At last the age of tyranny is over.'

Chapter Thirty-Seven

A long way down beneath the foundations of the barn the earth had shook and rock had started to fall from the top of the tall shaft. Those searching in the passage below were lucky to escape with their lives as the shaft quickly filled with black rock, coal and earth. This time however the mountain trogglebytes recognised that the collapse had not been caused by the dragon. Never again would they able to use the shaft as an exit out.

'It's the curse,' said one, coughing the dust from his mouth.

The one nearest agreed nodding. 'We said it was a bad omen and that Oyddiss should never have been made our queen. It was she who made the entrance collapse.'

A female standing at the back spoke rather hesitantly.

'At least the era of Trybulloc and Trygor has come to an end and with no successor to the throne, we should think of joining Selantra, Alburus and Marianna.'

*****

328

On the short journey back to Eira's cottage Gallius groaned and moaned incoherently, mumbling to himself through the pain and confusion of his wound. The only word that Behildwick managed to catch was when he mentioned Aurora, his beloved sister.

'Come on…' Behildwick urged, 'stay with us Gallius.'

Sitting alongside, as concerned Amanda turned to Master Hobble.

'Is there nothing that you can do?'

'Aye, he doesn't look good, I'll admit that, but your grandmother knows how to fix him.'

Amanda squeezed Behildwick's arm.

'He will live, I just know it…' she said.

Larissa and Daisy looked at the funny looking creature with the long rabbit like ears and top hat. 'And who exactly is he?' Daisy asked, screwing up her nose.

Amanda grinned.

'That is a garblewart, only stand clear when you're standing near because Master Hobble has a rather disgusting habit of spitting.'

'So does my brother,' replied Daisy.

'Yes, but not like a garblewart.'

Amanda whispered into Master Hobbit's ear.

'How come they can see you?'

'Aye, they can.' He seemed surprised. *'I've no idea.'*

When General came to a halt outside of the cottage there was a flurry of activity, one holding open the gate, another the front door, with another the bedroom door as Gallius was gently laid upon the bed. Eira cleared the room allowing only Behildwick Jones the right to stay. She didn't know about Queen Erikka or Castilleon standing in the corner unseen.

Pulling open an old leather bag Eira went to work on the wound.

'It's deep, but fortunately it had missed vital organs only affecting tissue and muscle.'

'Will he live?' asked Behildwick.

'He's strong, and handsome,' replied Eira with a wink. 'We'll patch him up best we can and keep a vigil at his side in case he wakes.

Behildwick held onto Gallius's hand as Eira bathed the wound then thread a length of suture thread through the eye of the needle whereupon she started to sew, pulling together muscle and layers of flesh. She finished wrapping a bandage about his back and front.

'That's as much as I can do now,' she said closing the leather bag.

Behildwick touched the gypsy prince's forehead. 'He's very hot.'

'That'll be the fever. He needs to fight that until any infection passes. The wound is clean and now it's up to Gallius and his will to live.'

Queen Erikka stepped forward placing her hand on her daughter's shoulder.

'Gallius has not come this far to leave you now Oyddiss.'

The princess put her hand over her mother's.

'I hope not mother. I love him.'

She saw Castilleon standing in the corner of the room.

'I'm sorry, but it has been so long and I thought you were dead.'

Castilleon stepped forward.

'I am Oyddiss. He's brave and he is a prince. If he lives you should think about discussing marriage.'

'Thank you.' She touched her chest. 'Whatever, there will always be a place in my heart where you belong.'

'Right, that's that settled.' Said Eira. 'Now we should think about joining the others, they'll be anxious to know what's going on.

'I'll stay here a while,' said Behildwick.

In the kitchen Mary Brodrick was pleased to have Amanda alone for a few moments.

'You've had yourself quite an adventure to remember,' she said giving her daughter a hug. 'But I am glad that you're home safe and sound.'

'I'll pinch myself soon and wonder if it was all a dream,' replied Amanda. 'It's the waking bit that doesn't make sense.'

'Beside the lake?'

Amanda felt her mouth open and drop.

'How do you know?'

'Master Hobble. I met him a long time back, when you were born if I remember right.'

'And Emma, does she know?'

'Yes, although of us all, it is you who has the *gift* the most Amanda.'

'Have you and Emma, and grandma seen the Lady Bleudele?'

'No. Master Hobble pops in from time to time, but only if he's passing. He just checks to make sure that we all okay and then he leaves.'

'He has a very disgusting habit.'

Mary Brodrick smiled. 'I thought you'd find it repulsive, but it's what garblewarts do.'

'Does dad know?' Amanda asked.

Mary Brodrick gave a determined shake of her head.

'No. The *gift* only seems to recognise the female members of our family and in time you'll learn that men don't always understand the secrets that women have.'

'I would agree with that,' said Eira Pryce standing behind them.

'Is Gallius okay?' asked Amanda.

'Resting, but the fever needs to pass before he is out of the woods.'

'That's where the trogglebytes snatched Behildwick. Is she okay.'

'Yes, she's tough and over the years she has had much to deal with. Perhaps now she too can settle.'

'Something happened at the lake grandma, only I haven't the foggiest idea what other than Behildwick and Gallius got younger.'

'Maybe one day Master Hobble will explain what.'

'What... you too grandma.'

'Aye missy, I knows them all.'

Amanda turned and to Master Hobble's surprise she hugged him tight.

'Don't you be so long in turning up next time, do you hear?'

The garblewart doffed his hat at Eira and Mary.

'Aye, I'm sorry missy, but I got delayed en route. I'm here now and that's all that matters!'

Mopping his brow with a damp flannel Behildwick looked at her mother standing at the end of the bed. 'Queen Avallana, she said...' but her mother stopped her.

'What was said, was for you only to know Oyddiss.'

'But father...'

Queen Erikka smiled.

'Your father loved you very much and nothing you would do, concerned him. His spirit lives inside you Oyddiss and it always will do. He would approve of Gallius.'

'But I cause so much pain and suffering.'

'No. Not you, the trolls that went inside the mountain. Trybulloc, he was to blame. We cannot change history Oyddiss, but you can change your destiny and with the man whose hand you hold.'

The princess looked to see Castilleon nodding his approval.

'Soon, Castilleon and I will have to leave to rejoin your father, but we will all watch over you. Don't waste any more years being lonely and learn to trust again Oyddiss. Gallius has our blessing.'

Behildwick stood and kissed Castilleon him on the cheek.

'Thank you.'

'If we could reverse time I would still meet you in the castle garden.'

Fading into the shadow in the corner Castilleon disappeared.

'Will I ever see you and father again?'

'One day, but not for a very long time to come. Your youth has been restored and for a reason. Use it wisely. Come, you should speak to the children. They are anxious for news.'

There was a murmur as Gallius opened his eyes momentarily. He blinked clearing his vision smiled seeing the queen and princess standing side by side, then fell into peaceful sleep.

'The fever will pass soon Oyddiss, then perhaps a little soup to help build his strength. Let Gallius sleep now.' She smiled. 'The children!'

Chapter Thirty-Eight

They entered the parlour where expectant faces were pleased to see them.

'Gallius is sleeping now, but he did open his eyes momentarily. He'll be alright after a long sleep.'

There were sighs of relief all round mixed with smiles.

Queen Erikka looked at ghosts of the children from nineteen hundred and five. For once their faces were a multitude of smiles and knowing.

'We're free at last,' she said, 'thanks to Amanda, Gallius and Master Hobble. Our spirits can move on and be with our ancestors. We should say goodbye to loved ones as the time is drawing near'

All around the room there were tears forming and children hugged one another.

'You're getting ready to leave, aren't you?' said Behildwick.

'We have to go Oyddiss, it's the law of the universe. Our time together was always going to be short.'

'Give my love to father please, tell him that I love him.'

'He already knows.'

Queen Erikka looked around the room at each and every one, including the ghost children.

'You are all so brave. A long time ago with what started as a rebellion turned quickly into centuries of terror and heartache. Such a tyranny has been crushed and now the time has come for those of you left behind to enjoy your lives, have families of your own and accept everything that the world has to offer. There will always be a Mud Island and children to occupy it, and fight for the right to say that it belongs to them. Always remember, what you love most is worth fighting for.'

Amanda felt a kiss land on her cheek guessing that Master Hobble had left the cottage. She saw Eira Pryce smile.

'He'll be around again soon,' she whispered. *'You mark my word.'*

'Why is it called Mud Island?' asked Albert. 'I never have understood why?'

Queen Erikka grinned.

'At one time the knights would practise their fighting skills on the land beyond the castle walls. Rough and unspoilt, the land would be a challenge that they had to overcome, knowing that the battles to come would be fought on such a terrain. When the rains came in the early spring the knights named the boggy terrain Mud Island.'

The queen looked specifically at Mostyn, Albert and Jonathon.

'When you fought the trogglebytes at the crossroads, you did so with the spirit of the knights in you. My husband, King Felman would have been proud to have had you in his private guard.'

Albert nudged Daisy sitting alongside.

'You see Gethall, even the queen thinks I'd make a knight.'

The room erupted into laughter. It was a good time to say their goodbyes. One by one they started to fade and soon there was only Eira Pryce, Mary Brodrick, Behildwick Jones and the children left.

'We will ever see them again?' asked Larissa Driscoll.

'Oh, perhaps from time to time.' Behildwick replied. 'At least in your dreams. Loved ones never really say goodbye, more like 'see you' which I think means they'll be back.'

There was a groan from the bedroom and everybody rushed to the bedroom at the end of the hall where they found Gallius awake.

'Did we win?' he asked groggily.

Behildwick Jones kissed the top of his forehead as she made him comfortable pulling the bed cover up.

'We won and you killed Trygor, and thanks to you and Amanda I am safe.'

'I hope my father was watching.'

'He was watching, as was your mother. They are very proud of you Gallius. Now rest my love. I will be here when you wake.'

Many, many miles away Queen Avallana watched as the princess fussed over her prince. It was how it should have been.

Stood nervously, holding tightly onto his hat Master Hobble knew he was in trouble.

'Now about that unplanned visit to the mountain!' she asked.

Chapter Thirty-Nine

Begrudgingly they removed the bloodied clothes from the smelly, bulbous body of their dead king with the captain of his guard scrutinising their every move.

'*Be quick,*' he demanded, pulling the blade from his scabbard as a warning. 'I want the king washed before we bury him. Others are already chiselling out a suitable grave so that he lays alongside the tomb of his father.'

The oldest of the trio grimaced. Rolling her tongue over her rubbery lips she spat at the dusty floor pushing the damp rag over Trygor's limp body.

'Do I have to wash everything?' Marigold asked lifting his lower garments.

'*Everything,*' snarled back the captain.

'So what happens now Captain… do we get us a new king?' she asked.

'Maybe Dwyain could sit on the stone throne?' suggested another.

Dwyain had not given the idea thought, but who was there to challenge him. Gradually a smile replaced his sneer. 'That's not a bad idea,' he replied. 'I would have to have it approved by King Stelfor of course.' He rubbed his chin. 'Now who can we send with the message.'

Dwyain pulled the damp rag away tossing it into the bloody bucket.

'That'll do, he's dead and gone!'

Behildwick Jones and the Children of Mud Island

ABOUT THE AUTHOR

 Jeffrey Brett was born in London during the middle of the last century, where he lived and worked until leaving for pastures green and wide, with opportunities to write his fictional stories.

Writing is not just a happy pastime, but has become a way of life for Jeffrey Brett and without it he would feel lost. He feels that there are so many ideas that need to be written although he follows no particular genre creating short stories, romantic and psychological thrillers, and hopefully humorous books.

Now retired after a lifetime of public service he has found the time to make his dreams come true and enjoys writing and publishing his books. His good friend, award winning writer and author Kathleen Harryman is a great inspiration and encouragement, and through her recent creative artwork, she has helped with some of the book covers. Kathleen's artwork service and books can be found on her website —kathleenharryman.com

Jeffrey Brett wishes you many hours of happy reading. If you have any comments regarding any of his books please email him and let him know — magic79.jb@outlook.com

Printed in Great Britain
by Amazon

59541282R00193